THE SEA OF TEARS

THE SEA OF TEARS

Nani Power

COUNTERPOINT

A MEMBER OF THE PERSEUS BOOKS GROUP

NEW YORK

Copyright © 2005 by Nani Power
Published by Counterpoint,
A Member of the Perseus Books Group

Counterpoint books are available at special discounts for bulk purchases in the United States by corporations, institutions, and other organizations. For more information, please contact the Special Markets Department at the Perseus Books Group, 11 Cambridge Center, Cambridge MA 02142, or call (617) 252-5298 or (800) 255-1514, or e-mail special.markets@perseusbooks.com.

Library of Congress Cataloging-in-Publication Data
CIP TK

ISBN 1-58243-303-8

05 06 07 / 10 9 8 7 6 5 4 3 2 1

This is all about Love.

What isn't all about love? Every story we hear, every scrap of news, everything we arch our ear towards is ultimately all about love and how we ruin it or seek it or run for it, how we destroy ourselves or others when we feel its loss, or how magically we cure when it is attained. All the great tales are about love, even beautiful Sheherezade, who lives on as the great story teller, enchanted the heart of the cold and murderous Sultan of Samarkand with her tales and brought him back to the world of love, he who had been so betrayed he swore death to all women for their unfaithfulness. At the root of all evil is a heart denied love. At the root of all good is generosity and kindness. These are four tales of entwined lives in a hotel in Washington DC and all are about love, first and foremost. If you focussed on the other lives that weave through these hotel rooms, or through your lives in the countless cities and countries of the world, all of them and us are led by the heart, woefully, willfully, as we should be. In the end the heart is the ruler. Let it lead the way from me to you and back again and may we never part again.

THE BROKEN

you have set up
a colorful table
calling it life and
asked me to your feast
but punish me if
i enjoy myself

what tyranny is this

—Rumi

ONE

Jedra Abdullah has noone.

This is what he said to himself as he entered the building of the Royale Hotel, the grand elephant of decay, where he worked. Again, bypass the brass and fern lounge area, hear Josh Groban singing on the speakers about falling, and see the pretty women, Denise and Phyllis in Reception who did not even look him in the eye much less talk to him. They did not even know Jedra Abdullah except as the engineer from the boiler room.

I have noone. He carried his tools in his faded denim bag bought at an airport that said *Washington D.C., the Capitol*, and Josh Groban continued to sing. He liked this singer, except sometimes he would make him cry, holding his wrench in the elevator and hope that Phyllis or Denise would not come in and see his tearstained face, his small bald skull like a squirrel or the shouting loneliness of his dark eyes.

He knows today he will hear about leaks. This is a word always thrown in his direction. Secretly, Jedra knows that the entire hotel is under immense pressure which will soon burst in a roiling avalanche of liquid, filling the block like a tsunami. When he wraps his wrench around the tuber-thin brass pipes of its inner sanctum, he can feel the coursing pressure threatening their metallic interiors, can see how they tremor under the weight and how easily small fissures occur, everywhere, spritzing and fizzing behind the brocade, the velvet, the satin, the chair-rails. When this tragedy occurs, he knows where he will be: deep in the boiler, sitting on his milk crate covered in a towel, eating cheese balls and olives, listening to the sizzle of the heater. Suddenly there will be a sharp—*crack, crack, craqk!*— as the pipes snap and the flood gushes, and at that time in a very instant Jedra, Phyllis, Denise and all of them will surrender to a watery death.

Perhaps today is not the day, though, he thinks, and stands in front of reception and makes no jokes and looks at Phyllis and wonders why she is a jewel he will never touch or own. If a person can be owned, but in his heart he would like to be owned and cherished, like an object. He wished he could be only all to one person, a friend. And why does Phyllis lay with one man and not him, he thought. Why is it possible that I should not have a woman, and some other man will touch her and see the light of her eyes? But was Phyllis only a bauble who would sit bored in his small shabby apartment on Swann Street, picking at his plaid sofa with sad eyes? Would she wish for sweet, soft meat instead of the cheese balls and olives he lived on, would her long pink body look wrong next to his dark shadow of a body, a lean little course of sinew and unloved muscles, like a scrawny goat left to scrabble on an unlush mountain for too long, where he ate dry roots and finally, rocks?

With this image of a goat and her pink body, Jedra goes down to the boiler room, the hot oil smell hitting his face harshly, and yes, he sits on the crate. He is comfortable in a prison, that is true, all space he fashions into a cell, with makeshift chair, bed, cold food. He decided long ago he would deserve warm food only if it were cooked by the loving hands of a woman, and this will never happen. So he chews on an olive pit. After this, he knows he must stop the leakage. He is sure he can hear the pressure already. He only does the basic with his wrench, a few twists, nothing secure.

All the pipes will soon start to shake, like his small legs in the cold water surrounding his home. The way he was shaking and shaking, holding his brother, through the water on a frosted early morning, when all was still dark, right before the rooster called. The gun he left behind. He didn't need it anymore. He would get him safely to his mother. He feared her face. His brother was too heavy. Wading through the oblique wall of water, the dank smell of sour mud and his brother's hair in his nose. Out of the water, the sharp air hit him, slicing as brutal as metal. He couldn't bear this, but he did. He walked only a bit, before they were there. They came swift and bruising, like heavy shadows. They left his brother on the side of the road, face down, his only brother, who he shared a bed with all his life (a small bed at that, with a faded red plaid comforter and two pillows, the blue one being his. It was jammed against a wall, a dusty soccer ball underneath). Jedra was thrown in a truck. His legs shook and shook. Like the brass pipes tremble within the quaking heft of the heavy metallic water. The pressure will climb. It will all blow.

Upstairs, he stands at reception.

Phyllis at once addresses him, her wet lip-glossed mouth skillfully avoiding, by a twist of the chin, her permanent headset. Oh, Jedra?

Yes, Mum.

Leaks again, uh, room 642, and 3, 3—

—320, reminds Denise, with obvious irritation.

—Yes, 320. *Sorry*.

Jedra wants to sharply admonish Denise for her rudeness, but fingers his wrench instead. He does not understand anybody, much less himself. Perhaps Denise has lost a brother. Who knows. Perhaps she discovered this morning that she has cancer. It is possible.

Ok, Jedra?

But still, Phyllis is kind and not deserving of such. At Christmas, she was the only one, the only person in this entire world who gave Jedra a gift—such as this small teddy bear holding hard candy—that he has treasured beyond the seven natural wonders of the world. In his box apartment on Swann Street, a study in beige and soot, the teddy bear is by his mattress always. He will not eat the candy. He slept with the bear once but feared it would become dirty, so he wakens sometimes and looks at it. Dusts it with his small embroidered handkerchief. He does not want to sully such a thing with dust or greed. Noone has given him a gift in many years. His mother was the last. Her last gifts to him before he was captured in the murky water were some socks and a book of Rumi's poetry, leather-bound in red, on Ramadan. He remembers her sweet, creased face coming closer to kiss his cheek, the lentil soup steaming up in his nose, the cheese on the table at the break of the fast. Lanterns glittering at the dark door-way of their cement house greeting the year. Do not think of this, he tells himself. Josh Groban is singing the Falling again. He must go to the leaks. Tears starting.

I am a breaking man! I am a brass pipe!

Jedra clutches his own bony shoulders.

His first stop is room 642, where a man in an immaculate suit lies on his bed, remote in hand, his soft naked feet appearing almost obscene entwined on the bed. Where are his slippers, his socks, thinks Jedra. The man is clean-shaven, highly groomed, he nods at Jedra, points to the bath-room with a simple hand flick, watches CNN. Jedra knows he is Iranian, from his clothes, and he is vaguely irritated. The man thinks *dirty Arab*, in Farsi, to himself. Deep within is his trained resentment of *these invaders, these bandaris*. He has cousins who were killed in the war with Iraq in the eighties.

The wallpaper of flowers in baskets has a tan cauliflower-patterned stain reaching around the showerhead, like blood from a burst capillary. Jedra cranks the skinny pipe a few times and the pipe actually talks, a *conk-conk* he has come to recognize as additional pressure. His job done, he leaves, *thank you so kindly*, says the clean man and Jedra leaves the room in a wale of sharp limey perfume from the man, lingering in the hall.

Why are some chosen for suffering and others not, thinks Jedra. Why am I in this land of shininess if I am the dull one? Why am I the starving mouth amidst the feast?

That man is loved by a woman, he is sure. All the men he sees are, and he is left out in the cold. Who cares what woman, a soft one, who loves him, who cares for him, so that he is not the scrappy goat scaling the hill-side, but the muscled lion lounging under the shade of the tree.

On the third floor, he enters a room strewn with toys and his feet step on some unintentionally, they squeak and snap. He picks up a clown, it's head pops up and Jedra does it over and over, laughing. Suddenly his eyes refocus in the distance and the bathroom door opens, a pregnant woman gasps.

—I am sorry, I fix the leak—

What are you doing.

I, I, he drops the clown. I am sorry.

She looks at him, looks down. Okay.

The leak, mum.

It's in the bathroom. In there.

Another singeing pipe, cavorting with pressure. He adjusts the mirror, to avoid his face.

Lately the lines have appeared too severe and scary. He is a skull. The bathroom is soft with her things, powder. He smells it. He hears the TV on. He must go. The powder lingers on his nose. His mother powdered her large, heavy breasts. She was a large woman, who smelled of lilacs and lamb stew. Her name was Zainah. His father was Abdul-Massud. They drank tea in a small table by the kitchen without words in the afternoons. The radio wailed with the singing of Om Khaloum. There was tea, there were cookies from an English tin, there was his mother's soup made of chicken and lentils, swirled with greens. His father's brown skinned feet, white from dry skin on the back, in his black creased slippers. He hears their names as well as their voices. He smells his mother in this room. He falls against the sink. He is dizzy. He wishes for his mother with all his body and he is ashamed to feel this.

Is everything OK, says the pregnant woman.

Yes, I am finishing fix this, he says to the closed door.

His voice is a hollow bleat, trapped in a wind tunnel.

As he leaves, more Josh Groban in the halls again. He knows the name of this singer because he heard Phyllis once say, *God, I just love Josh Groban*, while this song played and then he went after work to Coconuts and purchased the CD. But he hated it because it made him cry. Lately, it seemed he cried alot. What was happening to him. His eyes burn slightly. He must go to the boiler room. He walks briskly, the wrench swinging, the denim bag around his shoulder, passing the new young blond maid, to the elevator.

On this day of which we speak Phyllis does enter the burgundy velvet elevator as Josh sings about falling and Jedra Abdullah is there with his tools, the wrench en route to the boiler room and yes, he is crying. He looks down. She does not notice. They hear the *ding ding* of the elevator. Going to room 642, she says casually. Yes, mum, he says. That is where I am going. But when he looks up she looks scared to see his eyes are wet and she looks alarmed and he does the feeble, cracked smile of the crazy person.

It is at this moment the elevator decided to die and not work and come to a quick jump-stop. What is wrong she said, meaning everything, his tears, the elevators, all reasons for living. I am not sure, he said, meaning the elevator, his deep angst, his sadness, all reasons for living. He pushes buttons, repeatedly. Phyllis turns white and lands against the wall, and her eye whites surround the blue gaze. *You fix things you can fix things fix it fix it fix it, Jedra* and then she lets out a weird gush of wind and sits on her high heels oh, *I'm not feeling well.*

Mum, I am sorry, says Jedra. It will be Ok.

How do you know, I happen to be freaked out of tight spaces, OK, so, so give me some air.

Her nails flicked in the air, the plastic sound of petals.

Ohhh, God. She held her face. Josh Groban sung again of falling. It was repeating.

I am fond of this Josh Groban, are you, Miss?

She stopped whining and looked up. Can you *fix* the fucking *thing?*

He was shamed by her language. She saw his eyes, black as water in a canal.

I'm sorry, Jedra. Do, do you think you can fiddle with the, the, the controls—

I do not think this is the problem. I think it is shaft applicator because Montague said it needed to replacing it but Montague is not fixing on this day and this is the problem—

—I will *die*! She interrupted.

You will not die.

I will, you don't understand, and then she made a machine sound and he grabbed very quickly her arm and held her. Careful, please.

She looked up, grateful to be contained. She could smell Jedra Abdullah, he smelled like a dark spice she put in chili. It came in a small plastic pouch. She opened it with scissors.

He looked at her and gave her the crackled and heated smile of the adoring mother whose child is silly and yet very loved. And she felt that smile and looked down and closed her eyes to enjoy this tiny flash of warmth, in a secretive way, as if it were a form of emotional masturbation, because she had always pitied Jedra Abdullah or anyone who had to enter, repeatedly, the steamy, metallic boiler room, of rotten vegetable vapors and dark fumes of oil.

His small arm, brown and tendony, still gripped her hard. He saw a small tremble in her chin. He was too close to her, way beyond the conventional space standards he had respected in the outside world, but they had suddenly jumped into a closer, more dangerous space.

I am scared of being. Trapped. In places, sometimes. It's hard to explain.

Only the vague buzzing of the various machines of the hotel sounded in the space.

I can understand what you talk of, he said and she could fully see the deep black of his small eyes.

Jedra.

Yes, mum.

She wiped her eyes, her voice catching.

Can you get us out?

If it is the applicator, no. It is central. We must wait.

The smell of his sweat cracked through in gushes. It was brutal, animal. It comforted her.

He could see flaws. A tiny pimple on her forehead. Large pores on her chin. A feminine sharpness, like sour fruit came from her. Some deep fear. He held her hand.

We will get out, he said.

She was feeling dizzy and panic was rising. Her life had started an extreme curve suddenly to a different road. A man had just left her two days ago, dragging his suitcases in the dusty hall outside the apartment, leaving scratches. He had left things, shaving cream, beers in the fridge, vague thoughts and dreams he left as well, like the summer and the winter, and the very private air they shared, the naked hours, the confessions, the tears, his saliva he had spread on her body, his sweat which poured on her, his tears on her hands, the salt of his body drying on her, his breath on her hair.

She was a girl of shiny surfaces and baby powder dusted on her long body, a girl of sparkling lip gloss of clear peach, peach pantyhose, peach lace polyester bras, peach sorbet scented shaving gel, a peach, mind you, but even a peach has depth, sourness, pits, skin that feels too rough and grainy, furry, rotten patches, bruises. Everyone and everything have bruises, don't they?

Jedra Abdullah wondered of this, he who had noone.

I have noone, he said quietly as Josh sung of falling away from shame. Noone. First, you have the mother and you are happy. Then you grow and. Then, maybe someone comes. But sometimes no. So in this case, no. No. I have noone.

Neither do I, she said quietly, looking at his teary eyes.

The Peach had noone.

Where are you from, said the Peach.

Me? He looked up, fingering the wrench. I am from Iraq.

Oh.

Yes, he said breathing a sharp lozenge of air. Yes.

There's a lot of fighting there.

Yes.

Did you see, do, a lot of that, the fighting?

In uprising. In the south, you know.

I think so.

I am from island in Iraq. We eat fish.

I am from a town called Watchville. We eat, salads, usually.

In the camp, I was there, five years.

He looked at her with raisin eyes, eyes boiled in the juice of anguish, eyes so tired.

I am thirty-four.

He appeared one hundred years old. She appeared to be fours years old, her legs stretched out in front, peach-pantyhosed, not appearing to hers, they seemed odd in their sheer bareness.

What did you do in a camp.

In a camp? Just, staying there.

But like everyday. What did you actually, *do?*

Not much. Some days, most times, I study things, philosophy, science, ideas. Sometimes we talk, like about some subject: hope, truth, what it is, you know. Sometimes, always, there are sandstorms. The sky the floor everything the same color, just a brown. You can see nothing. Talk about Logic science, study English. Daytime, boiling hot. No air anywhere. Sometime, the air full of sand and you can't breath. Then, the temperature in the night, drop down, too cold. You are freezing cold. I was dead, down, sad. Bad memories was there. The sky is the color, one color, little bit light brown. You feel your head is gonna blow. You have no power. I play soccer. She looked up, her eyes were full of him.

Then, one day, it get over. And I come here. If I go there, I become killed.

Is it all about courage, as he says in that song? She said, is courage the key?

No. I think I have this, courage, he said.

How do you know?

I do not know.

She reached up and brushed his cheek.

You are Ok now, Jedra.

Jedra's face constricted like the shrink-wrap around a very tight gift package, like the ones which deliverymen often paraded through the hotel for important guests, his features tightened and frozen caught between a grimace and a scream. Only his small brown eyes, wet and light, moved as he looked at her. One less ounce of control, Jedra was sure, and he would be a lost man, a swirl of watery tears on the floor and his mind would leave his body in a fit of shrieks of agony. He pulled his eyes away from her kindness, and looked at the floor. She had touched his cheek. He found it extremely difficult to breathe. His hands were shaking. He battled with his quivering chin. A strange sucked breath broke out of his mouth, sounding desperate and bovine at the same time.

Phyllis heard the sound and said, are you OK?

I am very ashame, he said.

No, no, you have had a real hard time, what you went through, such a hard time.

Yes. I thank you. Jedra sat back. He felt himself coming back in waves of calm. He held his wrench again. He wanted to kiss Phyllis terribly, he had always wanted to kiss Phyllis, to touch her hair, to touch her body. He had thought of it many, many times.

He looked up at her through his lashes. She was staring at the ground.

I know how you feel, Jedra. Tim, my boyfriend, the one who comes sometimes, he, he said *to me*, on the phone, that there, there were *some issues*, some issues he needed to deal with about us, thing is, thing is, we've been doing this for two years and now I just feel like, you know. What's the use? What's the use? Because Denise is already mad at me, says I'm taking over her job and now that it's over with Tim, what else do I do now with myself. I can't stay at home, my mom's crazy. So I decided just today, Jedra. I'm going away.

Away? Where?

Anywhere. Just to go. Maybe Lake Placid. Or the mountains. Or an island.

But why not stay.

Ohh, Jedra. She brushed her hair back. It's not that simple.

When this man doesn't want you, you must go on. No need to run.

Jedra—

—Let rest for a bit. He is a foolish man—

I'm pregnant, though.

There was silence, the Josh Groban. The wrench. Peach legs.

Baby?

Yup.

I think I'm going to keep this baby. It's all mine.

Her eyes had courage. They were open as wide as they could be. She had life in them.

Jedra Abdullah wanted the good things: We all want the good. The sky as pure as the breath of a child. When people greet, they smile with kindness and kiss. When you speak, someone hears you and nods. When you hold a hand, the warmth is sweet. When a fire is lit, there is laughter swallowed by the black night. May all the ice of the world be melted in that fire.

Maybe the hotel will explode right now. He will grab Phyllis and they will be protected in the elevator. It will be fate. They will hear the water crash with force outside the elevator, and people swept along, screaming with their mouths full of water. *Craqck, crack, crakc!* All will pop and sink in the vast waves. The pipes flailing and snapped in the wet walls. This small room will keep them safe and, once again, Jedra will survive. He will sit up, and look around at what is torn.

The moment of courage is simple and direct. The heart is beating, the knees are quaking, but one reaches for it all the same. Like scrambling out the window at four a.m. with burlap wrapped around your legs to make less noise as you crawl. Bread wrapped in a roll stuffed in your pants. The water around your island appears dark and oddly pretty, as if beauty has no place in danger, and when you reach a boat, you are over there, and your younger brother laughs and cleans his tooth with his pinky nail, you see the same eye tooth he has flashed from that large-lipped mouth since you were very small and this is the same one who takes a bullet in his back—*craqck, crack, crakc!*—as you run in the alley of the town where you are captured and that is the end of him. The end of him. *I have noone.* So in the sandstorms of your captivity, as voices in the next room speak of logic science and philosophy and argue, suddenly you are whole and alive in another place, reaching again, despite all odds which say *never* and *foolish*, which warn of and promise you death and destruction, everything, everyone, everywhere, take notice, you must not fall in this trap again. There is no exit door. There is no safety net. We will all die. Do not enter. Do not ignore all the learnings you know. Do not break free.

This is all about love.

Jedra reached over, kisses her, his hands trembling, his eyes shut tight, the night beginning outside in a bold blue streak.

And then, in the next moment, the stiff metal doors of the elevator cracked open with a loud jolt.

Two

In his bed, hours later, when his brother, Jalil, appeared from the shadows and sat on the bed and looked at him with infinite kindness, Jedra knew he was in the world of dreams again.

Jalil sung a song, a little thing his mother would sing as she made bread in her kitchen.

How do you remember that, Jalil, he said to him as he lay down. How do you remember my mother's song. She sung that to me before you were even born.

Why do you not rise to greet me, your brother, said Jalil. I hear this song all the time.

I am afraid to, when I do, you will go and I miss you very, *a lot*. Where are you, Jalil?

Where am I, brother? I am lost in another land.

Me too. I am lost in a strange land where noone knows my name, where love doesn't exist, where all is cold, where I am a dog on the outside of the door.

I am in the dusty field.

Oh, Jalil, he said. He was crying. I am sorry. If it would've been me.

I miss you so much in this cold field.

Don't say this!

All the others, their tender faces in the dirt.

Jalil, please!

But we are happy, Zedra Abdul. And we haven't forgotten you, little bird.

Jedra couldn't speak anymore.

We shared our bed, remember?

Jedra looked up.

For years, I took the left side. I kicked you.

This made Jedra smile.

Your soccer ball was always under the bed. I had the blue pillow.

The blue pillow smelled! It smelled of your hair!

Where is that pillow now?

It is still there. In the house.

You can see it, Jalil? You can see the house? Is mother there?

I was small for so many years. When I lay on the field, I was almost your height.

Jalil.

All good things for you my brother, said Jalil. He kissed his Jedra's hand. All good things for you in the eternity. God willing. All is the will of God.

All of this was in Arabic, soft, windy Arabic.

It was then that Phyllis appeared luminous like the strangest apparition and he thought surely he was experiencing a miracle. Phyllis turned, naked toward them both and spoke also in Arabic.

She offered herself to them both. She said, her lips as red as a fresh-cut wound, I will take both of you as brothers in my flesh. It made Jedra inflamed with anger as Jalil bent to kiss, to touch her breast.

Jalil! I am first! He yelled loudly. Jalil!

He woke crumpled in his bed, damp, in the dark.

It was the same yell he had screamed the night they placed his younger brother on the dusty field.

I am first! Kill me!

They would do no such thing. His ankles were bound by telephone cord. They would not kill him. They would drag him along a road and spit in his face and lay him on wood and step on him until his skin split, yes, they would do that, but they would not let him be the first brother as his rightful duty and take his life first. So, he lay on his small mattress in the camp and talked in his mind to Jalil. At other times, he talked and argued with the other men to keep his mind busy. In the night now, there was no naked Phyllis or Jalil. The bed was empty. Outside the night was raucous, it was Saturday night. He heard revelers in the street. The clock said it was five after midnight. Tonight, after the elevator, he had come home, had cheese balls and olives. Listened to Josh Groban. He had watched TV. And he planned.

Jedra was tired of waiting. It was a new year. He wanted to find his old mother and father, bring them here. He couldn't bear to think of them suffering, him and them, in separate countries, without each other.

He lay on the pillow and sung his mother's bread song.

When the phone rang, he was already asleep.

His mother whispered in his ear, her lilac bosom crushing his face, *awake, little bird, your Mama's eyes will love you for the rest of your life, and sweeten your days like honey.*

Awake, she said.

Habibi, habibi, awake.

THREE

After the kiss, they had stood back, alarmed by the brisk crack of the door by Montague. Both were stunned by what had occurred, the kiss, which seemed the most remarkable occurrence that had ever happened in that elevator. Oh, there were other kisses in this elevator. They were:

A Mr. Frederick Ditchman, Jr. salesman with AMC cars, on conference kissed Connie Alderman, twenty-nine, an escort with Fancy and Fine Escorts, two and a half years ago. It was snowing and flakes lay on her purple wool collar of her coat, which he grasped and pulled towards him. it might be noted, Connie really was his escort. He only kissed her three times. She accompanied him to dinner (lobster, broccoli) and then lay down next to him as he fell asleep.

A woman, name of Mathilde Fracausse, kissed her child Matthau, on the cheek and called him *tres, tres bon* en route to the Washington Monument. Mathilde was to meet her husband, Jean-Pierre, there at three.

Mr. Claus Friedmann, kissed his wife daintily on the cheek, *Oh, Claus,* she said, smiling, *my*
powder. They were going to meet Dr. Kazan at Georgetown University Hospital regarding his (recurrent) colon cancer.

But this kiss, rendered with such immediate need, representing such a crashing breakthrough for Jedra, such daring, stood out. It warranted no slap or anger—it was pure. Even Phyllis could feel the utter pureness and sweetness coming through his kiss. And it moved her. She broke away at the flash of the door, got up, brushed off her skirt, said nothing. She looked down. To Jedra, it appeared he had done the unspeakable, he had sullied her. He felt beyond ashamed, almost as low as trash. He wanted to clean everything, scrub, do something. He could say nothing, She walked away. She had a child in her stomach, no less. Another man's child growing inside her and he had kissed her rudely.

Going by her desk to the boiler room—yes, an extremely out-of-the-way course since he could've just stayed on the elevator and gone down—he noticed she was not there. He went up to the desk. Where is Miss Phyllis, please?

Oh, said Denise, she had to go home. She wasn't feeling well.

Maybe, because of me, thought Jedra, she will lose her child. He felt terribly scared. He went to the boiler room and sat on the orange crate and thought. He would do something. He had all the employees number and addresses. He would send her flowers. What if she had roommates or the boyfriend was there? Would it seem strange to them. Perhaps. But she is a grown woman. It would merely say, Kind regards from Mr. Jedra. No, scratch that.

Going upstairs, the Hotel was being decorated for spring. Perhaps it could just say Happy New Year. That seemed appropriate, yet she did not celebrate the middle-eastern new year. Jedra walked briskly out of the building to the corner and took a bus, number 32, to his neighborhood. He didn't clock out. He stopped two blocks ahead of his apartment, on 16th Street, at a small Korean market. A Mrs. Park worked there, she knew Jedra. Her hair was thinning on top of her head, the fine wisps of a toddler covering her shiny skull. But her eyes were sparkly and pretty, deep-set and black against her opaque skin.

Mr. Jedra, hello, hello.

She was eating a deep red pot of noodles.

Excuse me, Mr. Jedra.

Do you have—he was out of breath and stopped, frowning with his exertion—some roses, please? White ones.

Yes. I got good ones back here. She shuffled over in her strange puffy boots. These good. There was one small vase of white rose, crumpled together in the case. The rest were red, but red was not good. Too showy.

I will take this one, please.

Mr. Jedra has sweetheart?

No. No, he said, appearing dismayed so she looked down, OK, only five ninety nine, please, Mr. Jedra.

Then he took the flowers home. Jedra was full of love. This was the problem he thought, I am full of love and nowhere to put it. My mother and father are not here. My brother is dead and I caused it. I love Phyllis and she is with the child of another man. I have noone.

Once again, Jedra sat on his mattress alone. There were two choices that lay ahead: he could go back to Iraq and find his mother and father and risk being killed. Or, he could kill himself. He had thought of this many times. It seemed the logical conclusion and yet even in this existence of sadness, Jedra kept hoping for more. He wanted to love something, someone. In all the bones of his little body, he longed for this. As he fell asleep on the mattress, a third option opened up to him, one that hadn't even possibly been considered:

As he just briefly slept, the flowers unsent by the bed because he was too timid, his eyes fluttering backwards, his dreams on the hilly island where he grew up, his phone rang and rang. Noone ever called him. He got up, still in his work clothes, terrified, picked up the phone.

Someone was dead. He was being fired. Police wanted him.

Hello Mr. Jedra, said Phyllis, to Jedra Abdullah. It is me, Phyllis.

Of course, Jedra heard the voice and knew it was her. But he did not believe it. He lay back in shock and looked at his cracked plaster ceiling.

Phyllis? Phyllis? He said over and over, as she giggled. *Phyllis? It is you, Phyllis?*

FOUR

Phyllis called him. There were awkward silences on the phone, where he could hear his heart pounding loudly through his chest and his breath brushed rapidly against the mouthpiece. He sounded like he been running for miles. He could feel sweat dripping down the side of his chest. He hesitated, then asked her to coffee. She didn't respond. He swallowed several times.

I am good cooker, he said. Very good cooker. Can you come for here to dinner? said Jedra.

To his great surprise, she said yes. That she would like this so much.

Jedra found even the water in shower felt deliriously sensual, his body felt different, his head spun. He sung. He danced. He relived the elevator scene, once again. How many times had the elevator scene replayed as a misty, rosy snapshot? Countless times, softly, intensely, with more passion, with more tenderness, with the culmination of her naked body in his arms, with endings of his eternal love, with tears. Always with tears.

Phyllis thought of it too, while she lay at home for four days in her bed of a thousand pillows, stuffed animals, embroidered puffs. She came home early that day because her stomach hurt. In the bathroom of the hotel, mirrory granite and limestone, her pregnancy dissolved away as she discovered bloody clumps falling from her. They fell silkily in the water, like beet-colored jellyfish bobbing gently down in the darkened water, and she searched for some sign of a child. More blood poured out, for days and she lay in her bed and watched TV, and drank tea. She cried for the child she didn't know, more than anything she cried for losing the specifics of Tim, the way he frowned when talking intimately, they way he sweat on her arms when she held him in bed, the flavor of who they were together would be gone forever, the package they created as they merged their tastes and ideas and proclivities (they like to make love on the couch, for example, not the bed, they loved to rent action movies and eat coffee ice cream, they liked to wear socks in the house). And she didn't even love him. But she mourned him all the same. The child, the man. They had been in her body and now they gone. Grayer and grayer became her eyes, her voice. The Peach wallowed. All the hormonal cocktail of the child came haltingly null, and she felt it, anxiety, loss and emptiness, more than anything, a minute cellular loss but a huge one, huger than anything one could ever expect. A frisson of life inside suddenly extinguished. Death, just a powdery whisper, but so evident and cold. She wore pads and every-day they grew fainter, pinker and the child left completely and went some-where. Where? Would she ever see it, on some celestial plane? Were we lost forever to each other? She rocked in the pillow and felt all this. She thought of acts of kindness, tenderness. She wanted to feel love. She thought of Jedra and the strange occurrence:

Phyllis kissed Jedra Abdul, to her surprise. The softness of his mouth completely surprised her. He caressed her cheek, touched her lips. There was no tongue. He looked in here eyes, blackened wet and tender, they looked into her and she was overcome. She pulled back sharply.

—I am very sorry. He looked terrified.

Jedra, she said.

She looked at him again.

They did it again. He grabbed her so hard she could feel the bones of his body like nubby rocks in a sack. Such power was in this small man, such intensity, Phyllis fell against the stainless steel wall.

The doors flew open, and Montague, the parking attendant whose sheer strength was sometimes needed for big jobs, stood there.

Ok. Ok. His eyes flicked around trying not to take in the scene, but he was shocked by what he saw. That little Jedra.

They sat up.

We thought you'd never come, she said. She was sad, nauseous from the baby, so tired. Montague kept flicking the doors, switching keys.

Got jammed up on fourth. Bad cylinder. You got your tools, Jedra.

Yes, sir.

He handed him the denim bag.

When you going to get a tool box, man.

Yes. Yes.

Phyllis got up to leave, awkwardly brushing off her skirt.

Uh, Mum.

Jedra,uh, thank you, for your assistance.

Then she was gone down the hall.

Phyllis was a girl who was not what she seemed. She was not really a peach, but a rough apple, hobbled about by life but her sudden soft beauty had taken her by surprise in the last few years and given her more attention than she was used to. A future was expected from her. The job at the hotel was a mere fluke. She had found it in the paper and suddenly Phyllis was a young pretty girl in reception. Before, she was going nowhere.

For a vague while, she lived in the apartment of a man named Tim, a waiter from the Cipriani Cafe, a dark studio on "S" Street, with a futon, a wall hanging of a Tiger, Sports Illustrated magazines. He pressed his cigarettes into a chipped tea saucer. He would lay with her and smell warm and slightly yeasty like cheese and then emerge from the shower artificially lime-scented. She lay more in study of him than in love with him, he was wholly unfamiliar, like a new breed she hadn't observed before. He would come to her apartment and decorate it with his odd totemic items, shaving cream, socks, condoms (which he wouldn't use). His Amaretto flavored coffee cream. He liked Diet Coke, bologna, hummus in plastic containers. These memorials lay about and she kept them out of some form of respect.

They seemed to buffer the solitariness of her choice. They proved she had been a we not just a she. This, she told herself, proved she was part of this world, was human. As she walked the streets, or lay in bed, she doubted she was the same as all of them. They did not seem to see or hear what was obviously all around on different realms. Noone heard the singing that came from the clouds at dawn, even beyond the birds.

Sometimes the sound of wings was so heavy, like cardboard knocking in a windstorm, but all around her in the street, all were unmoved. In his ordinariness, Tim moved through his life, carving a small life. As he lay naked in her bed, golden, sleeping, she felt his existence, saw his soul in it's journey from the marshland of Wales where he lay in battle. His teeth rotted, his skin pocked from plague, he left a wife and a daughter. He died at twenty-two, impaled on a rock by an English soldier, in a large muddied field, littered with other men in battle, twisted and stomped. The field was a lovely valley, speckled with mossy granite rocks. When she wanted to picnic one day, Tim said, I hate being just sitting in a field, doing nothing. It seems boring to me, and Phyllis blinked away the picture of his young Welsh face withering in the fog.

All these passings of her life and she arrived in the elevator nauseous, pregnant and being kissed by the engineer of the hotel. And now, this Tim gone, the baby he left inside her gone and she felt as empty as the hollowest paper bag, lying crumpled and discarded in an old parking lot.

Suddenly, she got out of bed and wished to call Jedra. Only one reason. There was noone else who seemed to care about her. And she wanted to be in the presence of someone who wanted her. It was an odd thing to do, a desperate thing to do. Phyllis needed to be cared for, adored.

When she heard his voice, it made her laugh, wheedly and tiny, his broken English. The very fact he would cook her a dinner softened her and made her feel teary, delicate. There was noone who had ever done this for her. How many times had she, Phyllis, steamed her face over pans of spaghetti, or fried eggs in her scuffed Teflon pan, or stabbed a steak with a fork to flip it over while Tim watched TV, and yet noone had as much as poured her a bowl of cereal. She wanted to go to Jedra's, to relax. To lie on his couch in a blanket while he cooked strange stews. To sleep and feel safe. She could tell him that she lost a child. Noone at the hotel knew.

Phyllis wore jeans, and a sweatshirt and purposely, but for what reason? She tried to look casual and plain. She thought about this. First of all, she didn't think Jedra needed anymore attraction to her. She felt he wanted her. But mostly, her womanhood went on vacation due to the death of the child. She would mourn it by her solemnity. She would forsake the heels, and the make-up (her face looked younger and soft, doughy) and the curling iron. Phyllis, all of twenty-four, had changed. She was going inward. Back to who she really was.

FIVE

Phyllis as a child had clung by the chain link fence in her dark jeans, a scrabbly reed child, a loner. She held twigs and made woven rafts and floated them in puddles, while the others gathered in pink-hued clumps and discussed boys. Phyllis was weird. She spoke to herself in small, mumbled sentences. Her mother, Francine, was called in. The mother slapped Phyllis in front of the principle and when he saw that she did not react, child services were called in. Phyllis' mother, it turned out, left Phyllis alone most days while she sold make-up at J.C. Penney. Phyllis got her own meals. She liked to open a can of Vienna sausages and eat them with ketchup. She would open a can of corned beef hash. She would cut up apples. She slept on the couch. She read voraciously. She stayed in the school library, hiding like a small colt with her wild uncombed red hair in the aisles and reading until the school closed. Then she would walk home alone through the dark streets, enter the cold house, eat cereal, lie on the couch and sleep. A fantasy life lived in her words, she would talk to herself through the school in hushed sentences, *I am magic and soon I will fly to the portal of all Dreams, and I will be the victor of the soothsayers*. Noone knew what she said by these magical phrases that came unexpectedly from her, like unleashings of some dark poetry she contained in her cerebrum. *He is the dark prince yet I am the changeling that will fulfill all the prophet's comings!*

Phyllis was crazy, was the assumption. Her mother was called in and the school psychologist and terms like psychosis and schizophrenia were bandied about and the mother grew suspicious of this small girl who she had hoped would have a normal future, unlike herself. But Phyllis grew more and more remote and lived in her dream world. She was put in a special class with a black boy who made chicken sounds and a large pale girl with no expression whose mouth hung open like a cow. Yet Phyllis knew she was in a wrong place. She was not out of touch with reality. At nights, she lay in her bed and wrote down what she saw and felt in different realms. If Phyllis had been born in the green forests of the Amazon, her cobalt eyes and frothy words would have been a sign of the curandera and she would've been revered, if Phyllis had been born in the craggy mountains of Tibet, they would've bowed down to her silvery mysticism, if she had been born by the beach of Bahia, tossing cowry shells and babbling in tongues and eating honey, they would've crowned her the offshoot of Oxun and danced in her shadow, instead, with her sensitive gifts, she was born in a gray world of systems and numbers and facts, and the heaviness of this dead world buoyed around her unknowingly. She buckled down. She soon learned that these visions gave her a marginal, unpleasant life. He mother would scold her, punish her. The teachers would appear angry by her strange words. She drew for hours and hours pictures of the beings and memories that flooded around her, and then, out of sheer desperate survival, started to talk of the things they required, of Barbies, and birthdays, and macaroni and cheese, and then dresses and make-up and boys. She became a normal girl, startlingly normal. She made friends and her old dreams and thoughts still were there but in the background. The starry dreams she saw, the realms, all faded year by year, until she stood, superficially clean and normal, in the lobby of the Royale Hotel. For these next years, she masqueraded as normally as everyone else. When ancients whispered in her ear, she would turn on the water in the bathroom loudly and drown it out. When angels brushed by her in the hotel, skimming the cool silk of her blouse, she pretended it was a gush of wind from the large lobby doors. When Tim said to her, you know, you speak some weird language in your sleep, she laughed it off, and didn't tell him it was Aramaic or Babylonian, or one of the other ancient tongues she just seemed to know. How many lifetimes had she lived, she wondered, but if she had really gone there, instead of quickly pushing this away, she would've smelled, once again, the ancient red dirt of Samarkand on the silk road, the quartz burned smell of Mesopotamia, the bloody metallic singe of a Mongolian warrior fresh from battle, the amber incense of Egypt, the sandalwood and acrid sweat of an sloe-eyed golden robed king who held her in his arms, she then a dancing virgin of fifteen.

Instead, she talked of silly diets and clothing she had bought, magazines read, restaurants which had caught her fancy, what to do on Saturday night, all the normal chitchat Denise and others parlayed about at the hotel. When she was with Tim, it was easier. She could sink into his mundanity and absorb it. She could cook chili while he watched football, and hum away any strange thoughts. It worked for awhile.

But when the child entered her body, this tiny body with an ancient soul, she felt in burning clarity the sense of its essence and it all came back, all the jabbering and images she had tried for years to tell people to their unlistening, confused faces, all the memories of before she was born she thought they must know, too, but this she learned was called craziness to know these things, who could know of different worlds besides this one? What was there beside this world than what we saw, what was there beside this country than what we had? Nobody believed.

The tiny voice of the child, the moment it was conceived was silvery and familiar, an angelic being she had already known. It spoke in Aramaic, it spoke in Farsi, it spoke in Pidgin English. She knew all the tongues:

Since she was born, she could remember heaven.

That was the problem. It was not an odd place. It was familiar and comfortable. She assumed everyone knew the same. When she said to her mother, at a young age, remember the lilies of Lebanon! And her mother stood back, spatula in hand as she fried bacon, I beg your pardon?

A golden haired Phyllis stood in her pink ribbed nightgown and said, *Thy teeth are as a flock of sheep which go up from the washing, whereof every one beareth twins and there is not one barren among them...*

Her mother threw down the spatula. *Honey! Stop being so, so weird all the time.* And she ran and hugged Phyllis, her tiny body to her chest and she worried about her girl.

Phyllis learned to not talk of this other world she had seen in some other realm. It occurred to her finally, when Tim left her, that it was heaven.

She saw seven feet creatures with skin as pale as columbine and veins clearly marked like wisterian rivers through their skin, and huge wings from their backs, etched and lined with small bones and pearlescent feathers. They flapped with a velveteen powdery hush when they flew. She lay in the arms of one such being, an *Angel it seemed*, who called himself Ismael, the Ancient who held her and they flew in layers of rain. She remembered the softness of his arms and his thoughts. She has not felt love like this, it is beyond love, it is regard, true and true. His brow was delicate and his eyes radiated a regal bearing and she lay there and saw the lights of the world below. Where are we going, my love, she said, and she was a child and an adult and all ages. The air feathered around them soft and blue in the darkness, and he let her go and she fell and flew among the clouds and then she was in a dark space, tight and boxed in, and she knew it had begun, the sea of tears and joy. The water in the box was salty and she was contained. And she fell asleep and those days were over, what begun later was a harsher world of strained lights and shouts and smiles and tears. Kisses, and frantic scratching. Love, as sharp as claws. The softness of heaven is hard to describe to we who only remember the arch panic and smack of this world. Both are beautiful. One is the beauty of shadows, the other like the shock and interest of blood.

In Heaven, it wasn't white, it was more shimmer, more shell. Sounds were the tiny voices pinging and she can remember the words, *I am the rose of Sharon and the lily of the valleys*, and the smell of burning Myrrh and the taste of figs and the shudder of an orgasm and smell of the skin of your beloved. Heaven is like the arms of the one you love, with his sweat and salt and love around you, and this Phyllis knew. And she knew, she could feel the essence of this all around her and she wondered why everyone else had forgotten.

She walked down the dusty streets of the city and felt the warm air and knew all was beginning. A child had left her body. The sky above she had fallen from. Was she herself an Angel, I ask you? All above and around her in the etheric field floated and confirmed this nature. Phyllis was a goddess, a magic being, dressed in the sweatpants and T-shirt of the mortal. But we all are the Phyllis of our generation. We are all queens and kings without a country.

Her hands were shaking as she came to Jedra's apartment and rung his bell. Before he answered, she started to leave, terrified.

A spirit came around her, a dusty boy shot in the back. He stood and stared and she felt his presence. She stood back and said, who are you?

He looked at her and he was sad.

I like to play soccer.

And you are good, I bet.

I set up cans of sand in the street, and made a goal, and I am the best of the boys.

Soccer is hard.

And now I lay in the field.

Are you a friend of Jedra's?

And then he was gone, and Jedra was there. He wore sporting clothes, of polyester and he held a spatula.

I am cooking *kibbe*, he said. I am happy to see you. His face was damp. He was out of breath. She walked in. Jedra's house smelled of coriander and grease. Candles were lit.

I have made a meal of seventeen dishes, he said. Tonight you are the queen.

My beloved is mine, and I am his: he feedeth among the lilies.

Phyllis panicked and felt herself wishing to run.

THE SECOND TALE: THE BRAVE

Everything other than love for the most beautiful God
though it be sugar- eating.
What is agony of the spirit?
To advance toward death without seizing
hold of the Water of Life.

—Rumi

SIX

The man was from Iran originally or Persia as he liked to say, which suggested a world of brocaded fabrics, amber, myrrh, dark-eyed shrouded women and the smoke of burning Cedar, but he hadn't lived there since he was seventeen so he stood in a Merino wool striped pullover and said things like *buzzword* and *target recognition*, which, he was trying to explain to the blond girl who was cleaning his hotel room, was what he did.

Already, before he came in from the big conference downstairs for lunch and came to grab his extra satchel, she had learned other things: that he wore Gucci for Men but it was almost gone, a mere droplet lay pinkly in the bottle so that the woman who had given it to him was no doubt history perhaps. That he traveled often, due to the fact his travel pak in the bathroom was chock full of free hotel toiletries. That he was small, because his extra pair of shoes by the closet were tiny, much smaller than her own sneakers. And that he was hairy, the bathtub had many squiqqly hairs she had to rinse and rinse again.

He had walked in the door and found this blond girl smoothing the surface of his large queen bed, much like one might stroke a large dog. So here he was now suddenly explaining neural networking to this young

35

maid who was in a poetry workshop at the local Y, this girl named Patricia who was considering changing her name to Jazmine. He was going too far, way into mathematical theories of pixels and vectors and kernels and the images he created in her mind were of corn, and tiny fairies and darts and a guy she knew named a Vector (a weirdo), and she must've looked clear-eyed so then he said, so you follow?

Kind of, she lied, and he smiled. Anyway, that's what it's about, he said. He wanted to sit on his bed but felt that would be awkward. There was the slight nauseating tension brought on by the fact that they were a man and a woman in a bedroom and yet didn't know each other and so it reminded him, with slight distaste but also a tendril of excitement, of being with prostitutes, of which he had tried once in London when he was in school.

It was for his initiation, as he called it. He was twenty-two. Before that he had been a studious and good Baha'i, and had come late to matters of carnal interest. But walking in the fog one night, he passed the women who lined the streets and he asked not one, but two, to come to his apartment. They followed him in their thin coats of fake fur to a small basement apartment with little more than books and a small twin bed, but a few rugs, Persian of course, but cheap ones that were not of good colors or hand-knotted, and he made them tea. The Persian style, very strong and very hot. He served it in two small juice glasses, and he was embarrassed that he did not have the proper glasses his mother used, with gold swirled around the edges, and then remembered that he was serving whores, and stared out the window at the street lamp shining in a golden blur through the mist. In his mind came the word *gendeh*, but it was a terrible, ugly word for these women, full of hatred, and in English it was so much kinder, the word whore. And in his heart he felt these women were not heartless.

He then walked from the kitchen to the rug area and taught them how to place a sugar cube on the tongue and suck the tea through, and then the tea was finished and he asked them about their lives. And one of them had a child name Simon, who had Asperger's Syndrome and she had to pay quite a bit for his special education, and when this woman, who had frizzy blond hair and dark circles and a red lace bra under a plain man's T-shirt reached over and touched him through his jeans, he felt sad. She undid his zipper and there was no response from him. They both pulled off his pants and took off his clothes and he had a beautiful dark body like some kind of lean, small animal who would live in shadowy leaves. His skin was soft and smelled green. Maybe from the cologne he wore or maybe he had an herbal part of him. He lay like a child, unaroused. And they held him and kissed him and said, no worries. The other was Australian, it turned out. No worries. They kissed his forehead and he felt ashamed and lost. They left back into the mist, these two women, who felt like angels to him, but he lost something of his manhood then and he wanted to find them, track them down and show them that he could—he used a brutal, violent word—*fuck* them very well. But he knew it was a lie. Even saying the word in his head chilled him and the image of gold falling from heaven filled his mind and the word he had used before became brittle and shattered into a million doubloons which whirred and scattered in the fog around the thin ankles of these blond women walking the wet streets and what was left etched on the dark pavement was the inner world of his beating lilac heart. It was too soft, a vulnerability he hid very well in the *buzzwords* of his profession, in the hyperlogic of engineering and how things work, and he worked hard to keep it locked away in layers of metal, but sometimes it leaked through, as it always does.

I wonder if you would like to go dancing with me, he said impulsively. She looked at him and felt pity at his eyebrows that suddenly slanted downwards and trembled slightly.

I'm the cleaning girl, she said, holding a broom.

I know, but, you know, you seem nice. Anyway, I'm not proposing to you or even hitting on you (he lied), just since I am from out of town, I know noone. And think maybe I would dance tonight.

She straightened the bedspread. Dancing? What kind of dancing?

Salsa.

That's, that's some kind of Mexican dance?

Suddenly he felt deflated and foolish. She appeared to have no idea of what he meant and he actually was quite skilled at this latin dance, haven taken classes for four years, a master of *the cross body lead* and at times, when he danced with a good partner, he was fluid and sensual, a man of passion. He looked at the girl, she was very young, maybe twenty-four, a simple face, perhaps a peasant, he thought. He would do better to call in an escort, if not for the embarrassment of his colleagues seeing her in the lobby and chiding him or disrespecting him. But this girl seemed simple and friendly, unthreatening.

I can teach you, very simply—

I don't know—

—it will take a few minutes, that is all.

He put in a CD and instantly the room was filled with the latin blast of drums and horns, chanting in Spanish. He held out his hands to her.

Keep a box pattern with your feet. Like this. Back. Now, front. Back. Like this.

Exactly.

They shimmied back and forth and at first, she was stiff, but she started to swing more and enjoyed herself, her blond hair falling slightly from the rubber band, the broom laid across the bed. He was getting sweaty. She could smell his Gucci for Men. The song ended.

She stood, pulled her hands back.

That, that was fun. But I think. I think I should, should go back to work.

She gathered her hair back in the ponytail and tried not to see his eyes.

So, will you come tonight?

I. I don't think I can.

This man was well trained in the ancient art of Persian etiquette called *Ta'arouf*, which will insist three times until a person accepts, it is a well-known pattern as predictable as the reciprocal box pattern of salsa, and he would ask her one more time, though it did occur to him that she is American and does not know this pattern but never the less —

It will be fun, I promise.

I. She picked up the broom. I have a kid, a baby, A boy, you see. At home. So.

There was a long silence, cold as metal. And then she said, *so, you know.*

I see, he said, of course.

She continued to clean in silence. She tried to keep an amiable smile on her face as she did. He said, excuse me, as he went to the dresser, awkwardly wedging by her closely.

Then, he was in front of her, crushing something into her hand. It was some money, cold and papery.

Take this, it is a gift. For your child. Buy him something special—

—No, I can't—

—Please. I insist. Please.

So she said nothing and took it. And she went to the bathroom to clean and took the empty bottle of Gucci as well. And then went to room 342, next door.

And the next day the conference left. They threw away the posters in the Boiler room

downstairs and she retrieved one, bent on a corner, that said *Welcome Optical Engineers* in large letters and brought it home. Her small boy drew on the back of it with markers and made a large ship.

SEVEN

W hen he arrived home from the conference, the house smelled cold and wafted a slight pale citrine from the *khormeh sabẓi* he had made the day before he left for a woman named Carol from his office. The stew—a brackish mix of beans and meat in a sour green sauce— lay in a plastic tub and he heated it in the microwave. Outside there was an ice storm, the branches of trees randomly crackled and fell and, if you opened the outside door, which he did to feel the brisk air, the world was full of the pretty shatter of delicate crystals. It was a fragile and sweet sound, yet seemed dangerous. The man felt the poetry of such imagery, yet stood there, recognizing the limed stew smell heating up, the comfy feeling of his slippers, the solitude of his silent furniture, and all the mixed feelings they created: his mother making khormeh sabzi in her wildly patterned robe, the slippers of his family by the door, all sizes, the furniture of his parents house formal and brocade, untouched. Once again, again and again, he mourned them all of them, his sister, his brother, his mother, his father. He mourned a family. He said a small prayer in Farsi. Even though he was not Muslim, he mumbled the *Fatihah*, just to be respectful. He said, I miss you all. He missed his father's cough in the morning. The khormeh sabzi his mother made from fresh fenugreek leaves she grew outside.

He was an orphan.

The woman named Carol, from his office, had been flirting with him
for quite some time. She was a technician. She was small with dark hair,
feral eyes, a nose that was a tad too round like a daffodil bulb and very
large breasts which she kept strapped to her chest with the help of an a
powerful elastic bound harness some might call a bra, others something to
fear. These apparatuses were sold in a special shop called Weavers down-
town and cost a lot. They involved many rows of eye hooks and stiff elastic and hard polyester crepe material. She had four of them. They had
started to yellow around the edges. She looked longingly in catalogues at
the flimsy, silken and lace bras women who had pert French breasts, breasts
which sprung from their chests like new growths of some unsullied delicate mushroom, while her filled all directions, her armpits, her collarbone,
her neck with a silken mass of fatty tissue, suffocating and collapsing.

She kept the bras, the ones she wasn't wearing, on hangers. She wore
one at all times, even while sleeping. The woman was thirty four and had
made love to three men, all embarrassing situations she couldn't recall without hugely blushing, remembering the awkward slosh of her heavy flesh.

Driving in her car to meet the Persian man for dinner, Carole listened
to Josh Groban and in her mind she replayed the story she sought—*A dark
man of indeterminate birth—Mediterranean, Hispanic, Gypsy—asked her to
dance at a small cafe in an indeterminate windy seaside town (south of France,
Spain, Greece, the Abruzzi coast), pressing her large breasts against his chest,
whereupon instead of confusion, shock, dismay or unbridled lust, he is overcome
with love and adoration of her huge femininity—*

She came to the Persian man's house at his request for her attendance
at dinner. He made his mother's recipe for khormeh sabzi. She came to his
small townhouse surrounded by pert and flavorless boxwood bushes. He
was polite and kind, ushering her in to a beige living room of ornate roco-
co antiqued brass and marble furniture. Again we return to the concept of
ta'arouf, the corner stone of Persian hospitality. Mistake number one, she
did not bring flowers or a gift for this man, a shameful thing. He was
severely scornful of her empty-handedness. Two, he offered her a drink
and she did not refuse but actually seemed eager and wanted, actually

asked for, alcohol. And then she seemed to drink it thirstily. He wondered at the manners of these Americans.

She then sat primly on the edge of his brocade sofa. He offered her a nut. He noticed as usual how large her breasts were. She was an attractive woman, a slightly monkeyed face but her breasts he found lovely. It was then he led her to his table for dinner. She commented during dinner that the stew was unusually sour and what caused that. She spit it out into napkin and said, perhaps it has spoiled.

At that moment, The Persian man's hopes fell.

He was not picky about women. He thought he loved them. He did, in a way. He thought them beautiful. He liked their smell. He liked the softness of them, their hair. He wished for a wife, was the truth, a woman who loved him, who put up with his strange habits and complaints, like going to the bathroom for an hour at a time and did not complain. A woman who would have a dinner he enjoyed waiting for him. A kind face meeting him at the airport. A woman who vacuumed and kept his rugs fresh. But this seemingly slight comment somehow deflated him-it was so benign—yet sourness almost single-handedly defined the entire palate of the Persian kitchen and without a taste for that particular sour flavor, she would never be able to accommodate his Persian palate. It was quite simple. She was very nice. Very nice. But would never do. Sourness is Persian food, dried lemons, dried lemon powder. Let me explain.

Khormeh Sabzi, A Brief Tale:

It is an average night and since he is without a wife, and eats on a daily basis in the take-out kebab shop where they know him well enough to prepare his kubideh and serve it with the sabzi (parsley and greens) and the bowl of tah-dig (crispy rice pieces) for him alone, he sometimes craves a home-cooked meal. He will usually have a desire for a sour green stew called khormeh sabzi. In Iran the women clean and dry and then chop all the herbs for this in the whole day, but his time is limited and they now sell a dry mix in the Persian store. His mother, with her brown dyed hair and dark, sweet eyes, showed him her favorite brand in the dusty shop run by a woman named Mitra.

The Persian man starts by frying meat in onions. You must let the meat smell and taste go away, he would think, as his mother would say. Whatever that meant. Perhaps it means to brown very, very well until no blood lasts. Get rid of the blood. Fine. His mother taught him this. He was alone, frying this in apartments, since seventeen. This smell of khormeh sabzi lingered in every hallway that he ever inhabited. How terribly specific is the chemistry of love and homesickness, that khormeh sabzi, a sour mix of greens, meat and rice, would cause such a mixture of nausea and love in this man's stomach, a longing both of heart, and body and soul. It will bring him instantly into the kitchen of his childhood where his mother and sister would chop the massive amounts of herbs needed for the recipe.

Next, you fry in some oil chopped spinach and other chopped greens, garlic chives, fenugreek leaves, and scallions but most Iranians use the dried "sabzi mix" which you buy in a Middle eastern market. (As Carole left from his house after the date, she asked herself: *Am I meant to be with a Persian Man? I had always heard they were difficult. My friend said, they will treat you like a queen and then as soon as you are married, they change overnight into monsters. Why did he serve such sour food? Never marry a man from an "I" country, said her friend How many prejudices we all harbor against each other. I am at one time intrigued by his strange culture, at times scared. Will he expect me to give up my friends, my identity? Another friend said if you marry him you will need to buy a second refrigerator you will keep on your porch for all the stinky food you will need to cook for his huge family who will always be around. But this man's family lives in England. And he is not Muslim, so they do not wear chadors.* They are Baha'i.)

At this point, you must let the greens brown slowly in the oil. The dried ones start to come to life. They smell like tea. If later on your khormeh sabzi smells like henna, then you did not burn the herbs enough. Burning is important in Persian food, somehow they have acquired a taste for it.

Take, for example, the prime example, the ne plus ultra of Persian food, the *tah-dig*, the hard, browned pieces of rice on the bottom of the kettle. Developing this is a skill, and highly regarded. In Persian restaurants, you can buy bowls of crispy tah-dig pieces, and you will notice, all around you, people are eating them. This man then took a bag from his cabinet of small hard balls the color of walnuts, but they were smooth and when held, lighter than walnuts and emitted a husky, citrusy tinge. They were dried lemons, and he cracked some with his hand and made a rough powder and added it to the meat—and added about five of the lemons whole, and water to cover. And then the browned greens. And he let this simmer. He was excited to offer this to his date, Carole. Little did she know the entire courtship and marriage was sabotaged by her simple dislike of this dish.

Let us notice his face. He has a wonderful, unique face, a large nose, elegant dark eyes whose lids fold slightly above his lids, covering them and giving him an Asian look, a spectacularly royal gaze. And his mouth, his mouth is soft and curved, pursed, sensual, and when he smiles his teeth are perfect, white, gleaming. His jawline is slack, falling slightly with age, but it lovely still. His hair: black and speckled with an occasional squiggle of white, not gray. But most of all, observe his feet and hands: They are dark and soft and perfect. Uncreased, unworn. They are the dark, soft hands of a scientist. His feet, when he lies naked in bed, are tan against the pillow, lying casually a pink brown the shade of a young Moroccan boy's cheek, the color of dried lemons. The man is royal, he is always elegant, scented, soft, strong. He favors silk.

After Carole left, he roasted chestnuts in his toaster oven. He was not unnerved. Love was not his good fortune. It was impossible to find someone to love. He would not give up, but it was extremely difficult. He even allowed himself to entertain the fact that perhaps he had unintentionally accepted the wrath of the evil eye, *chesmeh bad*, no doubt caused by all of his work success, all the awards and fellowships and now he was cursed to be unloved.

And anyway, he is glad. He is a reserved man and dreads losing control of his emotions. He does not want to be a fool. He cannot bear to break his heart again.

Love is uncontrollable, unsatiable. There is an Arabic saying, *you cannot hide a mountain or love*. His heart is about to break.

I am sorry, but this is true life and all our hearts get broken, in the end.

The khormeh sabzi makes the house stink for weeks, the sour green smell like spring forcing it's way in every corner, will fill every crevice, corner. Under his neck, in his collar bone, his chest hair, will smell of khormeh sabzi. He will ooze his spiciness from his very cells.

The Persian palate is about sourness. You have to enjoy the bracing quality of the sour dried lime. You have to crave it.

If you don't, it is not for you.

EIGHT

That night, after Carol left, a brief time after the dinner became awkward and still, The Persian man lay on his sofa, ate the roasted chestnuts and watched the History channel and felt the sadness of his life. It was a special reenactment of how Genghis Khan invaded Persia and killed village after village, pillaging, burning, raping. Samarkand in flames. He drank tea and watched the people fleeing and screaming. Fifty thousand killed they said. How did they dispose of the bodies, did anyone survive?

He wonders this, not knowing that a pocket of his mother's family came from Samarkand, that indeed the youngest child and the uncle had survived that very massacre. The Persian man drinks the tea and eats a chickpea cookie with it. The uncle's name was Khour and the child was Roia. She had been stuffed in a closet. The uncle had been behind the mud house, peeing. He had crouched in the bushes when he heard the screams. He recognized the screams of his dear wife. He cried in the bushes and lay there for one whole night and day. He was forced to pee and shit in his own clothes, and he dared not move. When he was sure the invaders were gone, he entered the house. His family was strewn about, dead and bloody. He cradled his dead wife who lay in a ball, her back split by a large slice. Harsh sounds came from his throat and he looked for a blade—his brother-in-law kept a sharp one—to cut his wrists. It was hard to even think in the blackness of his mind, he was so torn in grief and filled with disgust.

The smell of the room was of rusted iron and old meat, and he threw up on a animal skin rug. Then, he heard something and it alarmed him. Maybe they were back. His basic survival instinct prompted him to buck up like a bear and sniff the air. He listened. A child's feeble cry leaked from upstairs. He went and found Roia in a pile of blankets, dehydrated and yellow. He picked her up and ran to his goat flock in the field. With his desperate, ragged breath, he passed the houses and streets filled with dead friends. The baby felt unnaturally light and passive, yet still mewed occasionally. Fires still burned and he had to climb mountains of fly-covered bodies, recognizing many of the faces of friends or merchants. He clawed his way through the scorched fields. He finally found what was left of his herd down by rocks in a neighbor's meadow. The baby wanted to sleep as he ran and he would beckon her awake by whistling. Some had run away, some had been killed, but a young Nanny goat, her teats almost bursting because the kids must've been stolen, came to him. He milked her into a leather bowl and fed Roia dribble by dribble and drank two bowls himself. He then returned to set about cleaning the house and others started to come out as well. They cried and wailed as they took their families to the field to burn. Some of the men had been captured and taken by Genghis Khan for their skills. Several beautiful virgins, daughter of the local tailor, had been taken as lovers for the mongols. A young girl of fifteen, whose newborn child had been stolen by the Mongols, came stumbling out of a crushed house, her face puffy with grief, her eyes permanently wide and terrified. Her wavy hair was matted with blood, mud and twigs. Her breasts had leaked two wide, wet stains on her burlap shirt and she ran to Roia, who sobbed the hungry ragged lurch of the new baby. The young girl's face was wet with tears and she reached for the baby, she screamed for the baby in guttural cries, and he gave it to her and she pulled her shirt up and attached Roia. A farmer wiped tears at this. The Uncle looked down and prayed to the god of life. This young girl, named Cedra, would lay in his bed of goatskin at night. He sucked her breasts full of milk. He took her as his wife, and she became Roia's mother and the mother of two others to come. And so from the deep hollow of butchered pain, came a sweetness and light once again. The tears were dried and the blood was saved.

And from this pairing came the family of this Persian man, from a village two hundred and fifty miles from Samarkand, his family of building contractors who built offices on the edges of Tehran and with these incomes, sent him with two suitcases to London to study engineering in the large city.

But he doesn't know all this bloody history. We are born of blood and tears and sweat and spit. We've cleaned up considerably and lie in clothes of gold and rubies but underneath we are still dirt and blood and tears.

As he sits there, he remembers the cleaning girl in room 342. In a compulsive and utterly uncharacteristic moment, The Persian Man decides to go back to the Royale tomorrow.

He wishes to see the cleaning girl.

He calls and books a room.

Arranges a flight.

Sometimes you change.

In an instant.

The Persian Man has a name. It is *Khouri Karimi*. His Uncle's brave name, Khour, has traveled down the family line. The name, Khouri, is the name of the angels one first sees when you die. They are half-naked and beautiful. The name of the baby, Roia, has been repeated, again and again, in various females in his family. It was his mother's name and it means, quite beautifully, dream.

NINE

He arrives at the hotel and finds it sparkling and green. The lobby is full of people, clean, happy people laughing, smiling and in the middle is a large bouquet of Spring flowers and branches, cascading in every direction, Roses, Lilies, branches of Sumac, Cherry blossoms—

Lilies:

My beloved is mine, and I am his: He feedeth among the lilies. Khouri learned this from the Song of Solomon, in school. To him, it the most beautiful of love poems.

Roses:

In the summer of Tehran, a young Khouri would buy saffron-and rose water ice cream to bring to his mother, lying in her bed. Her robe was silk and paisleyed. The ice cream was sweet and perfumed, and melted in crystals of frozen cream in his mouth. His friend's wife showed him how to make a pseudo version in their suburban house. She took vanilla ice cream and added saffron water and rose water and mixed it with a wooden spoon. She froze heavy cream on a sheet pan and brought it up into crystals and mixed it with the ice cream and they ate it after dinner as they all watched CNN, and watched the about the earthquake in Iran, which killed fifteen thousand people in the city of Bam.

Branches of Sumac:
While his mother was ill, his grandmother cooked the meals. He would sit at the tin table in the kitchen and eat steak kebab sprinkled with sour, dried Sumac. This he liked with a cold Coke. She liked to smell the top of his head and call him a *sweet fig*.

Cherry Blossoms:
It was early Spring in Washington, which meant it was cold but the light was becoming more golden. Driving in from National Airport, he saw the crowds of Japanese under the Cherry Blossoms, on blankets, the petals falling on their heads, children running. Smiling. Picnics.

In the lobby they are playing some beautiful music which he enjoys. A man singing, asking permission to fall. He enjoys this concept. At reception, a pretty woman takes his name. He asks if he will have the room 342, which he requested. She says, of course, it is ready for you. The woman, whose name he notices is *Phyllis*, smiles at him sweetly. He can tell she is a nice person. Khouri has always felt he can read the soul of a person in their smile and eyes. Hers, he feels is kind and hurt, and there is a touch of artifice in this environment.

In the elevator, he notices an odd Arab man, clutching a wrench. All of prejudices ooze out at that moment. He remembers his grandmother's sharp voice, *crazy Arabs*! The two men eye each other, aware that they hail from the same part of the world, yet speak different languages. Jedra Abdullah knows this man is Persian. He can tell from his clothes, his jewelry, his shoes, and the shape of eyes. He has the slight essence of the Mongols in his eyes in the slight curve of the lid and the heavy skin of the lids. Khouri guesses this man is Iraqi, since many of them live in Iran. For eight years in the eighties, these two men's countries fought each other. They are enemies.

Jedra coughs. Khouri shifts his feet.

The elevator opens and there, standing with her little bucket and her cart of soaps, shampoos and shower caps, is the blonde young girl. She looks up, recognizes him as he comes out.

Oh, she says, hello again.

Well. Hello.

Is there a conference again?

No, I had to. Visit a friend, in town.

Oh. well, I guess I'll see you around! She goes toward the service elevator.

Jedra had in the meantime disappeared behind the closing doors.

Wait, says Khouri.

She stops.

How, how is your child?

Good. (She frowns slightly).

How old is the child?

He's. He's seven.

(My goodness, she must've had the child early).

Would you possibly allow me. He comes up to her, smiling weakly. To maybe take you and your kid to dinner? Anywhere you like.

She doesn't say anything. She looks down at the cart's wheels.

Well, I guess so. (She wonders if he is weird). Sure.

Well, then, may I pick you up.

No, we can meet you at the restaurant. Which restaurant do you want?

Khouri thought. He wanted to make sure it was a good one.

In his collective unconscious, was Khouri reenacting the spirit of Khour, his ancient ancestor, who saw the young mother who had lost her child and saved her and bedded her and married her? Did the young girl, remind him of her, her hair caught with twigs and blood and mud? It was obvious she was lost, this girl with the cart. Her shoes were old and worn and she had had a child at a very young age and her hair was caught in a real rubber band, the kind used for mail. He wanted to take out the rubber band gently, wash her hair in resin and myrrh, and let it dry in the warm wind of summer. Then he would braid it many times and spiral it atop her head, like the empress she should resemble. Then, they would lie under the cherry trees and let the blossoms fall all around, as he had seen driving to her in his taxi. It was a beautiful site what he saw: two young lovers under a tree, the spiraling pink petals whirling all around them, like soft snow. It made him ache to love someone. He was made to love someone.

She laughed.

He smiled.

How about Moroccan food? Do you like Moroccan?

I don't care, she said. She had never had it, more truthfully.

She had never really done anything.

TEN

His mother was dead. She had died three years ago due to a heart attack.
One day driving in the car, in California where she lived with her oldest
daughter, she had fallen over on her chest while talking about the next
door neighbor, a woman named Agnes Redfield, whose dog annoyed her
and ate her Delphiniums. She was speaking without rancor, or emotion her
daughter later recalled, simply stating that she had had it with her. And
then her head fell forward softly. Meryem pulled the car over and her other
fell onto the dashboard and Meryem screamed and dialed her husband with
shaking hands.

As the ambulance and her husband's shiny black Mercedes both simul-
taneously screeched into the side of the road, she sat on the passenger side,
cradling her mother's yellowing face, tears in a slick wet line down her
face. California was relentlessly sunny and bright and the persistent cheer
of the surroundings pained her heart and she studied her mother's old face,
a line for every occurrence in her long life—marriage at seventeen to her
husband Hamid, the birth of three children, all the deaths she had heard of
or mourned, all the pain her heart must've felt—she lost a child when she
was twelve to a strange fever— all the life she had seen and felt, her moth-

er's face now a crumpled washrag of flesh, all the pulsing mystery gone. All the snap of blood, the blossoming stream hindered and fled. Her husband lifted the body from her arms.

Then, in a freak accident two years later the same sister and husband were hit on route one by a drunk driver and the black Mercedes fell over the rocky cliff, spun and flipped several times and left them dead and mangled on the shore of the ocean. Khouri got a teary message from a good friend of the family and then he lay in his bed for three days. His sheets are trimmed in lace. He cried and stared at the ceiling. Masturbation was useless. Food tasted like paper in his mouth the futile time he tried to eat a bite. And he spit it into the sink. He lost ten pounds and his face became a hollow expanse of lurching bones. He barely recalls the airplane ride or arranging the double funeral.

He was an orphan: his father had died years back. His young sister, from the strange fever in Iran. Now his sister and her husband and his mother three years ago. Can anyone truly understand the feeling of the orphan?

You are above the world on a tightwire, bending foot in front of foot on the thin line, while the audience watches. You hear the roar of the crowd, in the corner of your eyes you can see the blur of their shapes, heads, bodies. You are aware of them but you are not one of them. You could fall at any moment but who is there to catch you, but the net? Not one of them will run to catch you.

You are sick at your house. You lie in your bed and get up shakingly to visit the doctor. Who drives you there? Who picks you up from surgery? Who meets you at the airport? Who gives you money when times are desperate? Who chides you for foolish behavior or reminds you of tendencies you've had since you were a child, playing soccer in the dust outside, a goal created from tin cans of sand, when you won't come in for dinner? Who reminds you how you never eat on time and have a tendency to become angry from low blood sugar but your mother, but your dead mother who now speaks to Khouri in her old husky voice as he grooms himself shakingly in the steamy bathroom of the hotel.

Eat, Khouri. You haven't eaten for hours.

Maman, I am going out for dinner.

With that girl?

Maman.

Are you sure she is good for you?

I don't know. It is not your business.

Don't be rude to your mother.

Maman, I am lonely. I have noone anymore. I want someone who will love me the way you do, father did, Meryem did.

Why do you not eat properly. At least, there is food in the mini cooler in the other room. At least, eat a few nibbles from there. There is yogurt.

Maybe so. Maybe so.

In his towel he goes in, finds the cherry yogurt and eats it while watching CNN.

From the window, more cherry trees are evident in the Hotel's lovely garden, their boughs brimming with pink petals, the breeze catching a few and tossing them this way and that.

Maman.

Yes, my son, my son who I love.

Life is so beautiful, isn't it.

It is.

When he walked into the restaurant, the young girl waved shyly, her blond hair atop her head, her lips shiny, and her small child, his hair in blond ringlets said *who's that, Mommy* and she half stood and then sat down on the pillow and the strap of her sun dress slipped for a second on her strong shoulder. She was beautiful. He was happy again, Khouri Karimi. At this moment, aside from the life he lived which felt frozen, he was in one of the warm moments, living one of the golden times, that one that memory pulls out and relives, the snippet of time standing still, the essential being, the now, the fiery sizzle of life and joy. A yellowed snapshot it would become shortly, drawn again and again as music played— Josh Groban and his falling—to relive, rethink, refeel, the brocade of the Moroccan pillows, the smell of cinnamon, the amber of the candles they

burned, the curve of her still rounded by youth cheek, the child's impetu-
ous bounce, the souk music, the waiter's black-eyed grin of greeting, the
tightness of her eyelet sun dress, the strap coming down, all of it too sweet
to truly experience in that very moment, it raced by
staccato and sanguine and fled like paint in water and each sense fled by on
their own circuit, the blurred lights of the city as the car races by, but when
it was too late, when all had faded and life had became gray once more, and
the heart sobbed, it would live again. Life as a painting. The angst of loss.

To Khouri, everything, everything is loss.

ELEVEN

Friends had set him up with various women in professional fields. He had envisioned a marriage with an attractive, educated woman, a woman who could teach him things, who knew history, who wouldn't watch soap operas on TV and answer dully when he explained simple concepts like the binary code or algorithms. He envisioned a woman who cleaned and folded clothes, wiped counters as he sat standing over them dropping crumbs. He envisioned a smart, clean look, silk scarves, well-manicured nails. Fresh make-up, glossy and lined. Hair highlighted, sculpted, sprayed. He envisioned a woman, soft and naked, lying in silk, smelling sweet and intoxicating, calling his name. He saw dark hair spread against his pillow, bathrobed in the morning bringing him tea. Singing in the shower. He saw a woman in his kitchen, stirring khormeh sabzi, he saw her bejeweled wrists flipping out of a pan the hard-crusted dome of golden Persian rice—the crusted, prized bottom called tah-dig—which any Persian wife knew to make. Maybe occasionally she would dance salsa with him, his weekend hobby. She would wear a flowered dress and he would swing her in circles on the floor, her dark hair shaking. Or perhaps he would let that go and stay home and live a quiet life. They would drink tea. He would read his papers in the evening while she cleaned the kitchen, the soft clanking of dishes while he read through his computations and dissolution's of algo-rithmic neural networks. His wife needn't know anything of these figures, this inner world of his. His daily life consisted of algorithms, of figures and codes written neatly in the countless papers he devised concerning the main theme of his working life: <u>Target Recognition</u>

This was essentially his life work, he was an electrical engineer for a firm contracted by the Army and he worked in a laboratory devising new ways to detect tanks or military bases. A satellite picture, a blurry code of infrared presented an unclear scene and it was his job—along with a team of others in a large white space of a lab full of computers and blandly dressed coworkers—to find methods to clarify the position of the target. One had to move and redetermine the vectors of space. One had to go into the square, blurry world of pixels and redefine vision. One had to think carefully how the human eye worked and try to replicate this.

In the meantime, Khouri tried hard to repress how the human heart recognizes it's target. Think of this: Khouri worked with neural networks, taught about neural networks, thought of them, yet was clueless to how they maneuvered his world. These neural networks were mathematical symbols, carefully scripted, to mimic the pattern working of the mind, and in his own brain—although he thought otherwise, he felt himself logical and systematic and fairly emotionless when it came to deciphering this world of love—yet his neural networks fell into a pattern of blinking obsession when it came to this hotel maid. There was no logic here, she was not educated, she didn't possess what he had thought of earlier as suit-able wifely attributes. No doubt khormeh sabzi to her would be repugnant, she had a child, yet he felt all the stimulation occurring, the limbic brain was cracking and snapping in joyous harmony. Unbeknownst to him, she possessed the exact facial balances as his mother, the same arched nose, the same full, bow lips. Her vulnerability echoes on some level the ancient Roia, twig-snared hair Roia, her smell, which he imperceptibly swallowed as she moved by him in the hotel room, was heady and horribly familiar and panicking. It was the candy sweet waft of a childhood room, of the cir-cled arms of someone who loved his baby self, it sung of violets in spring and dark warm oil, it besieged him by it's unctuous butter of youth. It, in short, sent genetic coding whip-snapping along his senses and the match came up perfect and right. Love.

And anyway, this is how his job sounded in words. In real time, he often sat at his desk reading e-mail, sending slightly misspelled responses to girls he had met or Persian friends. Forwarding large mass jokes about blondes to friends or soft-porn pictures of jokey buxom women. Or responding to offers of Persian activities, movies, concerts, Nowruz celebrations. The Persian New Year was arriving, festivities were planned. Then he would pause, go the bathroom. A lengthy procedure for Khouri. Or would get some tea and eat an Apple he had brought in. Go and talk or *schmooze* as he liked to say, with a coworker. He liked to wrap himself as an American, Polo clothes, catchy slang words, jokes, salsa dancing. Underneath, he was as Persian as saffron, dark and fragrant, staining everything it came in contact with.

All night in the Moroccan restaurant, she coyly accepted cinnamon scented dove in a small parcel of bread and neat spoonfuls of couscous with butter-soft lamb and smiled graciously. She was chewing gum and stuck it in the glass ashtray and occasionally he strangely stared at it and knew it had been in her mouth. Her child whined that he wanted a Coke and she said *no*, and Khouri said *that is no problem* and raised his arm and she said, *no, it's, it's*, and the boy, Trevor, said *I want one, Mommy* and Khouri said, *really, it's*, and she said *no, it's the caffeine*, and Khouri said *Oh*, (how little he realized he knew about children) and then the child was happy and quiet with a glass of orange juice. And he looked at her soft hair. He asked her where she lived and Trevor said, *on Kimble Street*. And he asked her what she liked to do and Trevor said, *Mama likes to play with me*, and Khouri realized children could be a problem. Patricia, though, did the careful talk of the parent when another is watching, *well, Trevor, Mama likes to play with you and other things, too, right? Doesn't Mama like to work on her computer, too? I like to write poetry sometimes. I'm taking a class at the Y*. Poetry, and therefore Khouri said, *do you know Rumi?*

Rumi, that's funny, Roomy, Roomy

Hush, Trevor, that's rude. Who's Rumi?

Rumi well, he was a, a Sufi poet—would you like some more of this lamb,
it's quite good—have you heard of Sufism?

No, can't say that I have.

Well, it's a branch of mysticism that is Persian in origin.

She was noticing his strong, chopped accent, he elongated vowels and
substituted "w"s for "v"s and said *braunch* for branch and *Pair-jhian* for
Persian and that his hair was thick and black, coarse and sprinkled with
gray hairs, and she too noticed the Asian influence in the eyes—*he almost
looks Chinese*—the way the heavy lid folded down across the lid and
curved. When he laughed, which he did often, his face broke apart and his
teeth flashed white. He had many faces: The sharp look of a dark bird,
tearing out of a closed space. The soft flashing white of his smile, when his
face became round and kinder. A sad, pitiful look when worried. And the
pillowed, regal air he carried when simply walking without expression. At
this moment, the pillowed look was starting to carry the worried look.
Time was running out and he didn't feel he had accomplished much. They
had eaten pigeon, lamb, chicken. *Bastilla.* Eggplant and chickpeas. The
child had enjoyed the baklava. She had eaten heartily. She said, *this is actually good.* She said she often ate pasta because it was easy and cheap. Her
shoulders were freckled and when she laughed, her face broke into dimples. He was hopelessly charmed.

She was not of his class. She was uneducated. These were fiercely
unacceptable things to him somehow, ever since he was small his parents
were scornful and critical of the lower classes. A woman needed to project
a look of finesse and comfort, quality and adornment. This mere girl was
simple and ungarnished. This is perhaps a question of lust, thought
Khouri. He could separate these departments. Would she fit into the cate-
gory of lover or wife? He needed to court her. How to court her. The
evening was growing short. The child was yawning. She was rubbing the
child's small head and saying she had to go. He dutifully stood up and yet
he was panicking. He had not accomplished his goal, although he did not
know what this was. The mint tea was drunk, the hour was ten. She
reached up and kissed his cheek and thanked him. All at once, the smell of

her flooded him again. He was desperate. He held the door for her and she went into the dark. He put her in a taxi, he said, *may I call you, Patricia?* And he felt her falter and he was embarrassed, *I would like to get to know you a bit*, he said. She said, *let me think on that*, and then the car was off in the night, and Khouri felt ridiculous, a grown man of a fine Persian family, standing in the streets of the capitol city, his eyes glistening with unshed tears.

Twelve

He runs back to his hotel room, tears off his clothes, puts on his golden silk pajamas, does not want to cry, hates to cry, but the hot tears swallow his face as he lays back and looks at the ceiling. He wipes them sloppily with the silk sleeve of his pajama. Stop all this outburst. The tears will not stop. A sound comes out of him that is not normal, a groan. *Khouri, Khouri,* he says to himself. You will be all right. He wants to control all this outburst. He is an orphan. He has loved people other than his family. He has loved women. Of this, he will catalogue, Dr. Khouri Karimi:

There were women in my life. Some love, some sex, not as much as should be for a Persian man like myself, perhaps. I think I am a good lover. I think I am very good at this. I am sure. There is a problem, the women seem to have with me, long term. *Ola,* I seem to make mistakes. At the crucial time. I am not sure of what this is. What, where I go wrong.

I will document:

1) *The prostitutes for initiation.* How I wish I could relive this night, where I sat like an idiot as they kissed each other and were naked on my bed. I was scared of what to do. I know now how to do certain things. I was young! Inexperienced. A baby! I felt so shamed when they left.

2) After a few months, I meet *German au pair*, much taller than me.
This girl had a very strong body. Nice butt. With this girl, I learned the
basics. This girl was extremely kind to me, and we did a lot of hanky-
panky. From this girl I learned many things. In fact, this girl I fell in love
with, you know, like the love like a child. I was crazy for this girl, who had
to go back to Germany and left me feeling, well, killed. It killed me. I was
getting my Ph.D. at this point. I tried to remember my work and not her.
I lose weight, living by myself in a basement apartment. I would eat rice,
buy an occasional *kubideh kebab* but it would sit on the kitchen table uneat-
en, and maybe I finally I would tear off a corner of the meat and dip it in
yogurt sauce and then fall on my bed in sickness.

You were always like this, Khouri. A bit too romantic for your own
good. When you are five, you loved the daughter of our cleaning lady, do
you remember?
Nandideh.
Ah! You see, you remember her name.
Nandideh, she was, she was.
Seven. Older.
But then, she stopped coming.
Her parents were Shiites, they felt, although they did not say, it would
lead to bad things.
I missed her.
You were quiet and not eat for awhile. I worry.

Maman, I need a wife.
It is good to marry, Khouri, this life of going out meeting all woman is
no good.
I like this girl—
This girl is peasant! This girl has no education, unkempt!
Please, Maman.
You can do better, my Khouri-joon.
Who? I have to like first!
3) *My first wife*: then I decided, while I got my Ph.D., maybe I marry. It is
the best thing to do then. So I look around for a wife and meet this

American girl who is a secretary in my job. I am teaching adjunct professor of engineering of course in the university and at the same time, I am working like the dog on my Ph.D. Like I tell you, she is secretary, this girl named Pammy with brown hair, this one, and large hips the way I tend to like. A big butt. I prefer it. I like something to grab. This is me. My parents buy us a brick small house where we live. We make *love rrright and left.* To me, she is very beautiful. I know I don't pay enough attention to her. I know this is my damage. I am sitting all night at the dining room table reading my books for my Ph.D. I am studying just so hard. All day as adjunct professor I work and work and then at night until late I read and study. She is bored, she says, Khouri, I'm bored. So, pick up a book, I say. Read a picturebook, do something. She is uneducated. She is from a small town in Virginia where her father makes cheeses from the goat. She likes to go out, to have dinners. She buy curtains for our kitchen in a yellow color like the sun and she likes to cook things like chicken with a dumpling, it is food with no flavor and too soft as well. I am thinking maybe a baby will give her something to do, so I make this happen, I try to secretly deposit myself inside her though I lie and say, it was in time. Please, do you understand what I mean without detail?

This is a normal thing, I am sure. And then, surely, as I hoped, she is indeed pregnant with a baby, and I am happy for this and she is less than happy, she is too sad. Things do not get better, they get worse. She is sleeping many days, complaining of this and that. Here we go again. The baby dies inside her, so it seems. I am sure it was because it was not cared for by her. It was not a good time, these moments in the hospital with her family and tears. I was not sad. Because what is the point? Something must've been wrong with the baby. Things go down the hill from there. Until one day I see her friend pick her up and I ask, why is that? And then she calls and says I am not coming back and I start to get extremely upset and ask her why, and she just says she is not in love with me, that is that. That is that.

I am crying at this time and I do beg her then, I say, please, we can go to the counselor and fix this problem and she says what is there to fix, I am not in love with you. It is that simple. Oh please. Oh please, I was saying. And that is that.

I must lie in our bed after she leaves and smell her in the sheets. I must see her juice that she prefers in my refrigerator and keep it until it has become a disgraceful mold and even then when I put it in the trash, I miss it. I must keep her hairbrush, her book, her sock under the bed, her bathrobe left on the hook, and the dirty towel she last used. I must lay on the expensive Persian rug that was our wedding gift and put my face into it and know she did not even want to take this good rug with her and I lie on the rug for too many hours. And even, with shame, I will tell you, I must keep in an envelope in my pocket all of the golden hairs of hers I find in the bath because I cannot bear to let anything leave my life of hers anymore and then I run out to the car and get into the Transam I had at this time and drive very quickly to her apartment house where she has gone to stay with a friend, the same betraying friend who helped her leave, who had many dinners in our house, who painted Easter eggs in our house, who would come and eat chicken and the dumpling at my table, this friend who has pulled her away, I drive to there and wait for her to come and go, and finally after four hours and seventeen minutes later, they drive up, my wife and her friend, my dream, my life, my love, and I must lie my head against the steering wheel in the cold dark night, alone again.

Thirteen

Here we go again: Dr. Khouri Khagosian wakes to the sour smell of Khormeh Sabzi and upon waking realizes it is the citrus cleaner used in the hall of the hotel and then he realizes it is Nowruz today, the Persian New Year and a time for new starts and he has asked for three days off from his job and he calculates, as an engineer, a plan, a document, an implementation, for obtaining the preferential treatment of an American female, or in laymen's language, to win the heart of this girl named Patricia. He must implement a plan.

First, in the duty of his heritage he must acknowledge Nouruz because his mother seems to wish this. Even a poor orphan must always hear the voice of a parent somewhere guarding and advising at stressful times, the way an old injury throbs as it relives the break, and there is his mother, waking him with Khormeh sabzi. His erection is thrusting through the golden fabric of his silk pajamas and reminds him that, yes, Khouri, you are also a man and a man who desires a woman, and back to the Patricia plan. He wishes to make sure the door is locked and the curtains drawn and perhaps bring himself to his own needs on this bed, reenacting what a woman could do, and thinking of such, but experience has taught him that this usually leaves him feeling tired and old, his bones actually aching after the pleasure, and therefore he says to himself *no*. And then he goes back to the earlier plan of Patricia, which hopefully would serve to eventually bring her to his arms anyway, or ultimately, and perhaps this is where all the neural networking really brings him to. But Khouri, despite all scientific training, truly believes that this is human cynicism to think such, that souls touch souls, that love is an elementary, luminous thing, an etheric presence between two people that no chart or graph can invade, that no chemical can reproduce, that no coercing can invent. Yet despite this he is desperate, he is an orphan. So he will attempt a plan, if only in the light of the fact that for centuries, for eternities, men have fought for women, battled for women, and generally won.

FOURTEEN

It is of no secret that Khouri enjoys the dance of salsa, of merengue and also cha-cha. This started three years ago because he had dated a Persian woman for one year and then they were going to live together, but she insisted on marriage, and he was going to do this, going to Neiman Marcus for a proper ring but when he drove to the Mall, he passed a Transam of the exact color and type of the one he had when he was getting his Ph.D., a light gray, and then he was laying on the steering wheel again, night after night in his thoughts, watching the solid rectangle of an apartment building where his wife had moved, and the pain he relived felt like a man of huge strength had thrown hard ice against his chest and he had to stop his car (now a black Mercedes) and deep breath and therefore, he backed up and went to the Persian girl's house and she stood staring as he tried to say something. He became mean to hide his fear and she pushed him and he left.

And then he was alone without a girlfriend for quite some time.

He plunged himself into a dream of vectors and kernels and the recognition of targets and schmoozed with his colleagues—Aparjeet Parusuystha, Min Hao Cho, Massoud Parcho, Scott O'Brien—all the men who were senior research analysts and engineers like himself. He drank a coke or a tea, discussed the upcoming SPIE conference, a paper he would finish soon with Massoud Parcho, who was implementing the configurations and they could hope to have a poster on display at the show. But he was very lonely, as he heard these men night after night click their heavy briefcases and get into their Hondas and drive to their suburban houses to their wives—and he would drive his Mercedes to his small rambler and watch CNN.

So out of this boredom, this loneliness, Khouri thought and thought of a hobby that would keep him busy. He thought of a hiking club, a gourmet club, an acting class (an absurd idea), and then ballroom dancing. This made him think of gray-haired ladies and so he narrowed it down to the latin dances, perhaps Tango, but when he saw in the newspaper several ads for salsa classes at clubs, he decided he would try this. He purchased two bright colorful shirts, a few pleated pants, special loafers for a perfect slide, and then attended the class. There was a small problem Khouri had, an embarrassment: he sweats profusely. He could drench a shirt in a matter of hours, in hot weather. He worried about this problem in the class. To insure that it would not be an issue, he shaved his armpits. The hair on his chest was profuse, a thicket of tangles. He considered having electrolysis, but that would be painful. He came to the solution of a white T-shirt under the shirt as an absorbent buffer. Then, copious amounts of Gucci for Men. And then he was ready for the class, but not without his rituals for going out:

1) He would sit on the toilet leisurely, almost pleasurably. It was secret, secret pleasure and one he would never discuss. While he did this—and he did this up to three times a day—he would be in a world in his head somewhat like the old Tehran of his childhood. The song his mother played would fill his mind, it would drift from the kitchen where she *cooked khouresht badmejan*, his father's favorite, he could smell the eggplant frying. He would sit over the small pit they had for this purpose on his bent legs and finger the cold tile underneath, the small perfect octagons. This made him feel secure and happy, this physical sensation, this memory, and before he went out he wanted to feel cleansed and empty.

2) He would take a long, hot shower that often lasted for one hour. The hot water would land on his head, and on his head he wore a semi-permanent toupee. It was purchased eight years ago when he noticed he was rapidly losing his hair, a considerable amount, in the sink after showers and being single and considered attractive, he saw all his hopes for finding a beautiful woman awash in the hairs. He panicked, applied tonics, Iranian home remedies of hot rose oil mixed with olive oil, medical prescriptions, even sperm in a strange moment one day, to no avail.

The Hairclub for Men, which he saw on TV on a late night ad, provided a solution. He called the 800 number and came to their office, a small rented cubicle in a high-gloss building where a man with copious hair, which was real (thus seemed false advertisement) showed him various options with different brochures. He chose the semi-permanent black with a tiny bit of gray model and it was custom made for him from real human hair (Korean) and it cost him 1,345 dollars. They had said it would cost only 895.00 dollars, that there was a sale but these extra costs included application fees, hairstyling techniques and adjustment, and maintenance equipment which Khouri knew was all pure bullshit but at this point they had woven the thing on his head in his natural hairs and applied the special glue in a small vial he would always carry with him, and he did see the magic transformation in the mirror as he lost fifteen years.

He became once again, the young Ph.D. student in Albany at SUNY, the face he wore before marriage to the young heart-breaking secretary, before all the hours he spent in the car outside her building watching her, waiting for her, this transformation astounded him. Women did react differently, they were more attracted once again. He felt lighter, younger, more himself. The problem came on the rare occasion he was with a woman, kissing her and they would inevitably reach to tousle his hair and hit the hard edge of the toupee. Some would recoil and say, what's that? or simply, snap their hands back fast and pretend they hadn't discovered this flaw. He preferred to not mention it until it was brought up. He would shampoo this lovingly in the shower and most of the time he enjoyed the water hitting his forehead in a wet stream and would stand under the torrent as long as the hot water would keep up. Then, he would shave, which was lengthy because Khouri had a very coarse beard. After this procedure, he was ready for the next part of the process

3) in his towel he would go to his stereo on the third floor of his rambler house, a darkly carpeted room with all his countless books on the Baha'i faith, of which Khouri believed in vaguely, having been raised as such, and his CDs, and various framed snapshots of his travels or smiling groups of his family, and put on a Persian CD, rather loudly, usually with a canned sounding disco back beat, which he liked to rev up for the evening, this time he played the music of Sea Amin, which sounded very eighties, and the words were always sad love musings on broken hearts which just seemed to echo the general feeling that surrounded this man, Broken Heart.

But did he seek out this condition? Did he find the woman who would never love him or her, him? Did he secretly revel in being rejected or rejecting and was the real issue that Khouri had a part of him that was impenetrable? Even his wife who left him, did he leave her first? Did he retreat into the studies of his Ph.D. and ignore her too consistently? Did he not lie to her as well?

He never told her about the night—he worked as a taxi driver for awhile in London—when an older American woman with reddish blond hair, freckles, had him drive her all over the city. Then she asked him for a Coke at a cafe. He agreed. His young wife sat at home cooking shepherd's pie. The older American woman sucked the cold ice and asked him many questions in the cafe, where he was from (Tehran), what he studied (electrical engineering), if he was married (no, he lied). Then she asked him to drive her home, but at her house she asked if he would like coffee and he said, that would be nice. But within fifteen minutes of arriving, the woman was kissing him against her kitchen table in her friend's flat. She peeled his clothes off him like he was an exotic fruit and smelled him all the way, noticing and savoring the Khouri scent, the green smell he emanated, and he passively accepted all of this and thought not of his wife and the Shepherds Pie. His penis came pronging out of his pants and she grasped it in her bony hands, with her long coral nails and licked him and Khouri felt he would pass out. His knees were weak and he felt almost nauseous. She pulled him over to an old brown corduroy couch, where she rolled down her pantyhose and Khouri briefly saw her vagina, neatly trimmed in a triangle, as she crouched over him backwards. He lay there passively while she waddled her hips around his penis, moaning and heaving in pleasure and still he lay there, captivated by the pleasure. Do something, do something, don't just lie there, she said, in impatient huffs, and Khouri felt true embarrassment flood his being, he felt his penis deflate, he felt redness invade his face. Slowly she moved slower and slower as she realized he had gone down. She said, what happened, and he said, I am very sorry, and got up from under her.

You are very nice, but I, I must leave now. She pulled her skirt, pinched it around her butt, that's really nice, isn't it? Just start something and, and just take off, just like you fucking foreigners, she said. I am sorry, he felt so foolish, standing there naked and shamed. I am sorry and he feverishly put on his pants and forgot about the huge fare she owed him, and ran to the car, his whole body reeking of this woman and her sickly sweet perfume and the overtones of dark sexuality, and he pressed his head against the steering wheel and felt sick—was this the key point of departure away from his beloved Pammy, this act of betrayal with the traveling American?

And here he was in the grieving spot as well, in the car, his head against the wheel, where he would come to rest for many more times when Pammy left him to live in her friend's apartment.

3) with the Sea Amin blasting, he often like to do a bit of Persian dance on the carpet, his arms outstretched, his face joyful, touched by tiny spots of shaving cream. It was OK to be happy again. Despite all the hardships, the death of his mother, his father, his sisters, the loss of his wife, all the heartbreak, Khouri always felt it would be alright: *He would love again. And this time it would last.*

Then, he would dress and prepare for the night.

FIFTEEN

The salsa class was packed, and Khouri noticed there were lots of beautiful girls, though too young for him. He stood awkwardly in the back and they all went through the basic movements as a group, back-1-2-3-4-5, front, 1-2-3, and Khouri was stiff. He could see the way the male instructor, Umberto, easily swiveled his hips and he wondered if he would be able to do that. He tried and he lost the sense of the step so, rigidly once again, he stepped in the pattern. Then they called to pick a partner and he rushed up to a young redhead of twenty or so and held her limp, white hands in his dark ones and tried not to look her in the eyes as the instructor went to push in the CD. *What is your name?* she said in a voice as light as a nightingale, *I am Khouri*, he said and she whispered, *I'm Kelly*, and he said, *well, I hope I am not too*—and then suddenly the music crashed into the room, all vibrant and snappy and wildly emotional, *Te quiero! Te quiero mucho!* the cocoa-voiced singer crooned, and Khouri snapped into the rhythm and she followed him gracefully and it felt so perfect—at that moment a whole new world opened to Khouri, a world of dance and laughter and life renewed. The music was so cheerful and innocent, always singing of adoration and longing, even heartbreak, but when it did, it was with joy, innocence, and such zest. God be praised for music! It is a freedom, a cure for all ills. At the end of the class, he was wet with sweat, aching in his legs and his feet hurt from the new shoes, but he felt reborn. He could learn this dance and be with women, he could have something to do on Saturday nights, it would make him happy. The whole of Khouri was always about bravery. No matter how low, how abandoned he felt, he always charged forward, finding a new tact. He wanted to hold onto life to the last minute, he wanted to be loved, he wanted to smile. His dead family surrounded him like a shawl of guilt. His mother's voice in the car, returning from salsa, admonished him:

What kind of thing, this, this crazy Spanish dance? Are you not lowering yourself, acting lower class, dancing all over, with whoever?

It is Ok, Maman. Please.

Find a wife. Get married. Settle down.

I am trying! all the time!

In this way you'll end with some low class latin girl. It's no good.

Maman.

A Persian girl.

I don't want a Persian girl. They are gold diggers. Some at least, listen. I just want to be loved.

Is it wrong to want good things, nice things?

Maman.

Go back to your Baha'i. You are a bad Baha'i.

Maman. Maman.

By that time, he was only looking at the picture beside his bed of his mother and father on their wedding day, wondering why he had strayed so far from his culture. Where was the young Persian woman he almost married, the one who requested a ring from Neiman Marcus, the one with the long golden-brown hair, who threw things at him when he wouldn't marry her? She lay in his bed a few times, idly accepting his overtures, coldly taking him inside her with little passion. He would move on top of her and he wished she would moan or yell, wished she would wrap her golden legs, perfectly waxed and smooth, manicured feet with pearly pink polish, buffed heels, around his hips and buck against him, but she lay there quietly, her arms above her head, her hair spread on the pillow as he moved faster and faster and as he reached his moment, she would issue a few dove-like coos to encourage him but afterwards, as she tore up to shower, he knew it meant very little to her, this act, many things were more pleasure, even brushing her teeth, or combing her lovely hair, lying naked with him meant very little indeed.

No doubt she had found another good Persian man, another engineer or doctor, married him and lived in a quiet suburb in Maryland, a glacine and glittered living room, Persian carpets, shining floors, *khoresht-e-badmenjan* bubbling in a pot somewhere, small dark-eyed children running through the house, and the memory of the sweating Khouri above her long gone, replaced by finery, Mercedes benz, Cartier Jewelry and a husband moving through her life like an expensive shadow.

Sixteen

Pomegranates are a commitment of time. They are contemplative, and insist on the quiet involvement of all your senses and your time. One will sit with the task of eating a Pomegranate for quite some time. At this moment, Khouri remembered he had brought a pomegranate, it sat on the gleaming wood of the hotel desk, plump and deep russet, an orb of delicate red and gold, a sculpture, this fruit, an amazing gift of a battery of juicy seeds. He would eat this fruit and decide what to do about Patricia or more specifically, how to invite her out for salsa. He was sure she would enjoy it. He could call her or he could find her in the hotel.

And then all of sudden, he felt full of doubt for his actions. Why was he pursuing this simple girl, this peasant, who worked scrubbing the floors of the hotel? Where, why couldn't he find a Persian woman of a suitable background. There were web sites. There is a shortage of men in Iran due to the war between Iraq and Iran in the eighties. There are scores of beautiful girls, virtuous girls, fertile girls who would long to live in this country, to marry Khouri and give him sons, and pass on the long lineage, the original lineage from India that his people possessed. The Persians were the lost Aryan tribe, a complex mix of savagery and refinement, a long genetic passage defined by opulence from the silk route, by royalty, by breeding. All this sacred blood he would waste and merge with the harsh white Viking blood this girl owned, freckle-shouldered, ocean-eyed, in her beauty she seemed pale and insufficient next to the bloodiness of his own people, the tribe with beauty at once fierce and amazingly, tragically beautiful, dark-eyed and blackened like iron. But he would. Yes! Yes! Throw me to the lions! *I will go this way because, my lovely Maman, in my heart I have no choices.* My heart is a willful master.

Each seed of pomegranate exploded in his mouth. He remembered the Fesenjan his mother would make, chicken in a thick paste of pomegranate molasses and walnuts and rose water. This dish had been hauled out by slave boys in golden beaten plates for Genghis Khan, it had been served on silver tureens for King Darius while girls with shining sooty eyes had spun on the rugs by firelight, coins hanging from their bodices, their tanned stomachs gleaming with sweat and amber oil, and his mother, her arms covered in her turquoise bracelets, often stirred this dish on a Friday when he returned from school, carrying the sack of the barbari flat bread he was supposed to pick up. *Maman*, he would say, *can I have some with bread*. No, it is not ready she would reply. She would give him some honey in a small dish, his grandfather would cough in the other room while he watched TV. He was old and dying of heart failure. Little did he know this woman would die of a heart attack on a California road, in a Mercedes, held by her grown daughter, in a state of sun and palm trees. Here, outside on this day in Tehran, it was snowing in large flakes. The people walking back from school were covered with the downy pile. The bread had to be shaken repeatedly so it wouldn't get damp through the paper. His mother gave him tea, boiling hot, and then, with a smile a small bowl of chicken *fesenjan*, a sampler and the taste, so familiar, so sweet and sour, burst in his mouth with each crunch of Pomegranate on the hotel couch.

Who would ever know him, all these memories? Who could replace the feeling he had in his home, his mother, his father, his sister, his brother, the smell of the food he loved, the life of his country, who could replace all this love he had lost? An orphan sitting in a hotel hoping for a girl who was so foreign as to be alien, was he so desperate he would take anything?

or was an etheric miracle occurring, was his old soul, mangled and hewn by Genghis Khan and Darius and countless blood-smeared Aryan warriors going in it's normal course, toward the next victory the next conqueror, bred of the clan of Celtic savagery?

But he wasn't thinking this. He was thinking of where to take this girl for salsa as he crunched each seed. He knew a smoky place called Havana Village. He must go find her now. She was working today, no doubt.

When he found her on the third floor, scrubbing a toilet, her blond hair scraped back and he asked her to salsa, and she said yes, Patricia herself knew something had been breached, changed, altered. Her hermetic life, diapering, cleaning a child, watching cartoons, cooking hamburger meat, doing laundry, would be changed. She felt it in the way he looked at her. She was a woman again. There would be no return. In the night, she would dance in his arms. There would be no going back. She would go to that dark place, but with trepidation, feeling with her toes along the dark corridor where he stood at the end, holding out her heart in her hands toward him. Is that what he wanted, her heart?

It is what everybody wants. Your heart, all of it's blood and tears.

Give me your heart.

Khouri picked up his cell phone, which cackled with a jaunty tune and put it near his mouth. He spoke quick, mumbles of Farsi in its most abbreviated form. He was holding himself up straight, his eyes glaring in blank warrior mode into the hotel. When he turned to look at her, they were so glittery and black, the white window's light bounced back in them like two miniature rectangles. A new world danced in that light, where things acted differently, where physics became so miniaturized it lost all sense of our normal physical laws, where neutrons and gluons broke apart and danced in waves and particles and nothing was until you decided it was, until you saw it, in his black Persian eyes, that moment, her child was safe, her home was safe, her heart was safe. Khouri's eyes, reflecting the windows of the hotel, were safety.

*   *   *

As she watched him on the cell phone, she felt happy. Just this morning, she had woken early before her son woke up and lit candles in her small living room and incense and put on her fluffy bathrobe of yellow chenille and held her arms tightly. She shivered. She felt reckless fear swimming in currents throughout her whole body. Who was this man who pursued her, this dark foreign man, this Middle Eastern man, this man from the land of women in veils, where, according to television, women were stoned and punished for looking like women. What did he want with her? Would he seek to impregnate her and carry her off and steal her baby? Would he marry her and keep her wrapped in a shroud, like a precious jewel one took out on occasion to marvel at and then put away for safety's sake?

Or did he only want her, naked in his arms for a few night's pleasure, and then he would toss her aside like a common street hooker. She had worked hard to make her home with her son and safe and sweet. She cooked him his meals and bathed him and worked hard at the hotel and saved her money. She said no to the busboy Rodrigo who asked her out, his eyes hungrily devouring her hips as she walked, who crowded her by the small entranceways and breathed on her with his hot, cumin scents, *please come with me out, Patreesha*. She said no to Leonard, the black man who worked in room service, who cracked jokes with her and they talked of poetry, because she knew he had been with Seville, a girl in laundry and had gotten her pregnant, and even though he talked of poetry with her, he wrote it himself, she shunned his overtures for fear.

She felt herself terrified of this man from Iran, terrified of where he came from in her ignorance, terrified of what the television and newspapers had made her believe about his people, but deep down Patricia really was a poet, it was no mistake she sought this world of symbols and whispers of the heart, deep down she knew the language of the heart, the truth of it's pulsing.

Like a road of rocks and roses, where would this man take her, to sorrow or to joy? At this moment, she blew the candles out with short, hard puffs and through the smoke saw her child's chest gently rising with each gust of air.

THE SEVENTEEN DISHES OF
JEDRA ABDULLAH

Tonight Jedra Abdullah has prepared a feast for the queen of his bidding. Her robes were of gold and her eyes shone as emerald amongst the dirt. She stood alone in the field, powdered with all the scents of the merchant. The honeycomb dripped from her lips and her lips were as red as the juice of pomegranates crushed by the boots of dark soldiers and all the pain in the world, all the dead brothers, all the lost mothers and fathers, even all the lost countries and youth, could not thwart the intense beauty of this moment for Jedra Abdullah. Phyllis, the queen of destiny, enrobed in purity at his doorstep. Her small stuffed animal lightly laying on his small bed in the left room, the hard candy intact, her place of employment, the Royale hotel stood alit as a brochure tacked to his wall, it's gleaming walls lit and garnished with italianate font. At this moment, all was well. And then:

Crack, craqk, crack!

The sound made Abdullah pale and ill and he stumbled.

I think something exploded in the kitchen, she said, still standing in the door.

They both ran over and a kibbe had exploded in the grease, his pans old and dirty around the edges, and it had left a mark on the wall. He turned it off and sat down, wiping his head, shaking.

I am sorry, one minute please.
She stood there.
I am a little. What is it. *Freak out* of this kind of sounds.
She was cleaning it up with a paper towel and Windex and he sat shaking, and she felt strange and out-of-place. Remember, she had lost a man and was still losing a child—another man's child—and this meant she was in mourning and he was in mourning too, she sensed. When she was finished, she went over to his living room, for the rooms had no dividers, and sat on his couch and thought to herself,
I lost my child today, Jedra.

More than the loss was the loss of her childhood. It was sad to be the weird girl. It was hard to always be an outsider who somehow looked normal and sweet and cute yet inside she had the turmoil of strange knowledge that was impossible to relocate. When Kara Thompson was rude to Phyllis and called her a *freak*, and dumped her tray on the ground in the cafeteria, Phyllis, her hair in plaits, leaned down to clean and saw clearly the golden feet of Kara as a mistress in the gardens of Babylon, where she served the king. Kara had been Mestisalah, the red servant. Her palms were died cinnabar and her feet as well from bright henna, and the king had loved her for eight months and then discarded her for another. Mestisalah took her own life with a stone in the river, tied with hemp, and when her soul shot up to Heaven, where Phyllis and the tall angels were, in the section of ashkanic records, she was told she had done a good job. Her eyes were clear and celery and sparks came from them, and there was nothing of wrong in Kara, not now or then, and Phyllis could see that too clearly.

So loss was for not knowing all these hidden journeys we all took but had thankfully forgotten. Phyllis had tried so hard to be normal with Tim, to forget these images but now it was impossible. The child had spoken to her in Aramaic from her tummy before it left. It said,

I am Ismael. The voice was pure and sanctified. She recognized it. He was fleeting and gone, a momentary blip of consciousness.

Phyllis pushed her head back on the couch and Jedra came over.

I am sorry, I have done this terrible thing to welcome you to my home. You come here and I, I freaks out. I am sorry.

Jedra.

Well, please, welcome to my home. Phyllis. Welcome.

She stood up and glanced around.

It's very homey, Jedra. Comfortable.

Well, It is Ok. Please. Come in the kitchen.

He went over to the frying pan, with a spatula. What happen is, this pop here and make that noise and I freak out, because you know, I hate guns sound. That is all.

What is that, Jedra?

This? This is kifta, a like a meat ball, kind of. You mix hamburger—(he said *haam-bour-ger*) with spice, parsley (*paar-se-lay*), other thing, onion (*oh-neeyan*). Mix like *thees* and fry, just like this, fry. Tonight we have seventeen dish I make for you. I make (*and he lifted various lids*) this kind of soup (*a soup of chicken and greens and lentils*), this chicken (*roasted and brown in the oven*), this kifta, lamb and the rice (*fragrant and sweet*), this brown bean dish, is good for brain and for muscle, like from the bean you call the lima, maybe?

The Lima bean?

Ok, maybe it is what you say is fava bean. You know the fava? You know *foul*?

Foul?

Yes.

Phyllis' senses were returning harshly. Outside she could hear a stampede of thundering elephants in the dust, their large voices squawking in the streets, she could hear thousand flutters of angels wings, what was all around us silently, crushing, harkening souls on all levels, etherium and materium, were quaking and spilling around her. The last bit of the child, Ismael, was leaving her body, the last cluster of cells, the last minute tether of flesh, the whisper of the soul, the Ismael she knew. She heard his descent throughout the clouds, the sky, then silence, sweet, pure, vanillic silence.

What I am saying is, you call it, maybe, fava bean.
Jedra.
Yes, *habibi*, he kissed her hair impulsively.

I just lost the child. Saying this, tears broke from her and she sobbed.
Oh, he said. He held in his bony shoulders and rubbed her hair. Oh, no, poor one. Poor one.
He led her to the couch.

How it happened noone knows. It was one of those strange moments lost in time and space. It would not serve well to analyze it in our poor, cynical world where romance and love are treated so badly, where cupid gets tired of springing his small tortoise-boned arrows, that quiver with rose petals and powdery tears toward people that pull them out and smash them on the ground, and prefer to track down their matches on the internet, than see those who stand before them with eyes of love. Cupid was surely in the room, though, at this moment, yea, he had followed these two all along for days since the elevator, where he crouched in a corner, uncomfortable, cold, but unwavering. Cupid is a small fellow, chubby, beaded dark eyes in a face of pillowy flesh, he's not exactly good-looking, he's intense. Cupid is fierce-minded, like a carnivorous beast seeking a hot-blooded prey, cupid does not accept the thought of no, Cupid has no concept of compatibility, Cupid pulls the arrow in the direction of inevitability. He has a plan. And you will fall. The elevator felt cool against his back, it smelled of human food and sweat and metal. He disliked the smell, preferring if he had to have a preference, the fields of Lebanon in high summer or Egyptian roses by the Nile or Persian orange groves near Bam, these had the scents that Cupid enjoyed and many frolicked in those areas and he had pulled his bow back many, many times through the trees. But an elevator, in this cold gray city. Ugh, he was busy in this hotel. He had flown all floors and his arrows hit target after target. But stop pulling them out. Let them sink in, let them permeate. Here's the thing, *he only comes once.*

Thus, he did his thing: pulling back his bow with acuity and stealth right into the chest of Jedra Abdullah, where it sunk with a satisfying *crack-craqk-crack!*

Maybe Jedra should've gotten to know her better, to talk for hours, to date her quietly for months, discussing politics, theories of evolution, mysteries of the world, maybe they should've attended movies and plays or eaten in Chinese restaurants or French bistros and slowly unraveled the braided incoherencies between them, before he moved her to the couch and kissed her neck like the sugared column of some divine entrance to mystery, but that was where Jedra was now, kissing all of her neck and wishing to wash away any pain she felt or he felt, and how painful his life had been. This moment was almost too sweet for him and her, too and the intimacy, though too fast, too quicksilver, meant something to these two battled soldiers of life. Her sweatshirt fell off her head in a tumult of her orangey blond hair and then she was in a white lace bra and he could almost not breathe. And then it came off, the bra and he beheld her pale, veined breasts as delicate as lily petals, as soft as warm air, and he sucked them with all his mouth and in his pants he felt a gush, a buckling and knew what had occurred, the same bleating animal sound erupted from his mouth, and as he enjoyed the watery intensity of it, he begged Allah that she did not notice, he was overcome, so completely excited beyond his life by her beauty, her smell, and the truth is Jedra Abdullah had never seen, touch or held the body of a woman.

He had seen a picture once. Some boys in his youth had showed him a French postcard of a woman with dark brown nipples and a triangle of hair between her legs and he had masturbated to this many times, to the woman slowly lying back and opening those legs, but he couldn't really imagine more, for he knew not much.

He once walked in the shadowy door of a strip club, and wanted to press through the bamboo hanging door, but grew afraid and left.

He passed prostitutes on the street who called him *sweetie* and *darlin'* but he was afraid of what they would do and say and see.

He wanted to buy a magazine but the Korean woman might tease him, so he did not.

In the night, in his bed, when he touched himself, moaning low and soft like a mountain goat, he thought of Phyllis, of the curve of her breasts, what lay between her legs, and now as he discovered, it was too much.

Her nipples grew hard in his mouth and he sucked on them and she sighed and tossed and he prayed to Allah to allow him to carry on without explosion again. He was delirious with pleasure and fragility. He pulled her pants off her hips and it felt like a dream. The chiaroscuro of flesh and bone and curve against his own rocky, sinewy body was shocking, abrupt. It was like the mountain against the ocean, water against rock. He lay against her and smelled the world, the ground, the sea, animals and flowers, all of it blending and steaming forth, he somehow sunk against her body and in seconds felt contained in a hollow, a vacuum of her flesh and he looked into her eyes as he held her face. They were whirlwinds, transparent geysers of ultramarine and teal, and the liquid around them sparkled like stars. He tasted her mouth, marine and carnal at the same time, and they both murmured sounds from some other language, from a world men and women know exist but have not named. They stayed in this world—cloudy, persimmon kisses, sweat and salt, all locks cracked open and destroyed— for an hour, a minute, days? Who knows.

In the end, the countries gate had been trampled and all inhabitants had fled. The evening light grew as dim and blue as plums, and breath came rapidly like horses' hooves knocking in a canter from their chests.

Across their noses, as they lay flesh to flesh, eyes sealed by exhaustion, confusion, bliss, came the cinnamoned scents of lamb and rice, kibbe and kifta, wafting, enticing, and begging that there are more earthly pleasures to enjoy, more joys to share, here in this apartment on Swann street.

EIGHTEEN

He brought her a tray of delicacies, balancing on his arms, over to Phyllis on the couch. He had displayed them on a large beaten brass serving platter, a little of this and that, with warm bread, and Phyllis and Jedra lay amongst their clothes and ate them, bits of lamb and kibbe and tomato and cinnamon, garlic and lemon, all the flavors melded, and they ate hungrily. But how to begin talking? Should one talk of mundanity—boy, *this is yummy.* Or profoundly? As in, what occurred just there? What exactly transpired? This is what Jedra wanted to say. He smiled continuously. He must ask. So he did, he broke all rules and got to the point, the deep, intimate point.

(Intimacy is always the problem of the world. First of all, it's an annoying word. It just seems to whisper sex in a vaginal deodorant kind of way, perhaps advertisers have abused the word and made it seem incoherent and slightly vague and fluttery. What is intimacy? Perhaps if I have to ask it shows my cluelessness. I am clueless. One thing: It feels like we are scratching and gnawing at it's door in fevered desperation, then backing away as the door promises to be

87

opened. Why is it so terrifying to know another person, without judgment and expectation? To simply be in their presence and let truth occur?)

·Phyllis, he said, breathlessly, this was amazing thing, I feel. He stopped, I don't know. Just this was amazing thing for me. Something just really, really something.

Oh, I know, said Phyllis, sitting up, petal-pink, hair askew, this, this was *heaven*.

Heaven? Maybe like what heaven is like. This may be so.

No, it is. This is heaven. This is the closest thing to heaven, this time. I know it. I remember it.

Remember it?

I remember heaven. I really do.

From when.

From before.

Really?

Really?

Heaven in the clouds?

No, further. Yet closer. Heaven is someplace different. I can't explain. But, it's just like, just like what you feel. That closeness. That is it. All the time.

And Phyllis proceeded to tell him the whole story and Jedra listened to every detail, all the angels, the smells, the sounds, being carried on the wind, the smell of the wind up there, for it is different, the languages spoken, the music—oh, the music, it is indescribable, sonorous and longing, delicate as daffodils, archaic, medieval. Jedra listened, struck, with awe.

And all around us are them as well.

Them?

The others, who have left, who are leaving. There is a dusty boy here, a soccer boy.

Tear's pricked Jedra's eyes.

He is my brother. I see him too.

Jalil sat on the rug and spoke.

We used to play everyday!

I would play better, actually, said Jedra. I am older.

Yes, but I learning fast. Over here it is different. Nothing ever changes.

Over here, everything changes all the time. Nothing stays the same, so you have nothing you can stay with, it feels.

Yes, said, Phyllis, life is like that.

This is the pain of life.

I don't feel any pain, you know. I should go now.

No, Jalil. I miss you.

Goodbye.

Jedra went and lay on Phyllis' chest, and closed his eyes. They fell asleep like that, on the couch, in each other's arms. Jalil back on the dusty field. Jedra dreaming of his mother and father on the farm in Iraq by the river, with the palm trees waving in the hot breeze, where they grew fifty one different types of dates. Yellow ones, amber ones, red ones, brown ones that fell on the ground and attracted bees. Jedra and his brother argued over the best ones, and in Jedra's mind it would be the deep yellow ones that grew down by the left of the river, the ones he often ate under the tree as he watched his brother kick the ball on the field towards the goal, over and over, on hot summer days.

When he awoke, Jedra Abdullah had a plan to save the world.

Nineteen

She lay curled in his bed, her downy hair twisted and burnished and she actually lay in his bed, and Jedra would marry her today if he could and wanted to. When she awoke he planned to ask her, beg her, to marry him, and then take her down to the town hall and sign all the proper papers and make her last name his and own every inch of her, if a person can be owned. If not, then she could own him, every inch of his flesh and intention and he would sing in Arabic the wedding prayers from Islam, and he would give all his body and love to her forever.

But first, he had been terrified for sometime now that there was danger in the hotel, imminent danger. That the pipes were too fragile and were going to all blow soon and implode upon the hotel and bury it all in a crescendo of damaging combustion. He was sure of this, he heard the cracking pipes daily and knew they all were in danger and he needed to warn the chief operating president, he knew where his very fancy office was up on the top floor. He would walk in there and tell him of this terrible thing and he would be grateful and maybe then Jedra could say, *and do you think I could be promoted, by any chance, sir, to chief technician of the hotel? I notice this position is open since Mr. Parks left two months ago, and you have advertised, but I could fulfill this position. I maybe would need a few make-up classes in air-conditioning and heating technology, easily to do at the college around the corner. I can do this, work very hard.* Please. And since Jedra saves the hotel and all are very grateful, the president would say, anything you wish for, Mr. Jedra Abdullah, we are happy to help. And then Jedra would tell Phyllis, and they would proceed to plan their wedding feast.

Thinking this, he has on his pant and nice shirt, his only nice shirt, a striped pullover. He writes a scribbled note to Phyllis:

Dear Filis,
Please to tell you I go to hotel to talk to Mr. President. There is crisis in the hotel, it will explode if I do not tell of this problem with pipes. it is urgetnt. Please to sleep as long as you can wish and please to eat something good for you. it is you I love with all of my heart. Jedra.

And after writing this, he darted out his doors and leapt onto the street, eager and pinched, like a small sparrow alerting to the urgency of spring. His face was conular and pointy, and he thought only of his mission. He took a cab, a luxury. He carried a briefcase, a cheap plastic one, but it looked official. He wore a dark colored jacket for seriousness. He was terribly excited and a bit scared, for he felt, he knew, he had that twisting feeling in his diaphragm of serious action, that all would be changed. It was the same feeling he had the night he went with Jalil in the water, to fight with their brothers, when all went wrong, but instead of heeding this warning tension, he thought it meant simple excitement, not that his instinct was in a flurry, knowing that his choice could lead him in a terrible way.

In the soft brocaded lobby of the elegant hotel, there was a problem. His brother Jalil stood in the middle of the floor and stared at him. He stood white and heroic and pale as morning light, his eyes watery and a hole so neatly through his thin shirt where the tragic bullet had slid.

I am not sure what it is you want, my brother, said Jedra, in fast, hushed Arabic.

I have come to tell you not to come here, said Jalil.

And for what reason? I have lost you, I have no country, my mother and father live without my knowledge, and I wish to do something of good for people. *I am in love, Jalil.* This is something you never knew.

People he knows at the hotel, coworkers, look up slightly frowning as Jedra rushes by, dressed up, mumbling to himself.

What you are doing is no good, said Jalil. Please stop.

I am saving people, out of my way!

Jedra is flailing his arms and the concierge looks up alerted.

Mr. Abdullah, is. Is there a, problem?

No, sir. No. I am sorry, there was a fly.

A fly, I see.

Jalil, he whispers as he dashes to the elevator. I wish to do something right. Something of good. for the woman I love. It is all important. Too many people see danger and let it stand by, say nothing. They are cowards. Danger is everywhere and needs to be fought and destroyed. Like an insidious force. Bad things happen. You can sit and let it just happen or you can fight, Jalil! You can fight! I don't have to permit all the bad things to occur to me or to others. I can do things, stop things. I am not with no power.

You are not aware—

Hush, Jalil! I am aware of everything! You are dead, my brother, dead in a field my brother and it is my fault and I am sorry so sorry I will always be. So very sorry.

Jalil stood crying.

The elevator dinged and opened.

There is one more thing I must tell you, my dear brother Jedra.

And *what* is *that*. You can tell me nothing that will stop me to save people now. I lost you, my brother. I will not lose my Phyllis, I will marry her and I will rescue my mother and my father and we will live in a house all of us, and I will revere your memory and you will rest in your green field. We will never forget you for the rest of our lives. It will pain me to hear our mother's cries for you.

There is one more thing.

Then say it, brother! The elevator is leaving (he held the doors). Say it so I may do my duty. I am not afraid.

Jalil cried more.

Say it.

What you are doing is not good. Please stop

Out of my way!

Remember, I didn't want to go.

You're lying. It was your idea.

I said, I didn't care. I said, we could die but I didn't want to fight them.

You are a liar!

I remember. You made me go. I only wanted to play soccer, brother! I only wanted to play!

Lies!

Please listen to me, I have to tell you something.

I don't believe in you anymore. You are a phantom.

Jedra stood. The elevator closed. He could hear through the doors the *plaintive my brother, my brother*, in Arabic, soft and muted, a prayer. Jalil stood in the hall, the dusty soccer boy, already fading and dim. Jedra could hear his soccer ball hitting the wall still.

Through the speakers, he heard Josh Groban singing again, the song about falling.

TWENTY

Phyllis slowly lay amongst the pillows on Jedra's couch and deliriously awoke to his small apartment, still and sweet from last night. Somewhere, maybe on his patio, wind chimes slowly twinkled on the soft wind, and in the air cinnamon hung as sweet as candy. She was naked, under a covering, and as she lifted the blanket came all the smells of her and Jedra, the scent of a pure, basic throb, of leather, of blossom. She arose.

Already, though, the flush of wings held her attention, and she heard the cacophony of voices and then of screams. She heard screams for help, and terrifying speed. Angels fluttered all around her, hushed whisperings, thunderous footsteps, sirens, crashes. She held her hand to her head, am I simply insane? It was a rhetorical question, she knew quite simply this was all real, just unheard of. She knew something was going down. She called out, Jedra?

There was silence. A faucet dripped in time with a limbic heartbeat somewhere.

Then, she saw Jedra's small, neatly written note, lying on the table.

Small cold hands pulled her up quickly, Okay, she said, I'm going. The small, cold ethereal voices giggled and said, *quickly*, in feather sounds,

94

quickly, Phyllis, quickly. A shirt was draped on herself, she sprung into jeans. She stood. A warrior, leather-willed. Phyllis had changed again. She stood strong and auburn. Amazonian and all-powerful. Where was she going, anyway?

Something told her, *the hotel. Stop Jedra.* Looking up through the ceiling, she saw the edge of her kingdom. Rain fell on her, as soft as touch, or gilded sighs. She smelled roses through the walls.

The fields of Lebanon were swaying in the breeze. Lillies blooming forth, pushing their scent sickly through the breeze. The roses of Sharon dropped petals and in the gardens of Shirazi grapes were full and juicy from their vines. People danced in the streets and heaven smelled of a thousand blossoms and horns blew and drums pounded. The clouds, Phyllis noticed, sped by the window in macrospeed, pulling birds and blue sky. She felt pushed out of the apartment by the hands of the baby angels. A female angel—Uriel?—whispered hurry, hurry in her pink ears and she found herself in the street, the normal street, gray and metallic, people rushing by in khaki and linen. A huge wind came and a sea of cherry blossoms spun around her, and intoxicated by their scent she whispered, *where do I go?* And again the voices, all million bell voices had no problem responding through the petals, *the hotel. The hotel. Go to the hotel.*

Followed by a sea of petals, she as if flew, so fleet did she run.

THE THIRD TALE:
THE LONELY

I've heard of living at the center, but what about
leaving the center of the center?
Flying toward thankfulness, you become
the rare bird with one wing made of fear,
and one of hope. In autumn,
a rose crawling along the ground in the cold wind.
Rain on the roof runs down and out by the spout
as fast as it can.
Talking is pain.
Lie down and rest,
now that you've found a friend to be with.

—rumi

In room 320 at the Royale Hotel, lives Daniel Espirito, a loner whose only contact with the world is his room service delivery. Daniel was hospitalized a few years back for a messianic complex, for lack of touch with reality, for schizophrenic tendencies. Later he left and lived with his family, a rich scion of Washington law and politics. Daniel is the black sheep, the odd one.

In his early days, they lived in Rio, on the Pao de Azucar in a large mansion on the hill with a maid named Esperanca. Daniel can't forget those days, from age fifteen to seventeen, right before his illness came bounding forward. Daniel's mother, Lucy, became desperately lonely. Her husband, Maximilian, preferred men, something she had always known but chose to overlook. Perhaps she thought of it as a tendency that might wane over the years, yet it did not. Daniel felt the distance between his parents. He became very close to their maid, Esperanca at the same time he became more and more out of touch with reality.

Esperanca, a firm believer in local Candomble, felt he had been possessed by the evil spirits because he had stolen from an altar of Iemanja, goddess of the sea. Esperanca, in desperation, stole him away to cure him. Lucy, his mother, was terrified and scared. She called the police and met Officer Terinho and their strange story follows. The loss of the family seemed to send Daniel over the edge. In the end, they moved back to Washington. Daniel seemed saner, he attended college. Then towards the completion of his thesis, he lost his sense again. He retreated into himself. They had no choice but to hospitalize him. During this time, he was beaten and starved, hovering for hours in the corner like a small dog. His mother cried when she saw him like this, because she loved him desperately. His mother came one day with a plan. They would put Daniel in a hotel to care for him. He could stay there safely and they would pay all the expenses. She would visit him weekly. He could live in his fantasy and be happy. The hotel, though they did not tell them of his illness, was happy for the income. And so Daniel moved into room 320.

Daniel, in his mind, lives in Brazil.

He is obsessed with recipes of Brazilian food. He is very bright, poetic. On the verge of his insanity is his amazing brilliance and they feed each other. This is the story of Daniel and his family, another tale of love, unforeseeable, unpredictable. It is a huge spider web of lies and betrayal, but beneath it all is love. It begins in Brazil and ends at The Royale:

Twenty-One

<u>My Life in Recipes</u> by Daniel Espiritu

From the window, all is blue.

A miraculous, cutting clean edge of cerulean slicing each window in half. My shirt sticks to my body and I tear it off and stand pale and damp on the small veranda.

It has been a long journey and I am tired, weary and sad for my physical vulnerability.

A knock on the door.

A small woman, the cook. Her name is. I've forgotten. I light a cigarette, a stubby French brand bought in the airport.

Her eyes are turtle green and speckled like the sun has dappled amongst the irises.

For your refreshment, she says, in Cariocan Portuguese, full of soft shuffles of the tongue.

I thank you, I say.

She hands me a tray, a scuffed tin number with a bowl of quail eggs and an Atlantica beer.

I thank you. An odd way of saying that. As she leans down, and she is young and strong, her white beads flop out over her shirt.

I like your beads. Oxala. His Portuguese is so good, it surprises her.

The senhor knows Oxala, does he? she says, referring to the God of peace and mercy, is he your orisha?

No. Mine was cast, as, as Shango.

Ish maria, She laughs, oh, Lord.

Where can I buy your beads, anyway?

You can't, boy. You have to earn them.

When she smiles as she leaves, her teeth are long and have a large gap in the center, a small white gateway. I haven't held a woman in a long while and even a woman's smile makes me feel sad and as I smile back, I can feel all the skin on my face reach for the crevices. Not knowing what to say, I cough. She stands. She smells like oranges.

This is the place I live in, this orange-scented world, this place by the window. This is where I have never left.

My mother says I live in Washington. Esperanca is long gone and she lives in Brazil, she says. But it is a lie. I know it is. I haven't seen my mother in quite sometime. She had to go to the north, to Bahia, for some business. In the meantime, a servant boy has brought me some wretched approximation of American food, some beef stew and I reject it. It sits on a tray and I am outraged that here in the heart of Brazil I cannot get a decent acaraje or a decent Moqueca or even Feijoada. So I call room service.

Hello, this is Wanda. Can I take your order?

I'd like acaraje, please, With Dende oil on the side.

Acara—?. Is that on our menu?

I have no menu.

I can send one up—

This is the only thing I request.

Well, sir—

May I speak to the cook?

To the chef?
The chef, whatever.
Well, she's very busy.
Let me speak to the chef at once.
Sir, I'll try, but. Ok, I'll give her the message.

Leslie Downing was a recent graduate of the C.I.A. (The Culinary Institute of America). She had studied in the four years all the proper techniques of butchery, measurement, pastry-making, sauce preparation, menu planning, innovative melding of ingredients, even delicate candy making. She had been hired one week ago at the Royale restaurant "Cipriani Cafe" to update their tired northern Italian cream-and-veal cuisine and bring in a trendy, upscale crowd. Her recent days were spent improvising in the kitchen, trying new flavors, spices, concoctions. At nights she went home reeking of garlic, oil and bacon and collapsed on her futon in her Dupont Circle brownstone apartment. She would take a bath of Lavender salts and put on her comfy silk bathrobe and sit in front of the TV and watch the food channel and read cookbooks and scribble down ideas for the restaurants new trendy change. She had until Friday to come up with an idea, when she would meet with the various managers, catering executives, general managers and president of the hotel to present her idea. So far, she had to admit she had nothing. Bistro French was tired and old. She went on a mad goose chase evolving a Russian idea until it boiled down to too much sour cream and heaviness. Middle-eastern provoked her, but a fabulous one already existed three blocks away, according to Achmed, the waiter. At this point, she was desperate. She cried in long jags and thought of how this was her big break. She had to bring in tastings, menus, a whole design concept in a mere week or she would be fired. Already she could feel the presence of doubt in her abilities when she turned a hollandaise yesterday into curdled lemon butter and when the special she chose for the evening—mahi-mahi in a pecan crust—seemed lackluster and stale. She knew it was. Her mind was too preoccupied.

It was her lovely father who started her interest in cooking. He would get up early with her and they would make his famous orange pancakes, with Cointreau and orange peel. He would make a syrup of orange juice, maple syrup, Cointreau and cream, and they would soak the pancakes and bring them up to her mom. She began experimenting and invented many dishes, sausage pie, chicken with cinnamon, egg pie with smoked salmon, at age twelve. Her father reveled in her dishes. Even now, she thought of his reaction first. What you gonna make that's good, Leslie, up there at the hotel?

Was it a coincidence that since her heart had closed up in the area of love her cooking had failed her as well? Were these two things related in her neural networking? Does good cooking insist on love? Does everything we do insist on love? How much better does food taste when stirred with love than with stress, or fear or contempt.

Sitting at her desk, wearing her stained chef jacket in trendy denim, her pink chef clogs, her red hair scraped back in a chignon, Wanda the waitress sheepishly gave her a pink memo.

There's this guy, up in 320. Wanted to talk to you about some, some dish he wants.

Oh, yeah? She was reading an article about Peruvian potatoes.

Yeah, says he wants some acara-jays, something like that.

Thanks, Wanda.

She was having her lunch, a broiled piece of salmon, some salad. All food was losing flavor. She was tired of grilled food, healthy food. She wanted ugly food that tasted right, that cooked for a while, that had sauce. She wanted the kind of food cooked in a bad kitchen, a kitchen without granite or stainless steel or numerous assorted perfect drawers and latches or subzero refrigerators. These kitchens were monuments to people that didn't cook, that picked up various pre-made dishes at Sutton Place Gourmet and reheated them because they were busy. They didn't want real food, they wanted the essential protein and carb to ingest and move on. Preferably, fat-free or carb-free or flavor-free.

She wanted something ladled out of a badly battered aluminum pan with dark stains on it. Something that had been cooked for hours with real food and oils, fish with bone and skin, meat with sinew and fat, with no parsley or tomato rose or cluster of sautéed zucchini or decorative baby eggplant on the side, just the food.

She finished her salmon and started to call room 320. Anybody that cared that much about a dish she would meet with. Nobody here gave a damn about her profession. She could use talking to someone who liked food. She went to the elevator. In the elevator was a dark man holding one rose wrapped in decorative paper. His eyes were beautiful and mysterious, folded and curved. He smiled and pressed the button three, your floor, miss?

Three, as well.

He had a lovely accent. She wondered where she was from.

It was Khouri Karimi, on his way to court his future love, the young Patricia, and request an evening of salsa dancing.

The rose made her think of all her failed romances and she pushed them out of her head. She would concentrate on her career now. Friday's meeting was coming up.

Khouri left a lime and herb scent wafting from his well-cut suit and she appreciated that.

She loved the smell of a man. Sometimes, it was so good it almost made her hungry.

TWENTY-TWO

In room 320, the door was slightly ajar. She pushed it open, and called out, hello? Is anyone here?

There was silence. Then she heard a small twinging sound coming from her right. It seemed to be some drum-laden music playing from a boom box. A man sitting in shadows by the drapes, a terribly thin man, in an orange Hawaiian shirt, smiled at her.

I have a visitor, he said.

Hi, uh. My name is, uh, Leslie Downing. I'm the executive chef in the Cipriani Cafe. I understand you have some specific requests—

Esperanca, my dear.

I beg your pardon.

I called you 'Esperanca.'

It's not my name.

If you insist—

—as I said, I am happy to discuss your specific requests—

—Miss Leslie Downing, just play along with me. Just play my little game.

Listen—

—I am so very lonely.

He started to cry.

Leslie downing stood there, in her denim shirt. One thing that characterized her was her soft heart. She hated to hurt people's feelings.

Oh, um.

He wiped his face with his sleeve. God, I'm sorry.

I should maybe go.

Sit down. Please.

I guess, she sighed.

Ac-ar-a-je. Ac-a-ra-je. A fritter, delicate, of black-eyed peas. Lightly battered, micro-fast fried. Served with fresh neon orange oil of the palm, dende oil and pepper vinegar. Street food of the Bahian region of Brazil.

Leslie's mouth was watering.

I should write this down—

I have it all for you.

Next, Moqueca. A stew of cilantro, onions, peppers, coconut milk, dende oil, garlic—oh, sweet bulb of life! Cooked down and heavy with shrimp and fish.

Oh my.

Vatapa—a ground stew of dried shrimp, coconut milk, peanuts, dende oil, oozed onto white rice...

This is too much.

Can you bring me these foods? Can you take away that, that beef blandness and just bring what this country is known for, for real food?

This country?

This country we call Brazil, *nossa pais*, this lovely South American haven.

We are in *Washington, D.C.* Oh, you mean like a state of mind...

My mother has you involved also, I see. What's the point, exactly? To frustrate me, to anguish me?

I'm not sure I understand. I *wish* it were Brazil.

It is Brazil.

OK.

Can you make that for me, the good way. Can you make *Acaraje* for me?

I don't see why not. I'd like to try it anyway.

Look the ocean's turned green. It's the afternoon light that does that.

She looked out the window, saw the edge of trees by the Washington Mall. Saw the Washington monument in the background.

Some start to leave the beach now. I hear them, tired, sun-scorched and brown, returning to their apartments. There's a place around the corner, you can get a good *Milanesa* and *suco de caijao*.

She looked confused.

Cashew juice and sautéed steak in breadcrumbs. Come on. Aren't you a chef.

I don't know these things.

Too bad. In Brazil, they are common.

Give me the recipe for the Acaraje, and I'll make it, and the Moqueca.

And when you make it, let's go eat it by the ocean out there.

She laughed. Out there, is the Washington Mall. You want to eat it out there?

Oh, you like to play with me. Listen up! Here's a pencil and paper (hotel stationary), to make:

ACARAJÉ

First get yourself 2 cups of black-eyed peas. Not canned, fresh. Are you writing this down? Good. Then soak overnight until soft and the skins are loose. Here's what else you will need:

1 cup water

2 cloves of garlic. Real garlic.

11/2 tablespoon ground pepper

1 teaspoon baking powder

1 teaspoon salt.

Then you are going to rub the skins off the beans with a cloth. You will put them in a blender and mix everything together until you get a dough. This takes about 4-5 minutes. Heat up some oil and dende palm oil, about three tablespoons for color and flavor, until it is 350 degrees and fry a spoonful of the dough until dark red. Dry on paper towels. Keep mixing the mix so it doesn't separate.

PREPARE:
To taste something unlike any other. This is mystical, prepared only by women. It is the holy food of Candomble, Africa's Yoruba religion mixed with Catholicism, an animistic religion set upon appeasing the whims and ways of the Orishas, numerous gods and goddesses that are in charge of our world. There are ceremonies and rituals and foods that they each like. There is Shango, god of thunder and the color red. There is Oxun, the sexy one, goddess of the rivers, who likes gold and honey, and my favorite, Iemanja, goddess of the ocean and mothers and every year here in Rio there is a ceremony for her on new year's day. Everyone goes to the beach and sets little boats out on the ocean to request a wish, and if she takes it, it comes true and if it doesn't, she rejects it. She is my lady, that Iemanja. But before you even make the acaraje, you have to cook the vatapa and when you fry the acaraje, split it open and fill it with a spoon or two of vatapa and enjoy...

VATAPÁ
(Spicy shrimp puree)
INGREDIENTS:
1 Loaf of French or Italian bread, soaked in water (small).
2 tablespoon peanut butter
1 lb cooked shrimp
1 cup dried shrimp
Ground seasoning with parsley, onion and ginger.
Salt.
2 cups coconut milk
1/2 cup palm oil

Combine in a blender all the ingredients except the cooked shrimps. Pour the mixture in a large saucepan and simmer for about 20 minutes or until you get a thick cream. Add the shrimps and cook additional 10 minutes.

There you go. You got that?

Here. Take this samba CD, as well. I'll be here. I'll be waiting. I never go out.

Do you. You. Live here?

Yes, I live here. And I never go out because I'm afraid of Brazil, too. But I'll be waiting. I'm working on a grand scale book of recipes and life observations. And then I plan to kill myself.

What.

I'm joking. Anyway, I prefer to control all aspects of my life at this point. So, food is one element. Please, I would like all this for tomorrow. On a linen cloth. With a few limes. And if you can find pepper oil, any tienda around the corner will have it. And if you are by the beach, pick me up a *caixinha de siri*—

A what.

Stuffed crab. Oh, well. I'll tell you about that tomorrow.

Thank you. This has been most interesting.

They call me Daniel Espiritu.

They call me Leslie Downing.

It is a pleasure.

I will see you tomorrow, Daniel Espiritu.

Coming down the hall, she passed Patricia, the housemaid, her blond hair falling out of her rubber band, wearing gloves. A rose wrapped in tissue lay on her cleaning stand. Leslie remembered that the dark man in the beautiful suit, who smelled of herbs and spices, had carried that rose.

All around us there is mystery and life, she thought. For the first time in a long time, Leslie felt happy, excited. She had a new idea, something new to cook. She was going to the store, she was leaving early. Outside it rained soft petals as she left, and they smelled like Frangipani and the air was as soft as skin, and there was no reason to believe that this wasn't Brazil after all.

Daniel sat at the window and watched her walk out the door, and in his mind she ran towards the sea. In his heart, he ran towards the sea as well. In the dark tropical night, he closed his eyes toward Brazil and stayed there, the palms rustling, the ocean still and cool.

Twenty-Three

They call me Daniel Espiritu.

I remember when I was taken in the night. It was the most beautiful time of my life.

At first I thought it would be scary. She woke me in the night, I smelled her velvet smell in the dark. She said wake up, wake up now. She had told me for weeks what was wrong with me, why I wouldn't eat. She said hurry up, and we left in the dawn rain. The roads were slippery and drenched, it was a typical Rio downpour. The leaves of the bananas were wet and black and the jungle steamed. In the sky it was red along the Pao de Azucar and Esperanca said this was good, Shango, would come out tonight. I felt almost nothing in those days. Esperanca was the only thing I really trusted. Basically I just needed to be loved in any way. My mother was too sad, sleeping in her darkened room. My father had left and we were not close. I lay in the hammock in the garden most days.

We came to a corrugated tin building down by the ocean on the empty side of the bay. There were the sound of drums althrough the shore and people milled around in white. People were all friendly and they hugged and kissed me repeatedly. I felt welcomed and loved. There was peace.

They all wore flowing white dresses and multicolored beads. They put some on me. They served us rooster cooked in wine and on the altars the blood of the roosters lay. The drummers played the bateria. People started to chant. There was scented smoke in the air.

Esperanca began to tremble. Her whole body changed. I grew scared and tried to run. They held me down.

All at once they were blowing smoke from cigars on me, and the drums were loud and hypnotic and I fell into some kind of trance. I don't really remember. I must've danced like they said, like a crazy man, because the next day my muscles were so sore. I was scratched up. They said I danced and sung and I became Lord Shango. They said I chased every woman here and kissed them and grabbed their bodies. They smeared me with blood and took me to the crossroads down at the end of the driveway, by the shiny Rio moon, where Lord Exu lives. They said, rid this boy of the bad demons that possess his soul. Esperanca said they would leave one day, but she didn't know when. She said, They may return again. Where are they going in the first place, anyway?

That night she brought me to her little hut in the favela, and I was still Shango. She had a little bed in the back and she said I drank two bottles of sugarcane rum and I pulled off all her clothes and I made love to her like no man ever could or has in this world she said, she made love to Lord Shango that night. And in the morning, the police came in and found us, and dragged me naked to their car, and wrapped me in a towel. They took Esperanca away and charged her with kidnapping. I was covered in the smell of her body and blood and soot from the candles and the drums pounded in my head, and even though I still looked like a boy, from that day on, I was a man.

TWENTY-FOUR

A child was gone.

The mother stood in a robe out in the blue dawn, sobbing.

Birds clattered in the surrounding bush as police cars inched up the sandy driveway and the lights in neighboring houses flickered on and the milky white moon still glowed in the sky as the words fell crackling like pearls on tiles from her trembling mouth, *I don't know what to do.*

Peering from a sheer valance 100 yards away, breathing shallow, Senhora Vasques could even feel her pain, though she had no children of her own, even she could sense the hot anguish shuddering down the Lime treed walkway. The police stood helpless, though they spread their legs out like ladders to look strong. The air didn't feel serious, a moist fog from the garden that smelled soapy and wet, and faintly of honey and yet all involved ignored it's sweetness to the fact of what had happened:

The maid had stolen a young boy and disappeared in the night and the dog's incessant whelping by the back door woke them, and then they found the note.

Daniel and me go. Don't look because we hide.
—Esperanca

Twenty-Five

The day advanced and the heat came up and people drifted around the house like loose flimsy cloth in the wind, without purpose but always moving. A sickness spread in their guts when they sat so the newly recovered damask chairs and couch stood soft and insolent. The cook chopped a fish in the back in meditative slices and knew it would stay uneaten and the mother sat with Officer Terinho and answered his careful penciled questions, *black, or dark brown with maybe a slight red tinge*, and the questions about Esperanca, the child's maid, came up strangely blank and it panicked her. *Well, she came up from down in the favelas, where the poor live, she came recommended* but she didn't know the house or her people or even where she was born or her birthday or her age or if she had a husband or most importantly where she would go and why.

Why.

It stayed suspended in the air like a powdered slap and all in a rush she felt like a fool at the same time as she noticed from the window the garden hadn't been weeded in some time and the very chair she sat in was covered in a fine mist of pale dog hair and then all the inattention hit her forcibly, the adrenaline tore through her fleshy chest, her speedy heartbeat gulps, the hot spin of blood and then her cold hands flew up to her ears and she screamed, a broken guileless note of frustration that filled the house.

The garden boy cutting coconuts, the cook searing the fish, the gardener posed over the toilet, fiddling with his zipper, all heads cocked up one inch, eyes staring ahead at nothing.

Nobody moved.

TWENTY-SIX

Lucy, as the mother was called, found a new existence on the floor.

How she got there she didn't know. The transference to the horizontal plain was mysterious, but she accepted it, barely acknowledged it, instead she noticed the world of dusty particles that lay on her floors and that no amount of Brazilian maids from the muddy favelas would ever produce a floor that would gleam at this low level as much as the shiny, well-tended shoes of the policemen that circled her. They were miraculous, those shoes, spotless black mirrors in a circle around her. At night, she envisioned them beside their beds, or moving through the sand in the case of an Ipaneman beach murder or strolling through the sequined curtains of beads at carnival, these impervious, quiet shoes.

She wanted to be lower, to cover, to dig. A huge boiling need to bury herself, to hide from this anguish. Her cheek lay meatily against the cool floor and the sound was only a monstrous rip of a noise, which later she realized, came from her. All their strong arms grasped her, held her up and she roiled like a red snapper caught in the bay. Her skirt had twisted up, her underwear showed, a few pubic hairs twisting from underneath and this indignity was graciously ignored, and this thought even managed to get some attention, a fleeting instantaneous blip that men, in times of great trouble, would turn away from lust when heroism was another choice and as they grappled with her twisting, muffled body a totally inappropriate, she thought, and horrifying, sexual excitement came over her, these strong, honorable men assisting her, helping her in this bad moment, and she wished they would all circle her, hold her, tear her clothes off, and view the woman she was. Perhaps it was an unconscious need for cleansing, to recover what had been lost. T crape off the patina of peanut butter sandwiches made through the years, tears dried, diapers folded and retaped by her manicured hands, baby's heft destroying all her stomach's collagen, to wash away the knowledge and feel of mothering and return to the soft and pearlescent shape of her early womanhood, to stand in front of them, pale and free, pink and dappled, Venus de Milo in a shell of patent leather shoes.

But, she didn't. All thoughts made no sense. Instead they pulled her up and all other thoughts hit her.

Her son wasn't dead.

He needed to be found.

Composure, or some relative of it, pause, came over her as a hot cup of tea had been placed in her hands and she tremblingly held it and smelled the sickly sweet air from the officer who stood to her side. His black and oily hair thinning, his small, acute moustache, his dark eyes that solemnly regarded her, his smell oddly pine-like but with an irritating overcoat of sweet musk, and she was hideously brought back to a cotillion when she was fourteen. A holiday ball in December whereupon, as she stood in front of a mirror with her friend, she used her perfume, a seasonal bottle by Coty, bright green with a pine sprig floating in it's center, and the smell, sickly sweet with a pine essence embodied the night, the fog of young lust, the flailing tongue of her date, a cocky fifteen year old who strongly held her against a cinderblock gym wall and she remembered the heat that blasted from his underarms and then it became imbued with a sort of guilt, too, for no accountable reason, except that it felt strangely wrong.

They called this man Terinho, Officer Terinho. And from the way the words came haltingly from their lips, eyes down, he was the man in charge, the top dog. He stood squarely on the ground. His smell around him, confusing his solid profession. His face, without expression, yet she noticed his eyes. They were soft. Soft black eyes, if that is possible. As in dark fur, or a stain spreading on a cloth.

Terinho ordered his men to search the city, in no uncertain terms. To form squadrons and leagues, to search every favela, every bush, every pocket of the seaside port known as Rio de Janeiro. They didn't hesitate or ask questions. They took to the bush, calling out the child's name as the staff hunkered down and skittered like tiny bugs under a rock.

Lucy looked at Terinho's knees and asked, will she kill my baby?

And in his truncated English, heaved out in chunks of melded inappropriate vowels, he said, he was sure, *shore that this issa nod trooth*, and she was so comforted by such a word of absolute clarity, truth, it shone in her mind as a helpful beacon, he spoke of truth. He was *shore*.

The shore of the ocean circled the city like the sweet, pale arms of a lovely woman.

The flavor of this city was female, hot and misty under the sun, cacophony of sweats and sequins and riches and black beans in metal pots. The sound of eager bodies against adjoining walls during the day, in a bumped rhythm. Birds on porches. Wittled and gleaming bodies, cacao-shaded. Drums. Tin. Terinho.

Terinho pulled away from his woman early in the morning, answering his call.

His body was covered with a scratching pattern of black hairs against his body. He was slight and fine, a river elk, a type of capibara, which was a strange large rodent. He rubbed his nose doughishly, scratched his eyebrow. The woman, she was large and smelled warm. Her eyes still had makeup on them. She was a dancer in a bar by Baja. Her breasts were small, hard shells. She took him in her mouth as he spoke, only his staccato breath giving away her warm melon mouth, spreading warmth, he lays back. His shoes shining on the dirty mud floor. He got up quickly, before she was done, meu amor, she languished.

A child's been taken, he said. This was unusual in Brazil. People did not hurt or steal babies here. At this point he did not know they were talking about a young boy. He was putting on his clothes, mashing his hair down. This woman in the bed was a cousin of a friend. Occasionally, he lay in her bed. It was an act of kindness to each other. He did not love her. She did not love him. Sun was absent from the sky.

I am going to help Americans on the hill. Their child is stolen, he said. Roubada, he said.

Robbed.

She said, *roubada?*

Terinho stood immobile and solid in the American's house. Lucy looked at him as if he were a marble column or a huge unmovable wall of stone. He grabbed up his radio, which cackled with static, and put it near his mouth. He spoke quick, mumbles of Portuguese in its most abbreviated form. He was holding himself up straight, his eyes glaring in blank warrior mode into the garden. When he turned to look at her, they were so glittery and black, the white window's light bounced back in them like two miniature rectangles.

A new world danced in that light, where things acted differently, where physics became so miniaturized it lost all sense of our normal physical laws, where neutrons and gluons broke apart and danced in waves and particles and nothing was until you decided it was, until you saw it, in his black policeman's eyes, that moment, her child was safe, her home was safe, her heart was safe, Senor Terinho's eyes, reflecting the windows of her house, were safety.

Helicopters chopped the balmy tropical air, other characters in the lives of these people prepared for their role in the pivot of events, birds cackled in the garden, the cook tasted the vatapa she made from the fish and found it good, the couple next door made love in their big shadowed bed after lunch, forks tinkled on plates throughout the open windows in the clustered city as people finished lunch, and a mother, whose son was gone, looked up into the chief of the police's eyes.

All her life she had thought of love and it's meaning.
If her life had a theme, then this was it.

She would start by breaking it down, to textualize it's essence, to strip the extremely unfathomable into something palatable, understandable, acceptable.

So, in the beginning, to love someone is to really like them a lot. To find that a group of characteristics that they display are extremely pleasurable to you. Is it about gratification of pleasure then? Is it merely ego-driven? And then she would come back to square one. You like them a lot. When you see them, these characteristics please you (pleasure, ego...). If you like brown eyes, their eyes are brown and earthy, and twinkle with a deep Moorish sparkle, more so than all the other brown eyes. If you appreciate service and kindness, when they mention they volunteer at a children's hospital twice a week, your chest feels warm and saturated with some treacley goo. But it is beyond this she got confused, as she thought of the types of loves and the situational aspect of love—

All she knew really, was that were a series of small buttons, imaginary code openers which unleashed various responses in her and this coterie of tests lay in some etheric room in her heart, her heart which was muscle but also a vast veil which lay over her—

Lucy had never been in love. Poor Lucy.

Her husband, Maximus, preferred men. She knew it, he knew it, seemingly everyone knew it. She knew he pursued and hired ridiculously inept yet beautiful garden boys. The last one—Edison, dusty brown eyes, impossibly luminous skin as sweet and soft as what, some kind of honeyed batter which leapt all over his body and poured itself around the dipping and pulsing muscles of his active body. She had wanted him, too, all his sick cumin-like smells as he whacked down the brush, but she clip-clopped through the garden to the Rio ladies luncheon and he stopped and wiped his cheek, smiled, *bom dia*, strong Cariocan accent and her linen dress, (ironed dry and stiff by Esperanca) and his naked chest made no contact.

A rustle in the evening garden.

She was home early before the concert, though she said she'd be back at ten. A distinct ruffling of leaves and cooing sounds, she thought it was maybe the pelican family the older gardener Josue had said lived near the stream which flowed out back, towards the mountain and as she walked closer, she actually knew what it was somewhere inside her, but lies kept her going, falsehoods about maybe the pelican family until she was face to face with Maximus and Edison, laying in the grassy bank together. Maximus lay on his back, naked and soft, his blond hair tousled, and he said nothing, but looked up and there was deep sadness in his eyes. Edison dashed up, pulling up his pants. He rattled on in Portuguese, odd explanations that were meaningless and he tore off snapping branches in his haste and the boy never came back. Lucy sat on the grass next to Maximus and watched him lying there, all golden and aging, his hair a mix of blond and gray and his face, which always had a child pouch around the mouth, and looked pensive. He still said nothing. A tear ran down his cheek, silent, flashing like a trail of glitter. There was nothing to say. But he looked beautiful, he had always been beautiful. She leaned over and kissed him, wildly, madly, his hand held the whole side of her face. He rolled on top of her, crushing the linen dress in the grass, harshly shoving her breasts, his tongue all over her face, and throughout, as he tore off her underwear and ground her into the grass. She could smell the cuminy gardener all over his face, and then they collapsed in the grass.

TWENTY-SEVEN

I don't know why I am the way I am. I want to be different. But I don't know what it is, said Maximilian. He lay on his side, his arms wrapped around his chest. I love you, I love the children.

I don't like to be touched, he said, as she stroked his back. It makes me sick.

Maxy, she said. I understand you.

No, you don't.

Maximus left a few hours later. His face was wet with tears. He had taken a small apartment in Tijuca. Daniel asked him where he was going. He said he was going to get some air for awhile, and would be back soon, but Lucy knew that was not so. She knew Maxy would never be back.

This was only a month before the boy was taken.
Lucy sat at the table now with Terinho and her boy was gone.

Her life was this right now.

My husband, she said, prefers men to me, like some strange addiction.

Terinho looked up, those black eyes, shiny and dark like the wings of beetles.

He prefers to lay with young beautiful men than me. Occasionally he will, with me, but only when kind of desperate.

Senhora, I think—

He likes women, he can perform with women, but there is something wrong. Therefore I always feel, something is wrong with me. So, now, he has left me. And now my son.

She broke down.

My son, where is he?

Terinho looked around.

So, you see, there are many things wrong. A husband who doesn't want me. A child gone.

We will find him soon—

He is lost.

Terinho's eyebrows shot up.

Mr. Terinho, would you like coffee?

Terinho stood for a long moment.

The cafezinho pouring steam in a small brown mist. The garden through the window, soft and lush, a green haze. Tiles on the floor. It lifted slightly as they walked through the house and knocked pleasantly. The smell of the house: citrusy, moldy, the sharp cinnamon of woman, the powder of children. A cuckold's potpourri. Her skirt, its delicate flounces. She wore skirts of some soft fabric. Women in Rio, Cariocas, wore shorts or bikini bottoms or tight pants. All showing their hard, brown asses. She had a soft rear in a cloud of pale silk, shifting from side to side as she poured the coffee.

May I, he said. He used his bad English. Use your toilet?

She hated that word. He didn't know about Bathroom but she wasn't going to interrupt or correct anybody anymore. She was always fixing people, things. That was over now.

It's there.

He walked down, touching the sides of the wall, his face hunkering. He made it just there. He leaned over the sink, his face crunching and twisted, the tears burning out of him, his low sobbing muffled wrenches. He fell on the tiled floor. He was breathing heavy.

Parra. He screamed at himself. *Parra.* He pinched, slapped his face. *Parra.*

Then he paused. It was over.

He looked around. There was the smell of the toilet, a mushroomy wilted smell. The toilet paper, the underside of the sink (dirty). His shiny shoes. He lifted himself up. His face was a mess, his eyes deep red and swollen, his face raw from salt tears. He washed his face. Dried it. Coughed. He went outside, hummed an artificially bright samba then realized this was a house of mourning, straightened up. Get out, he thought. Get out. Avoid this woman.

Go back to stone.

He came back to her, clean, straight-backed and cool.

He stood drinking the coffee fast.

I need to go, to look for your child...

Her face was crestfallen, desperate.

She came over to him, stood too close.

Take me with you. Please.

His voice sounded squawking and shrill, a foreign language of strange sounds.

Please. Her hand on his arm. Her eyes, moony blue. Please.

He saw the tiles. The garden. Looked down at his shiny shoes.

She grabbed her purse.

Her skirt, silken folds, led him to his car, to the sunshine beginning to crack through the gray dawn. She thought of her son and Esperanca, trying not to think. How close they were. She blocked out these signs. He opened her door.

You actually should stay here. They may call. You should sit by the phone and wait. I will go, look around—

The woman started crying in her palms.

I am too scared to be alone.

Terinho held her shoulders and led her inside. The sun had cracked open upon the living room and he held her elbow and led her to the couch. She fell on it sobbing. Terinho stood above her like a tree. He wished her husband was here, comforting her. It wasn't good to leave a woman like this—

His mother, in a blue dress. Tears across her face. A frying pan in her hand. her mouth, red with lipstick.

—She crumpled her knees further. Terinho, his arms waved erratically above her. He finally held her back and then he cradled her whole body. She became a small ball. She trembled and sobbed, and the thing was, it wasn't even for the child. It was for herself.

Like everyone in the world, they each had stories to tell. Terinho was a silent, bursting envelope that longed to be opened, that went through life solemnly and cleanly and left little residue. He wanted to close his eyes and spew. Instead, he coped and maneuvered and shuffled. Once in a while, he felt a burst and he would run away to some corner and drain and hunker down with tears and then regain his shell and go back in the world.

What does it mean to be a man anymore?

They are damaged warriors that flee from women and then turn around and lie in their arms. Now Lucy was in his arms, but in his arms did not mean in a lovemaking sense that it has come to imply. His arms were a container. He led her in. She sobbed. He took out a tissue, and dried her face.

I will stay with you, Lucy, he said. His men were on the field. He would stay here as an outpost.

This Terinho, an older man reaching his fifties. A man unmarried. A man who lived in a small apartment in Ipanema.

She looked up at him and coughed.

I will make us some lunch, she said. I am not hungry but I will make lunch. We can sit in the garden. And I will tell you my story and you tell me yours.

That sounds very nice, he said.

In the garden it smelled of bananas and passion fruit. The sun was coming up hot. It smelled sweet and sour, like a woman. He sat there and heard her clanging pans. He felt the best he had in a long, long time. Maybe he wouldn't feel sad today.

Senhor Terinho?

His eyes had been closed, bathing in the warmth of the garden.

Could you help me here? Lucy was at the door, struggling to balance a tray as she opened the door.

Oh! Terinho bounded up, his short legs flailing through the green leaves surrounding the path.

I just made a little lunch, it's not much. Just something. I heated up some stew that Esperanca had made before, and some rice. A cloud went over.

It looks good, very good.

It's what they, what you Brazilians call, um. It's, it's—

It's Vatapa.

Yes! This. You like it, Senhor Terinho?

Oh, yes. It is a favorite of mine.

Well, I'm glad. I'm very glad.

Terinho smelled the vatapa and remembered:

One day out of the blue, she came back. Willy was in the garden, Fernandinho was taking a nap. Father was at work. Willy was outside in the garden and he was building a fort and he heard the gate swing and there was his mother.

Willy baby.

She stood there in a yellow dress. He stood up and looked at her. She had been gone a year. The Oranges were ripe again.

Did you miss me? Did you miss your Mommy, baby?

Willy didn't know what to say. He had missed her so sorely he wanted to run to her but he was shy, as if the fantasy of her was more his own than her actual being. He also was afraid she would go away again.

Willy.

She crouched down next to him and the smell of beer was over her, and blossoms. her make-up was smeared under her eyes, and still he could see she was beautiful. The skin on her face was smooth and brown and her hair had a lemony color and hung in a ponytail.

Willy, I'm back for awhile. I want to be with my babies. I missed my babies. Look what I brought you.

She pulled out a GI Joe doll, and a small red truck.

All these toys for you. She got up and her knees were dirty from the ground, oy, Maria. Dirt.

She brushed them off. How about we cook something. I cook you something.

She picked up a brown bag and took his hand. Where's my Fernandinho, eh? Where's my other baby?

She came in and called out Fernandinho, Fernandinho and the impregada, Dolores, came out the kitchen, shuh, shu, he's sleeping—oh, Senhora.

You can go home, Dolores.

I, I...

Go on home. I'm back now.

But, but, Senhora.

Go.

So the empregada left, who was mean anyway and made rubbery fish and bad beans, she left, mumbling some stuff. Willy heard it and he heard her say bad things and he frowned at her. And then his mother said, well, we let the baby sleep, little man.

And then she put Willy on a stool and took all the ingredients she had bought out of a bag carefully, one at a time.

If there is one thing your Daddy can't resist, it's my vatapa. You like Vatapa, Willinho?

I don't know.

Maybe you don't remember.

I don't know.

Well, when you taste this, baby. It all come back. All, come back to you.

She took out shrimp, small pink ones.

Now these. Do you remember when we go down to the shore, your papa and me. You were a tiny one. Maybe two. Or three, maybe you were three. We rent this little place, just a shack. Your daddy and I, we take you out to the marsh. You, me and him. We take these nets. We get close to the water and throw these nets out, they're these sheer things, clear plastic. Oy, mosquitoes bite us bad. All over our bodies. Big welts, xinginho. Your little body all bitten. We throw out those nets and, oisha! Bring it in full of shrimp, popping all over the net. Thousands of them. All pink and snapping and wet, so pretty. They're clear, you know? a soft clear pink. and then, I take them and I cook him like right now, and give them to your father and he, he is the happiest man I ever see. Ever.

The shrimp lie in paper, coral.

This now. Dende oil.

A dark orange oil in a Mason jar.

This is dende, meu bem. They take this out of a palm tree. They squeeze it out.

Soon all the food lay out on the table, fresh smelling.

And she began chopping and cutting and singing. She had Willy peeling shrimp, which was fun. Soon the house was alive again. The shrimp was boiling in coconut milk, and rice was steaming and filling the room with the smell of nuts. And his mother went over and put on a samba record and danced around, shaking her hips gently and smiling as the hair fell in her face, and fernadinho woke up and came down in his pajamas down on his butt down the stairs and he clapped his hands and she picked up Willy and spun him and rocked him and then the door opened, and his father, his big, tall father stood there, watching. He looked and looked as she stopped out of breath, her golden hair loose now across her eyes, Willy holding her neck, his eyes afraid, and he watched his father stand there and he watched his father with tears rolling down his face. And then, his mother put him down. The rice was steaming. The shrimp boiled. His father came and grabbed her and held her crying, his big strong father, and his mother was crying, forgive me, meu bem, forgive me, he could just barely hear her words over the shaggy beat of the old samba music she played. And then, they were silent.

They swayed to the music.

That was just that time, though. After awhile, she took longer to come back. He drove by a bar once and saw her standing outside, with some guys. He called her but she didn't hear. After awhile, she stopped coming at all.

Little Willy Terinho remembers his father saying, forget about your moth-
er, my son, she went bad. Nothing we can ever do, meu filho.

Strangely, you resemble my mother.
I do?
Well, she was blond like you. She was a blond lady.
The Vatapa lay on his plate, uneaten.
I'm sorry. It must not be good.
Oh no. It is perfect. I'm just not feeling so well today. I'm sorry.
He took a small forkful and put it in his mouth and he thought, the past
is over. Move on, you stupid old man.
And once again, what was he doing with this woman. He should be
taking notes. He should scouring Rio with her, in proper police fashion.
He was sitting in her garden enjoying lunch talking of his mother when a
crisis was erupting around them.
He should start somewhere. He looked over at her, her blue eyes
looked into his. He didn't remove his eyes. There was the sweetest air from
her eyes, a soft caress. He held it. It made her eyes pool up.
Senhor Terinho, she said.

He got up abruptly and the chair fell over, Senhor, she said again, and
he felt he couldn't breath.
Excuse me, he said. Excuse me!
He ran to the bathroom, his heels clipping on the tile, the French door
swinging and banging, sweet, rotten bananas in the hall covered in a sea of
fruit flies that flew to the air in a lacey hover as he darted by and then
redescended over the fruit, his hand on the brass door knob, the bathroom,
water splashed on his face, recovery, his chest bound by some emotional
straps, his face a mauled and soft thing in the mirror, a man without an
emotional map. The tears wouldn't stop. Like faucets, with a mind of their
own, the water flowed down his face. He had not cried in thirty two years,
now it was unstoppable.
Softly, from the living room he could hear Lucy had put on samba, the
soft, lush drums poured around his ears. Could he live his life without
hearing this beat, day in and day out. Each time, it wrung him, scorched

him. But he lived in a city of the beat. There was no place to go. He was alone, facing himself, at last.

Out in the back garden, by an orange tree, he played as a child. He pushed a small tin truck through the leaves and made a levee by the roots and piles of cicada husks fluttered in the breeze and his mother came out in a white dress and a trunk. He and his brother then watched as she said she would be back shortly. He got up to hug her and she held her self as a statue, protecting the dress. She smelled soapish and then oranges and the milkman was delivering milk and his brother was crying. A door slammed. And his father stood there, dark in the shadows. And the taxi took her, to go shopping. And then the oranges and the broken ones oozed under his feet and filled him with a smell of rotting fruit and all that was warm and reddish, like the inside of his eyes and he sat back on the ground, holding his truck, closing his eyes, knowing something was wrong but without a grasp. Oranges fell from the tree, he heard a shake and plop beside him, and his father was there, filling his lungs with some kind of swallowed sigh.

He saw his father's feet, atop a pile of old browned oranges and Terinho then started pushing his little truck through the roots of the tree, softly whirring as a truck might. The little truck came to his father's feet and he pushed it over it, then his father kicked it off, stop, he said.

His father went inside, a long whine of screen door, a sound that turns his stomach in homesickness and fear.

His mother never came back.

I am having a nervous breakdown, he thought.

TWENTY-EIGHT

She was outside the door of the bathroom, whispering.

Senhor Terinho. Are you OK?

Yes, yes, I'm sorry. I must've received a virus.

Received?

I must be ill.

He coughed.

Well, if you come out I could make some tea, you could rest on the couch.

He opened the door, smiling.

I am sorry for all this inconvenience. I come to find your child and instead I act like the child, and for this I am truly embarrassed and ashamed. I need to leave and do my job for you—

She could see his face was puffy and his eyes red.

—in the proper manner. So if you will excuse me, I will shortly call the office for news and dispatch myself to the search. This is a grave situation, a matter of life and death, of urgency, a matter of a child's life, a matter of the utmost...utmost.

He looked at the ground and sighed.

Importance.

At that moment Lucy lost her bearings. She reached up and grabbed the collar of his uniform, his eyes flashed up at her— the look of a door swinging open and locks clicking free—and she pressed her mouth on his and held him, eye to eye. They kissed.

Sighing, mashing, rustling.

Terinho and Lucy fell against the wall. His hands were in her hair.

Her hair, all is soft. If her hair was silk or strands of the softest flax or if her hair could be golden strings of beauty or her skin, her skin felt so soft as if it were air. I am touching skin that is powdery air.

His hands are strong and forceful. He wants me. He is devouring me. I am melting. His hands are in my hair. Maximilian. His tongue. His tongue.

My heart is opening.

He is laying against my heart.

TWENTY-NINE

She pulled back from him. You have to forgive me now.

You have to forgive me.

You don't understand.

She led him to the satin couch in the living room. Birds chattered outside the window, a dull cracking in the sun. The sun seemed insolent, loud. It was a day for rain, but sun in Rio was impervious to pain.

I have lied to you and I need to tell you the truth.

She sat down.

I have no small child. There is no small little child that I have lost. It is all a lie. What has happened is, my husband has left me—

I am so sorry.

—It was inevitable. He doesn't love me.

She wiped her face with her sleeve, sloppily.

So that was bad enough. But this morning I realized that Daniel, my teenage son, who is sixteen, has left. He left in spirit for some time. He has not been here. He has been a, some vague shadow in his room, and then, then this morning I did get the note. That Esperanca took him. And I don't know why or what is going on. And I thought, if I called you the police you wouldn't care, you would think they were together or something but I can't understand why or what is going on. And Maxy has abandoned me and gone to Tijuca and I am left with all this mess. What is going on. Please stay. Please stay and help me find them. I am so sorry I lied.

Just yesterday, Terinho sat in his dark brown leather chair in his office and watched small particles of dust dance in the hot sun flooding in the window. He heard the voices of the police station all around, loud grunts and mumbles in Portuguese, phones ringing, footsteps, and he overheard two men walking by, and then he distinctly heard, him? Oh, Terinho? and then laughter, light derisive laughter and he realized his career was over. Just like that. In one stained moment, all the work he had done throughout the years became useless and unrealized. He was a sidebar. He was a man people laughed at. He had lost power. This morning, he took the call from Lucy, in one last attempt to do his job well, but it was over. At the end of the week he planned to quit. His chest felt crushed and solid and what would he do? He would sit in his room and watch TV. He had no life. No woman. No children. No hobbies.

Terinho wanted to be happy with all his might. His body ached to dance, to make love, to feel life. But he was chained down by sadness. A drug could not fix this sadness. He wanted to erase his memories from his mind.

He saw Rio de Janeiro outside the garden, soft and hot, packaged in a quilt of all his memories of childhood and adulthood, good and bad. It all surrounded him, enveloped him. She turned toward him, I feel so comfortable with you, Mr. Terinho.

Why don't you start from the beginning, he said

Ok, OK, Mr. Terinho, I will. It all begins in Washington, D.C. where I am from. Do you know the states, Mr. Terinho?

I have never been.

Mr. Terinho, I am ashamed that I kissed you. I was very inappropriate and I'm not sure what I *am, was* doing——.

I also participated.

She looked at him. He looked at her. She stood up, took his dark hand, she led him through the shrouded hall of the house, by the carved crucifix, by the fountains, by the palms, by the kitchen, to the room at the end, her bedroom. She pulled him and closed the door. She held his chin and kissed his mouth. He grabbed her body and it became almost violent, their need for each other. She was so familiar to his mother as a child it made him love her desperately. He was so masculine and needy of her it burned her up, she had been ignored for years. She pulled off his uniform like it was the casing of a crab, a hard shell, and flung it to the ground and let it lie in the dust that Esperanca had failed to clean in the last week, as she conspired to steal Daniel to the hills of Brazil. Then he she pushed him down on the bed and he was dark and shiny and perfect, and her flounces he pulled off of her like flower petals and he loosened her yellow hair and almost instantly he was on her and in her and almost instantly they feverishly crusaded the territories of each other and then lay back in the rough Cariocan heat, sweatish and palpated. All the petals of the Bougainvillea fell off on the breeze and fell purple and pink all over their wet bodies.

And they slept. People worried and fret and cried in the world, but these two slept.

THIRTY

When I came home, all was changed. Officer Terinho was courting my mother. My father Maxy never came back. Esperanca was gone and forbidden to return. The drums beat outside my window and I longed to go back to the hills, but instead we packed our bags and sailed across the sea, to our home in Washington and that Terinho packed up his things and he never left my mother's side. But I never left Brazil. I am still there. Say what you want but it is all Brazil.

Everything is always Brazil.

I stay in my room and never come out.

You would say it is fear, I am sure.
But it is different.
From my room the moon is perfect and round. It sits in the sky like a vast round eye overseeing all the pain, all the cries, all the joy, all the beauty of this broken world without blinking, without tears. And from this room I can even hear the waves of the sea, crashing and lovely. You see the line of blue. At night the moon will dance on the waves. I will hear laugh-

ter. will hear singing. But I will above it. I will stay untouched by it. In my short life, life has touched me too much. My heart can't take anymore. I came to this country to escape the ruinations of my heart, for once, and here all over again it aches and longs. I want to stop the endless cycle. I don't want to feel with this mangled hunk of tissue. I want to fall from this window and know nothing.

This is no doubt my last entry into a journal of dubious import, but if you are reading this, if you have found this, under the rubble of this tiny cot or perhaps in the trash, please see that it could find the way into some publisher, somewhere. That these words of my journey can be understood at least by my family. And that the recipes I painstakingly compiled can be enjoyed by some.

I remember when I first came to Brazil, so many years back. I remember the airport. It had that smell that makes me happy, the smell of the tropics, the sweet rotten smell of too-ripe fruit. And somewhere, a bateria was playing in the airport. A bateria is the drum part of a samba band and usually consists of African instruments that rattle and batter and squeak. They sounded like a bobbing mass of animals braying for attention. I stood briefly at the clutter of all these sounds, played loopily and softly by a group of dusty skinned Brazilians and almost forgot my sadness. I knew I could live here. It was a love, a love of place. Love always feels right. It is a clicking in place, isn't it? I suppose.

(*The sun has popped through the trees from my apartment, I see. Down in the green shadows light has now dappled the stones. This is when Esperanca will arrive shortly. In ten minutes or so.*)

My mother said I could paint at her house in Rio after my studies, and I took up my other hobby or interest: the pursuit of unusual foodstuffs and receipts. And thus I keep them in my illustrated journal. And on my arrival, exhausted, I lay in my little attic room they had fixed up for me with some simple palms and cool linen sheets and I lay, dirty and fatigued from my travels, on the bed and from my window I could see the lovely line of the Brazilian sea, cool and green in the hazy heat and I started to drift. The smells were so different from Washington. They were fruity, heated rock, herbaceous resiny plants, women's bodies, surf all plaited into a lovely braid which assaulted my nose, and then a knock on the door.

As I opened the door noone was there, but a tray. And on the tray was a bowl, covered in a clean ironed linen, and on top were a pile of freshly hot *Acaraje*. On their side, a small bowl of banana peppers bobbing in oil. One bite. A samba started up in the street. Two men I saw as I tore to the window, two men in rags beating small tins, a woman in the middle, her hand on her hip, tossing her buttocks, laughter, a bite of Acaraje, intense burst of luscious flavors, the woman's eyes looking up at me, laughing, *ting-ting, ting-ting.*

Here's what reminded me just now. Even outside my room, I hear the samba. *Ting-ting.* Laughing. *Gente,* screams a man. People!

People. Life. I am going to die. But outside, life continues. So continue this for me, will you? Bring my words into yourself and hold them for awhile.

While I take my leave.

Ah, Brazil. Esperanca. *Acaraje.* I loved you so.

(*Where is Esperanca? Often by now I can smell her perfume, that's how sharp I am in my senses these days, as I stay alone. I can hear the tiniest sounds, moans from people's room clear across the city. I am on super alert when I hear the sounds of love. They force knives in my heart. I may never feel this again. Where is Esperanca? Usually by now the rustle of her skirt, the flip-flop of her sandals, then the powdery velvet of her voice, that browned palm honey. The spices that come from her air.*)

You know, like I said, I came to die. I was full of despair. My life in the states had fallen apart and I was weary. Everyone leaves me. Women leave me. Friends leave me. I fell in love with the secretary in my department, a young girl named Angela, when I was working on my Ph.D. in physics. She was much younger than me, only nineteen. I was twenty-four. I talked to her as I would come to work and we chatted, and one day we went for a sandwich. Just like that, a sandwich. She held the sandwich in her slim, white hands and her eyes shined and when she laughed, there was a tiny piece of lettuce resting on the corner of her mouth and she flicked it off with her tongue. And we were in a cheap Greek carryout, the walls were covered in grime, there were faded blue pictures of the Acropolis and old calendars and a woman with burlap skin behind the counter frying meat. This was my first love, this girl. Before that, all I did was study, from early on. I would read and study in my room for hours, outside I could see people walking in the streets, holding hands while I studied calculus. I felt safe in math.

Angela wanted to know what I was studying, what my doctorate was about. I tried to explain to her about quantum, how the quantum model for the atom is so small it works differently than the normal atom, but I didn't think she understood how the normal atom worked, either. I looked in her eyes and told her how the electrons don't orbit like planets, that instead they hover as invisible probabilities around the nucleus. She looked at me—(*her eyes were green, Esperanca has sea green eyes, there is something almost animal and scary about green emerald eyes and skin like here, the contrast is so strong and provocative. Esperanca is now quite late, the sun has shifted from the flagstones to the beginning of the stone wall, and my stomach is rumbling. Did I mention I avoid all clocks? I want nothing to remind me of my old calculated life, of science, of exactitude. I want to die in a world of poetry, of blurred specters of probabilities...*).

So her eyes were green, and pretty. Sparkling. She said, it's perhaps like hummingbirds as they gather around flowers, isn't it? You can see them, or know where they are. But because of their flight patterns, you could guess their whereabouts ahead of time. Right?

Science explains nothing, I sat there and thought. My limbic region, my neurotransmitters hurdled and collided electronic signals to and thro and the endocrinological system of my body spurted with new measurements, and as a scientist I could write these facts down, but they explained nothing. Only the poets explain, and I wasn't a poet.

But she was more right than my stupid thesis: *Quantum Query and nondeterministic Query on a Punctured Surface, with a long-range Electron-Phonon Interaction.*

I had been working on this for two years. It was almost finished. But it seemed meaningless drivel suddenly when the world became alive from this syncopated hormonal orchestra in my heart, loins, eyes, head, veins, mouth, eyes: Love.

What is love?

Can I explain that in a theorem? Never. I just want to die.

I want to go back to where I came. I will tell you a secret about me now and don't laugh. Please remember me.

Ever since I was born, I could remember heaven.

I never told anyone because I was told not to, and so I kept it a secret.

I remember everything: The smells of heaven, the light, the sounds—and they were amazing, soft, and delicate and loud and shiny. I remember the angels or whoever those people were. I remember one in particular, Ishmael, I found out is who he is, although at the time I only knew his name as something like isshhhhhuuuu, a soft trembling sound.

Ishmael was my guide, I suppose, the one in charge of me. I was a small, strange being, yet very purposeful. I had a strong mission, they would say, and they said this touchingly, and it was supposed to be very hard. I knew of it then and now, here in earth, I see it, though you have no idea how different thought is on earth and on the different plane I want to call heaven, but I rather think of it as the Place Before, because it's not about what we think of as heaven.

I have told noone of this. I live in a world of scientists and scholars. They would laugh me out of the room, the school, the world. And besides, I was told to never to tell until one day when the right moment would come. But you know when you are waiting for someone or something for a long time, and then you just can't? You break down barriers and leave, you can't take it. It is the rash moment that often defines a life. You leave. A marriage, a job, a person and go forth. So I can't wait anymore. Noone will tell my why I am to live this life of extreme heartbreak over and over, like a wound that never heals. I see happy couples in the streets outside the window, going to church. They have been married for years. Their arms are linked nonchalantly. They argue sillily over the wrong juice purchased, or the way they spend money, or who washes dishes, but the issue of love was long decided and sealed and accepted, and the eyes between the two still catch and burn on that energy and it lingers in their life. But I, I haven't gotten there, as soon as my heart opens it is flung back to whence it came, and can I tell you the pain is great? *The pain is great.* No pain is greater in this world.

So I want to go back where everything is light and warmth and kindness. Where my heart doesn't eternally break. And the reason I came here is simple. I want to be by the wide blue sea when I die. I want to hear the coastal birds in the sky cawing and smell the salt and wind.

My mother says I live in a hotel in Washington, and that outside is Washington and that Brazil is long gone and over and that Esperanca is back in Brazil, maybe even not alive, but I know my mother says that because she doesn't want me to break open this window, which doesn't seem to open, and fling myself into the sandy road of Ipanema, which I plan to do when I finished compiling all my recipes and writings and ideas. This was my plan. I did not tell my mother, but this was my plan.

But like all things in life, my plans were screwed up. I fell in love again.

And then love claws at you like a relentless beast with all its insane beauty and you are devoured again and again. Until you kill it.

I have killed many things. I have killed spiders, flies. I have killed deer, one groundhog, squirrels and numerous frogs with various vehicles through the years. I have killed Hope, with words, and watched it die in other people's eyes. I have killed an unborn child, as I consented to its death with my old girlfriend. It was only a mere sliver of tissue at that point, but holding her hand in the dimly lit recovery room (I being only a mere twenty one) I felt an immense sadness and loss. I killed ideas: quickly and succinctly with the lash of a few sharp words. I killed romance. But worst of all: I killed love, with that same girlfriend, poisoning our relationship with foul words and acts out of guilt and shame until she walked. I took life away from another. My hands carry the taint, my heart carries the shame. A day doesn't go by that I don't remember every visceral experience, the smell, the sight, the grasping last words we said to each other.

Sometimes I wish I could dance. That is what life is all about. Dancing. Get up and dance all of you sad people, cast aside your medicines and your drink and your food and your tears and your cold pursuit of bodies and your credit cards and your shiny cars and your treadmills and your grilled chicken breasts and your shiny loafers and your mawing words and your hemmed down feelings and your no no no and dance with yes yes yes.

Here is the bad thing about me writing down my life and my recipes: The only way to write anything is to get to a point of such desperation that the feelings inside feel trapped and burst forth and suddenly you feel my pain and you live through me and cry through me and sob through me and love through me, and then it is on paper and then you, reader, come and read it, and eat it, you eat my soul and you think nothing of it, you move on in your life but I'm in you. And you move on. I could be a plumber and be free. I could be a clerk in a grocery store and you would never consume me this way.

THIRTY-ONE

The teenage boy named Daniel had just turned seventeen. A large boy, awkward, his shirt always half-untucked and his loafers mashed to one side. His face has a beautiful curvy symmetry and his eyes are black around the edges and crisply blue. He liked ham and cheese sandwiches in the morning with cafezinho and he'd go to the beach with his friends and build bonfires at night and in the morning, Esperanza, the family maid, gathered his clothes, in a heap at the bottom of his bed, smoky-tinged still and his eyes smiled from a corner of the pillows and she pinched his toe. His hair is a shine of black wiggly curls. And soon, she thinks, when his awkwardness smoothes and his muscles and body clams out of the rubbery lankiness of a child, he will stand straight and smooth, an arrow, and girls will call. As she came in the beginning, he was fifteen. She gave him *Acaraje* fritters and *vatapa* and *guarana*, and as his mother slept long afternoons in her shuttered room or fought with the father, Esperanca lay with him in his small walnut bed and let him enjoy her body. It all felt good to her, his knuckly hands on her, the way he reached up on her and stabbed himself in, after she showed him how, how he sucked on her breasts that were so large they slipped to the sides. He was quick and happy. And then she'd would get up and let him sleep. She would start the wash. She would peel shrimp. And then she'd come upstairs to make his bed and there he'd be under the sheets, his eyes open, the sheet popping up, laughter, and he pull her down again, pull up her big skirt, and breathe raspily against her chest. They never spoke of it or said sweetnesses. She felt herself slide into pleasure in silence, squeezed her eyes shut and let it come on. Then she go downstairs and stir the vatapa.

She washed herself with orange water.

A few months ago, at the new year, Daniel found a group of his friends and they went in search of bonfires by the beach. During the day the beach had been full of throngs of people all in fluttery white, walking the shores in the annual Iemanja festival, the goddess of the ocean, the moon, motherhood. People came with tiny silver painted wooden boats holding offerings of perfume, soap and jewelry and it all glittered, everything shone along the beach, he could see it from his veranda when he took his coffee and thought the people looked like a large white snake.

But now they had gone and bonfires and offerings lined the night beach. He wore a pair of jeans and he found a large swath of silk in his mother's room, indigo-colored and wrapped it around his brown neck and they all ran up and down the beach drinking cachaca and Coke from coffee mugs and then they ran out of cachaca and Daniel found a full bottle of Pitu up on a sand heap, the red lobster on the label flashing up on the beach through the bonfire's spiky light. He screamed in his light suedish Portuguese and the others stood, a bit alarmed but bravely allured as he grabbed the bottle and downed a huge salty swig, *that's for Exu*, said one guy's voice, his aunt attended a terreiro in the hills, *you can't do that*. That's just superstition, said Daniel. He fell against the sand and noone would drink his cachaca, so he lay there and they turned on their boombox and the music swept over his head and he felt his head spin. As his eyes sunk low, he saw the water, dimly black in the horizon, heard his friend Ze running with Silvia, saw the candles flickering in the sand where the cachaca was, saw a small lump under the candle. He pulled it out and saw in the ragged candlelight, it said in tiny Portuguese script,

My dearest Iemanja,
My precious Lady of the water,
Accept this drink as a token of my esteem. Please save me from this terri-
ble love.
Yours in piety,
Marco.

He felt he might throw up. he stumbled over to the water, where it looked so cool and dark, like a soft hazy blanket tossed across the land and lay on the shore, and then he rolled in the water, and suddenly amongst him, cluttering the shore, were thousands, thousands of crushed mirrory boats, damaged and wet, some tangled with their offering or soggy paper notes, heaving in the swelling waves all over his body. He picked up one, tied a dangled necklace around his wrist. His friends voices danced down the beach. He was soaking wet, sandy, his hair flat against his head like an expensive animal pelt, holding the crushed silver boat, he went home.

THIRTY-TWO

It was morning and Esperanca squeezed oranges and in her body she felt the energy of Fufu and she went to the boy's room. He lay sprawled in the cover like a shrouded corpse and the silver boat came rolling out as she lay in his arms and she drew back in shame. He awoke with a start and reached for her and she cried, what did you do, fool? Why'd you pick this up?

His head was full of sand.
It's just a *boat*.
It's not just a boat, it's a dead wish and she stood up and shook her hands off all around him in the air, as if her fingers were burned.

But then, he was seventeen, she came by the door with the laundry to go to Lucy's room, and as she went by the door, she heard his soft stammering voice. And it made Esperanca smile. He had a girl in his room. A soft muffled stab went off in her heart, but it went into a quilt of a million painful encounters where men always moved on and noone loved her long and forever, until the ends of time, a phrase she felt on her tongue many times.

It had been a long time since they had lain together. Just weeks before she came in his room in the night and he just lay in her arms and nothing happened. He was awake all night. She asked him what was wrong. But he was silent. She could feel his eyelashes against her chest, and then she drifted off, and when she awoke, maybe an hour or so later, he was still awake, the eyelashes still moving, her chest wet with tears.

What's wrong, menino? She pushed his heavy hair back from his face. Maybe he had fallen in love with someone.

Tell Esperanca.

No, he said.

I can help you, son.

It's nothing.

Nothing is nothing, my boy.

It's, It's. (His voice was sweet and husky, a coconut voice), I am just scared.

Of what? What are you scared of?

There was along pause. Her chest was wetter with his tears.

He didn't speak. She waited.

Everything, he said finally.

Then she lay against his door, smiling, yet deep inside stabbed because he murmured to a girl in his room. She wanted to hear what he was saying, what sweet nothings he was using to ply her clothes off, what Esperancas had taught him and now no wonder all of their time was over. She was too old. A servant. Her ear pressed flat and his voice sounded stronger and the words hazy and then clearer. This is what she heard:

It was a dark place. Hair. Smell. Smell. Smell.

Smell of blood.

On my arms, face, me, all over blood, I am lying in blood, I am covered.

I am gnawing. I crunch bone. A deep growl emits from inside, an unfurling, an unhinging. I snap.

More blood.

The animal is dragged. I grab a leg. I bite a sinewy hunk, I snap. I push down the others.

There in the light of the mouth of the cave, I pull out the animal.

The dark is coming, pouring on the trees. I hover over the animal. My child gnaws on an ear. I want something, though I know not what it is, as the darkness, cold falls on us, we lie on the animal to keep it safe.

Fire.

Is what I want. But I don't know the word. In the dark, things happen. In the light of the new day, the animal is gone, the child is gone. I grunt to the wind. Caked blood on my hands. I walk.

Fire.

My child.

I wander alone now.

Another comes and takes me on the floor. I walk on.

I lie down and sleep. I catch a rabbit, later, but never find the child. A new one comes out later. We stay in the dark.

Fire.

A woman comes, and says things I understand.

All over there is fire. I take her coals. Fire.

THIRTY-THREE

Noone knows what causes schizophrenia. It is a heartbreak for everyone in the family because it tears your heart out to see your son, child, brother, sister, father, mother, torn by illusions and beliefs that have no reality. To Esperanca, Daniel had crossed a bad line with the Orishas. He had defied Iemanja, Yoruba goddess of the waters, by taking one of her sacrifices and mocking it, and drinking her cachaca, and by doing so had invited in dark forces. His heart was bent into a new shape, it leaned towards Esperanca now instead of his mother. Maybe such pain recreates the circuitry of the brain. She loved the boy and then watched him drift in his teens into a solitary island.

Or, is it that he was programmed to disintegrate at a cut-off point, seventeen, when the hormones altered the brain chemistry and then everything refired incorrectly, and would never be the same? Everyone had their theories. When the family packed up for Washington, Esperanca stood at the gate watching them go, crying, praying to Iemanja to free his soul. She never forgot that child. She thought of him often. When you think of an old love, how sweet and tragic is the moment: It's like the periwinkle shadow that moves across the flagstone garden when the sun leaves, acceptable, cold and yet a welcome break from the sun.

THIRTY-FOUR

In her little apartment, Leslie Downing wore warm fuzzy socks with tread on the bottom and a flannel nightgown and Samba music blasted on her speakers as she blended the black-eyed peas in her blender. She felt she might be on to something. Something she couldn't put into words but in her mind she saw the committee of the hotel bosses on Friday, their smug faces expecting foie gras and truffle and risotto and arugula, and she was going to give them *the flavor of life*. She didn't know how yet—she stopped to shake her small hips to the samba—but she wanted food that burned your mouth and came from dirt, that tasted of the ocean, that made people happy, and even though this Daniel Espiritu was strange and alarming, and smelled of onions and dusty tea, he cared about what he ate more than anyone in that whole hotel.

(Or did he, Leslie? Let's inventory so far:

Jedra Abdullah: cheese balls and olives

Khouri Karimi: khormeh sabzi

Patricia: we haven't heard from her but word has it her favorite is pasta with butter and cheese.

Phyllis: she likes a good crisp salad with ranch dressing. So, maybe she
has a point.)

The fritter batter was ready and the vatapa had become thick and
orange. She made sure the oil was at a proper stage and then she quickly
dumped spoonful by spoonful into the oil and delighted in the way they
popped up and buoyed in the oil and smelled like the peaty smell of
unearthing a rock. And then the smell changed and became hot and starchy
and they turned red and she skimmed them out on paper towels and eager-
ly, burning her hand, sliced one open and covered it with a bit of vatapa.

She took this over to her couch and listened to the samba and prepared
to eat. First there was the crisp outer shell which gave way to a mealy souf-
fléd center and then the sharp, oceanic brine of the vatapa, with a spice and
sweetness from the coconut milk. It was heavenly, earthy and light, dense
and poetic and it seemed like she fell to her knees symbolically because all
she had been looking for hit her mouth with force. *It is real.* She had four
in a row, gorging on them, happy, almost tearful, they were so good. She
wanted to call someone, anyone, at ten twenty two in the evening and tell
them how damn good these things were, but her mother and father already
felt she was on the edge. When will you just settle down, her mother would
say, *just find a nice guy, a Caucasian guy* (Leslie often went out with
Middle-Eastern men or Hispanic, not only did she like their looks, but she
tended to meet them as sous chefs, waiters, etc. Her mother didn't approve.
Her mother would've preferred Irish or English, someone ruddy and tall
who played football) and Leslie replied, I'm trying, I'm trying, but she
wasn't really. She was so caught up in her food, in cooking, in striving to
create an experience, a total package in a restaurant that she didn't have
much time for dating. She wanted the senses to explode, the atmosphere to
glow, to control every element. For a while in college she toyed with the
idea of inventing a restaurant with a made-up country of origin and cre-
ating their culture, inventing the language, food, traditions. She even
thought of the name, Trevania, a small island off of Africa, featuring
foods made of monkey, squash, coconuts and an invented sauce called
fer-hi-po, a potent blend of local herbs. She was fairly idealistic then,

not considering if Monkey meat was available even, or edible. She had worked for months on the language. But when she entered the C.I.A such foolishness would've been laughed at so she dropped the idea, to a pile of rubberbanded spiral notebooks pushed away in her closet and grew seriously engaged in French butchering.

There was one person who would care about these fritters, though. It was foolish and absurd, but she wanted to see his face as he bit one, to see if she did it properly. She fried up six more, warmed some vatapa for the side and wrapped it all carefully a linen cloth as he had requested. She had the pepper oil, called Amazonia, in a small bottle. She threw on some jeans and a sweater and flew out the door, to visit Daniel Espiritu.

THIRTY-FIVE

Daniel. Daniel Espiritu, she whispered outside his door. Please open the door.

Finally, after a long period of shuffling, he came to the door. He looked worn and old.

Tonight, he began, I have had the indignity of dining on chicken noodle soup, from a can. Here in Brazil, where soup is always homemade, they have the gall to open a can of imported hogwash and serve it to me. And by a non-Brazilian. It is always like this. Salisbury steak, chicken and ceasar salad, onion soup, all these strange, boring continental foods that are flavorless when I live in the land of flavor—

—I brought *Acaraje*, and, and. She fell into the room after he opened the door—they are magical, I think. Amazing.

He looked at her, at her package.

I don't believe it.

Please. Please try them.

They moved to a table by the window. It was dark outside.

The ocean is bleak and deep tonight. Still. She is solemn and silent. Deep inside, Iemanja broods and misses Shango. I heard the candomble ceremonies on the beach.

On the beach?

I heard the drums. You didn't hear them? Oh, they were loud. They were calling forth Shango. The sky was red, earlier. When the sky is red, Shango is coming. And I saw earlier, the dead chickens on the crossroads, newly killed, with candles and cachaca—

—cachaca?

—rum, bebe!

—Try them, try them, please. I know it is late. I couldn't sleep.

Daniel sat down, sighing. He opened the linen cloth slowly and smelled the fragrance and his eyes closed in pure pleasure.

Can this be? Ha, can it be! Oh, the smell of heaven. You used Dende, my girl, and good dende at that—

—Try!

He grabbed one, bit in delicately, chewing and smiling in delight.

Oh my. Oh my! You have the knack. You are Esperanca!

I am Leslie. Leslie Downing,

Please, suffer me and let me call you Esperanca. You are my Esperanca. You cook like her. These are the best Acarajes I've eaten since hers. You have made me very happy.

Leslie ate two more, soaking up the sauce.

When the morning comes, after the ceremonies, the smoke trails from the burned out fires on the beach. Once, I wandered out on the shore, lost and drunk in my youth. I fell amongst a group, worshipping by the moon. a young woman was jabbering and twirling, and in my naivete, I thought it was a bizarre dance, I didn't know she was possessed. Suddenly, she came running towards me, holding on her outstretched fingers, honey. She offered to me to eat. I was about to, when the crowd rushed in and grabbed me back, yelling no, no!

Why?

Well, she was possessed by Oxun, orisha, one of the goddesses of candomble, and a powerful one at that, and her offering comes with a price tag. She was offering me love but I would have been hers. And Oxun, they say is a possessive lover.

So what happened?

I didn't take it. I've never had love, successfully. Noone stays with me. Did refusing Oxun make me to live in this strange world, removed from all, yet feeling the pain of all? I wonder. It is Iemanja, the goddess of the ocean, of silver, of blue, of mothers, that I think of, that I worship. When I see that line of blue out there, the ocean, it is the color of her eyes, I think.

Daniel Espiritu's own eyes were brown as dirt, glinting with mica from the moon high in the sky.

Leslie noticed the dawn was breaking through the sky. Had she stayed up all night in this Brazilian haze?

I guess I should go, she said. Washington looks beautiful, in the dawn. Did you see the cherry blossoms?

Washington?

Yeah, Washington.

It is Brazil.

Oh, come on. You don't really think that, I mean—

—*It is Brazil and you are a liar*, he suddenly screamed and knocked over her plate of Acarajes and the sauce, all over the rug.

What the—

Tell me it is Brazil.

Leslie Downing was getting scared. She wanted to leave. She felt this man was on edge, dangerous.

It is Brazil.

Yes, it is Brazil.

You see? I was right.

I should probably get back, but we'll try and make that stuff as soon—

Lie on my bed!

Oh, I—

Lie on my bed! Now!

Let me go please.

I said do it.

Daniel had bounded up. He was strong despite being so thin and he pushed her down on the bed.

You can't go.

People know I'm here.

You will stay and we will talk.

OK. Leslie frantically thought of how to escape. Her hands trembled. If she could get to the phone, she could call. She had told noone she was going here, was the problem. Daniel's eyes were dark above her.

Esperanca, why did you go?

She looked at him and played along.

I, I had to go, it was time. It was time to go.

I waited in the garden.

I was there. I was cooking in the kitchen.

What were you cooking, Esperanca?

Those acarajes. Just for you.

Daniel came in front of her and slowly unbuttoned her denim jacket. Leslie grew scared and started to cry.

Hush. I love you. I will never hurt you.

Underneath she wore a lilac lace bra. He brushed it with his hands gently. The room was dark and a samba played on the boombox, it's boom, caach, boom, caach, moving with his hands.

You have the curvy body of a Brazilian, anyone can see that.

She could move toward the phone, and press the room service button somehow.

Oh my God, but you are beautiful.

He had undone her bra and her breasts were exposed. The nipples hardened in the air and he just looked at her.

Meu deus.

She didn't move. The last time a man saw her naked was eight months ago, a horrible encounter with a guy from Match.com, who she wasn't even attracted to. He worked for the Pentagon as an engineer, he was balding and slightly pudgy, he had troubling maintaining an erection and when he did make love to her, it was over in a few seconds, and she felt shamed.

Suddenly, this man was above her, his black hair falling over his face, his eyes blue and soft. He was smiling.

Please let me go home.

He kissed her neck.

Please, please, was lost in the dark dawn. His mouth was on her breast, his hand squeezing it gently.

The last time he was with a woman was years, years ago, with his first wife when he studied for his Ph.D. He trembled, he was terrified.

He remembered Angela, his wife, her eyes were green as grass, and pretty. Sparkling. She said, when he tried to explain quantum physics to her, it's perhaps like hummingbirds as they gather around flowers, isn't it? You can't really see them, or know where they are. But because of their flight patterns, you could guess their whereabouts ahead of time. Right?

Right, he would reply. She had figured out quantum mechanics, in her own way. They lived in a small one bedroom two blocks from the university. He liked to wake, fry eggs in the morning while she slept late on their futon, and wake his wife gently. They would eat together on the patio. His thesis was almost finished, coming to the end, when things went awry. He awoke one morning and sat in the black director's chair and looked out the window, staring at the pigeons. When she awoke, Daniel was carefully ripping up each paper of:

Quantum Query and non-deterministic Query on a Punctured Surface, with a long-range Electron-Phonon Interaction

And sending it out the window, watching each sheet float away on the breeze.

From then on, Daniel was lost. He called his wife Esperanca. His Ph.D. was incomplete, because he talked only of Brazil. His parents came in, after Angela's desperate phone call and found him as she had said— talking to himself, looking off in space, talking of Brazil or Esperanca, only. Delusional. They took him into the clinic and the doctors told them he was schizophrenic and that there were medications that could do wonders. They admitted him. Angela moved back in with her parents and divorced him a year later. Secretly, they were happy to do this. it was terrible stress dealing with him, and relentless. He would be caustic and rude or silent for hours. The old Daniel was gone. In the clinic they could be sure that he was taken care of and being fixed, like dropping off a small dog for grooming. He would emerge, they were sure, clipped and clean and new, back to normal. Let the people do their jobs. But when his mother came back, unexpectedly, months later, he had been beaten and was huddled in a corner. She tried private shrinks, nursing care at home. A nursing home took him in for awhile, down the road from them, but the food and conditions were horrible. I will put him in the hotel, for awhile, until I decide, she told her incredulous husband. I will work out a deal with them. The hotel, slightly European and slightly deshabille, was grateful for the money. They could deal with old money eccentrics. They pandered to his every need. When the mother returned, after two weeks, Daniel was happy. He was firmly in Brazil now, no leaks. Look how the ocean sparkles, he proclaimed when she entered.

Indeed it does, meu filho. Indeed.

Did you ever see such waves in Ipanema?

Never. I brought you some Moqueca de Camarao, it's good.

They sat around eating the shrimp stew. His mother could cook Brazilian food well. She went more with the theme.

You're going to have a great view at Carnaval from up here.

Oh, I know. Caiprinha in hand, I'll be perfect. Esperanca makes the best caipirinhas.

How did he remember that, she thought. Caipirinhas, the Brazilian drink of lime juice and rum, had to be made with a strong hand. She had long forgotten that, but it was true. The woman had such and could push the limes down into the cup with sugar and make a perfect mush, and then she knew exactly how much sugar and cachaca to add. She would bring them caipirinhas to the back porch, along with fried codfish balls, singing a samba along the way. Sometimes she would take a little sip herself and laugh and hold it back from them, her big gap-toothed smile, laughing, swaying her hips. Daniel would be on the hammock, watching. Get over here boy and eat something, she'd say.

The long-legged teenager would amble over, all sleepy-smiled. Brown-skinned, eyes like glass. Earlier after lunch, he had lain in Esperanca's maple arms in her little room, the smell of coconut oil and her grassy body, and now she laughed, a shot of white teeth and swayed to a samba that came from the transistor in the kitchen, and he loved her.

And now, in bed with Leslie Downing, he was with Esperanca. He loved her with the same intensity of his youth, his hunger was fast and desperate, her clothes he sprayed all over the room and he whispered to her in Portuguese and Leslie felt a delicate loosening in her body, she was losing the slow death that had pervaded her life recently, the sterility that she had somehow imposed in her need for respect. She said the words back to him, not knowing their meaning but loving the sugariness of the sounds, and the abandon of his voice. He was not the thin, ascetic looking man who she first encountered, he had become lithe and supple. He held her face with his soft hands and kissed her face, in all the hollows. Mostly, she felt softness from him, a new level of kindness that had been redefined from the tools of his artificial world, as if reality had very little power in the treatment of the heart. She fell asleep covered in sweat, the ocean in her ears, his breath in her mouth, a samba somewhere repeating itself, *welcome to the sea of tears, welcome, welcome.*

Thirty-Six

Leslie Downing awoke naked, in an insane man's arms but she felt happy. All trappings of her life had been thrown aside. She awoke with a vision, an idea.

She saw the meeting with the bosses, it would be in the executive meeting room at 3:00. There would Mr. Morgan, Mr. Bimbley and Mr. Feinstein. They would expect ideas, spreadsheets, architectural drawings, a menu concept. She would give them none of this. She would tell them boldly, it will be called *Esperanca's*. It will be sea green and turquoise and Aqua. The banquettes will be azure silk. The walls will be covered with flecks of sea glass, mired from the Ipanema bay. A Mural of *O Crest* will be on one side. We will have live bateria, samba. The menu will feature vatapa, acaraje, Moquettes and Esperanca's Caiprinhas, lime juice crushed with rum. This man, Daniel Esperitu (for she will bring him in to the meeting) is our chief consultant. And they will go with this idea or they will fire her. And if they do, she will go to Brazil and live on the beach.

This is how she woke on this fine day. Daniel, next to her, stirred and she kissed his neck. She was happy.

She reached over to the phone and called room service. Wanda answered.

Wanda, this is Leslie.

Oh. Leslie? Oh.

Could I get some room service, please?

Well, uh, sure, sure.

I'd like two cafe au laits. Very hot.

Yes...

And some bread. Some cheese. Some papaya.

The continental?

No. French bread. Plain. No muffins.

Scones?

No. Like in Brazil.

Like in Brazil?

From now on, don't bring anything to this room that isn't like Brazil.

Are you coming here later?

No. I am staying here.

She hung up. She was freeing herself. She put on clothes she had worn for days. Daniel woke up and looked at her for a long time. She beckoned him to the window.

The ocean is calm today.

I see. There are lots of people on the beach.

She held him.

Daniel, I have to go later, but I will be back.

OK.

His papers were strewn on the desk.

I will be working on my journals: *Quantum Query and non-deterministic Query on a Punctured Surface, with a long-range Electron-Phonon Interaction.*

What is that?

It was my life at one point, Esperanca, after I left you in Brazil. My brain became different and I went back to the world of science. And then one day, maybe Lord Shango took me back, but it made no sense to me anymore. What punctured surface? What is an electron or a phonon? And why do they interact? The words made no sense to me. My own words, which I had written into a thesis of 100 pages, made no sense. It was gibberish. Another language. I think my brain closed down like a suitcase and buckled away the information. I had a wife, I went to a university, I wrote a thesis, I was obtaining my Ph.D., I lived in an apartment, but I don't know who that person was, it's as if I am watching a movie of someone else. I can only know this one thing, where I am now, in Brazil. In this very moment. And I can only know of the times with you Esperanca, those I remember too well, perfectly. Like last night.

Only.

You are exactly like you've always been.

Only, I'm not Esperanca.

Lies.

I am an American chef named Leslie Downing.

Why were you in my bed.

Because I wanted you.

He just sat, blinking.

Then, what am I doing?

I don't know.

He started to cry.

If you are not Esperanca, then who am I?

You are always, Daniel Espiritu, no matter what. Esperanca or not.

Then where is my Esperanca?

Esperanca must be in Brazil.

But this is Brazil.

She was silent.

This is Brazil.

This is *Washington, D.C.*

Daniel said nothing. He looked at the ground and his face was crumpled. Then he opened the window, and started putting his papers out the window, one by one, all his recipes and journals.

Daniel! Stop.

He pushed her arms away. He said nothing.

Daniel! She pushed him away and he answered her with a muffled cry and then room service was there, and she went to the door to answer. It was Wanda, who looked at her aghast.

Thanks, Wanda.

Uh, OK.

I'll be seeing you.

Wanda left, stunned. She told Benny and Rhoda and Scott, all in the kitchen. She told Achmed and Sally. Everyone who would hear. *The chef went and slept with that crazy.*

Leslie grabbed Daniel and pulled him to the bed, and he collapsed and sobbed and she held him. He slept. But while he slept, the room changed. She thought she heard drums and she smelled a strange smoke, like burning herbs. The room grew dark and in his sleep Daniel's body started to buck up and down and move back and forth. He cried out:

Caboe, Caboe
Caboe, Cabiosile O

And he kept repeating this in some other tongue, and Leslie Downing grew scared and her worldview started to change again. What if, what if he was indeed possessed by this Lord Shango, not schizophrenic or crazy? What if a dark force had taken over his mind? She started to pray, any prayer she could remember, the only one which came to her mind, *The Lord is my shepherd, I shall not want...*

The room grew still. The light changed back to normal. Daniel sat up. He smiled and they went and ate bread and mango and coffee. The light over the ocean was bright and sweet, a pale yellow like gold.

They lay in the bed for a good long time and watched the light change and sometimes they would make love. She liked the way his skin smelled, and everything shuffled down in her life to taste, smell, sight and sound and she tried to leave her reasoning out of everything, because it didn't seem to help her much in the long run. So the skin of Daniel Espiritu had a low golden sheen which looked almost doric in the light and he smelled like a spice which hadn't been imported or invented and he said to her, when he moved on top of her, words that were from another language, and he seemed indefatigable, unstoppable. He concentrated on her body as if it was the only thing he would ever do, and she lay back and the wind again sounded like the ocean. And his mouth tasted light and pure, like the juice of a young peach. When he moved inside her, when he came close to the end, his physical strength was so intense, he bound her to the bed with the tension of his arms. He migrated from soft to strong in seconds and it vacillated between male and female energy and it all begged no comparison. And then it was noon and they slept and then they awoke, and when their heads popped up and saw each other, after sleep, it was joy. It was recognition and joy.

The boundaries and definitions of nationality started to seem irrelevant, to Leslie. What really was Brazil, a group of people, a language? What was the definition of place? What was it about Brazil that some part of his shadowed brain clung to so fiercely? Was it the soft moments of his adolescence, when he felt truly adored by this maid named Esperanca that he held on to? Was he really just insisting on living in an old memory of being loved?

As she perused these thoughts, she lay in the darkened room and heard his breathing, willowy thin, papery in the early morning.

In this way, who didn't insist on inhabiting a different country?

Khouri, did he live in the Tehran of the seventies in the bosom of his family all alive?

Phyllis, in the sanctuary of a heaven she knew before time?

Jedra, in a dusty village in Iraq?

Patricia, in a home she had not inhabited yet, of safety and courage?

And herself, where had she lived? She had lived nowhere but in the cold sterile light of the future where her life would magically appear when she succeeded at the dreams she sought ruthlessly. But what were these dreams, to be a famous chef? And why did this dream seem so cold and barren next to the fantasy of a simple South American country she had never known?

The warmth of Brazil was alive in the room. In the shadows, one could hear the rush of the waves, feel the heat splashing on skin like hot oil, smell the sweet bananas, the exhaust, the salt. There were drums from the corner somewhere. Chunks of portuguese flung on the breeze, punctuating the lull muffled in the halls of the quiet, serene *Royale*.

THIRTY-SEVEN

Khouri held her in his arms, a new Patricia in a shoulderless red dress. The meek washing girl had become a woman. She stood tall and her child was with a babysitter. The dance floor spun with circles of light. Her dress swirled open like a large balloon, and she wore red patent leather sandals and she looked like a star from the forties. She did not know how to salsa, but she moved the way he led her.

The dance of salsa is a mirror of the tensile flow of a man and woman. We have forgotten this dance in our world, a flow of opposites, of yin and yang, metal and fire, sun and moon. The man leads, the woman follows. It is quite simple. We are used to being partners, to doubly leading, to butting heads. The man leads, the woman follows. There is no loss of power. It is simple. When the man suggests a turn, by subtly lifting his arm, the woman turns. They move back and force in syncopation. The man must learn to shake his hips to the music like the woman does easily. It is the rhythm of everything. He moves back, she moves forward. The hips shift and wiggle, reminding us subconsciously of fertility, of the mating ritual, of love. Love is from the heart but lives in the hips as well. The hips of a woman are round and soft, they inspire attraction as well as promise child-bearing. A man's hips are strong and forceful, the engine of his love-making, during which and during salsa his hips twist and pump. The men of this world are experiencing a shift, no longer are they content to be cordoned to the area of non-feeling. They move their hips like a woman and feel the natural movement of the world, they feel the sensual flow of life.

Before this evening, Khouri had had dinner in a small Persian restaurant he found about six blocks away. Patricia had not wanted to have dinner, though he was ready to take her anywhere she wanted. There was a Tapas place he wanted to try, that served sardines and codfish balls with honey sauce, but she had wished to stay home and have hotdogs with her son.

Hotdogs with her son. Would this be his life if he pursued the winsome Patricia? Would they be sharing hotdogs on a tin table with that bright yellow mustard, with a large coke bottle on the table? If he cooked Khormeh sabzi would she disdain the sour flavor? Would she toss out the *Torshi* pickles his mother made homemade, a sour chopped blend of cauliflower, carrots and herbs? Khouri liked to eat them late at night with Feta and bread. When he did he thought of his family, the jokes they shared. He could see his mother's small dark hands, knobby with veins. All Iranian woman seemed to have low voices, he thought, like men. They were tough as men. His sister scooted through traffic on those multi-laned highways as aggressively as any *Irooni*. How would Patricia be, could she be a wife. He had a detailed idea of a wife, it was a certain type of force and strength, a power he needed to maneuver his life. The owner of the restaurant came over to his table, asked him how he liked the *fesenjan*, the house specialty. Chicken cooked in a paste of walnuts, rosewater and pomegranates. It was very good, lied Khouri. It was Ok, but his mother made this very well. She made her own pomegranate jam from pomegranates in her California garden and sent jars of it to Khouri—they lay now in his cellar, untouched miniature altars to his dead mother—with her curvy Farsi on the labels, how sweet of her to make this in her steaming kitchen, boiling away the juice of these fruits, just to make the occasional *fesenjan*, so that her children could eat good Persian food. How culture is lost, in every way but the food, which goes last. The tongue clings to the brain.

First the language slowly recedes, you mix the Farsi with English, until the juxtaposition becomes farcical, comic, a hodgepodge of clashing cultures. Then the Farsi fades. The next generation may not know all the words. English slang takes over, and the clothes and the dances. The dusty smell of a Tehran market is lost, the limes, the dark roasted sumac. In a strip mall, sprinkling the dried sumac on a kebab as the Iranian family stops shopping for lawn furniture at Kmart, the smell of the sumac rising is indeed like the hot steamy market in Tehran, with it's roasted beets the street seller hawks, their sweet iron smell mingling with the meats and the sumac, it all combines and surges forth as memory to the Iranian family and they feel the sensation, the history, albeit meekly, they are simply talking of the lawn furniture, their history wafts by unnoticed except for a brief quiver in the cortex. But they will eat the food. Mixed with cornflakes in the mornings, or dim sum, or hamburgers or Taco Bell, they will still brown the herbs for *khormeh sabzi* and marinate beef in saffron for the barbecue, or grind walnuts for the *fesenjan* or burn the rice on the bottom on purpose for *tah-dig*, because the food lives on.

The owner sits down, introduces himself. His name is Tooraj, he says. I just opened this place three months ago.

It is very nice.

We have belly dancing on Friday nights.

Really.

Beautiful women.

This is good.

And you must try our filet kebab. It is very delectable. Are you here for Nouruz? You have family here?

There is a Nouruz table set up by the front, full of the seven items required for the celebration, the sprouts, the egg, garlic, goldfish, candies, all dutifully arranged.

No, no. I am here on business.

I see. May I ask what field you are in?

I am an engineer for a large firm. Optics.

I see. I was studying Petrochemical engineering in Tehran, then I came here. I met my wife, she is American. And, well, now I own a few restaurants.

Tell, me, your wife is American.

Yes, yes. I have three sons.

Has it been, well, excuse me for being intrusive, has it been difficult with the cultures?

Hmm. Yes. They are very headstrong, these American woman. My wife is better. She is different. Before marriage, these American girls—my wife is different, very—they say these American women do everything, everything! But not my wife. She is very special, different. And the Americans, after marriage, they are very faithful. They don't stray.

I see.

She can cook Iranian. I teach her.

Really.

You'd be surprised. Although, we eat a lot of American food. Hot dogs.

Hmm.

The man got up, said we would bring him tea. He came back with a glass of hot boiling tea and a plate of two Persian pastries. We make these here, too, he said. He left, saying he would be back.

Khouri ate the pastry, it tasted sweet, with ground nuts and cardamom and roses, all the ancient flavors of the Persian Kings, who brought back spices from the silk road in the ancient city of Parthia. Walking after dinner through the streets looking for a taxi, the wind would knock all the pink cherry blossoms off the trees and spray them through the air, like pastel snow, and they landed on his clothes and face and made him laugh, it was so soft and sweet-smelling, Khouri Karimi thought, surely this is a good sign, I am walking in a path of petals, like the aisle of a wedding, strewn with roses.

Spinning Patricia on the floor in her red dress, she made the shape of a rose. Her face became shiny with perspiration and she looked glowing and pink.

They stopped for a coke.

Actually, she wanted a white wine.

Khouri didn't really drink. He was a good Baha'i. He would have an occasional beer.

She held it in her hands and Patricia felt so happy. This strange man was so kind to her. She wasn't sure how long this would last.

If you don't mind me asking, Patricia, but who is the father of your young child?

There was a long pause. A little smile was on her face. She didn't know whether she should say the truth or lie. She wanted to keep this man in her life but she wasn't someone who lied, she didn't have the heart for it. So her head felt hollow and she knew the truth would eventually have to come out. She wiped her head. Khouri felt panic, he knew there was something odd going on.

The father was. She drank from her drink a tiny sip, The father was, my teacher. In school. My gymnastics teacher. I guess I was in love with him.

Khouri was frowning, he heard a buzzing. He felt great anger inside, at this man for his infraction.

He was married and had kids and all, and it only happened. Once. On a trip to Philadelphia for the regionals. So, then, he was fired and moved away. My parents wanted me to give up the baby for adoption, but I never did. So, here I am. It's Ok, because I love him.

Who was Patricia? She sat there mortified. She was proud of her decision. She longed to have a real life. Lately, it was television and cooking and cleaning at the hotel and tired feet. She often took baths. She dated noone, noone seemed interested. She wore large white cotton underwear like a matron. She had no feeling of sexuality whatsoever. She would read stories to her son, wash her face, moisturize, and fall asleep, until work the next day. She cooked the food of her youth: hamburger helper, hot dogs, macaroni and cheese, pork chops. She dreamed she might marry one day, but with whom? She dreamed of being a poet and somehow artistic. She wanted to go to a coffee shop and recite them at an open mike. She wanted to publish them in journals but she wasn't even sure how to write one. It was an outfit she longed to wear. It would give her directionless life a bit of meaning.

Some of the boys from her high school had become successful. She met one, Mike, in Safeway. He was embarrassed and didn't know what to say. He sold cars. He fumbled around and said, take care. And now an Iranian man pursued her, a dark man, older, mysterious whofrightened her.

Khouri was bold. Empowered. He was an orphan who stood tall on the wire and wouldn't look down. He had no time for fripperies. He wanted what he wanted.

Patricia, I intend to marry you. As soon as possible. I wish for you to be my wife.

Adrenaline cascaded in her chest. She looked at him, incredulously.

Marry?

Immediately.

But, I don't.

You need a husband, I can see that. I need a wife. I will love you, I can promise that.

Again, Khouri was safety. His black eyes were safety.

I guess so then.

Then it is settled.

I guess.

Good.

He smiled.

She smiled.

Something was missing. It felt dead calm, emotionless.

They both stared off in space.

The salsa bombarded off the walls and the crowd moved like snakes, slithering to the rhythm. But they both sat there, dumbfounded. They had nothing to say. They might as well have been old people, waiting to die.

In his mind, his mother screamed at him. *You fool, you little fool, you fool.*

In his mind, *khormeh sabzi* filled the house with its lime pitch.

In her mind, she saw a white wedding dress without her in it.

In her mind, she saw herself falling off a cliff in slow motion.

He wanted to hold her hand, to kiss her. She wanted him to say something of love, to tenderly stroke her cheek. The moment was gone, the ceremony aborted.

He wanted to take her to his hotel room. He was terrified.

She missed her son. The place lit up, the party over. Her dress looked like blood in the gauche lighting.

Thirty-Eight

Back in his hotel room, she stood at the mirror. He had ordered coffee. They had drunk it with some small cookies found in the mini refrigerator. He played no music. She was afraid he would try to make love to her. The bed loomed like a giant sign, reminding them of the next step. He was also afraid to touch her. He discussed where they would live. He would sell his house and they could buy a larger house. He would like them to convert to Baha'i. Patricia listened. He told her how he had no family. The air conditioner was cold and it buzzed. The pipes in the wall made strange conking noises. Patricia looked at Khouri, who was so unfamiliar and dark and shiny, and longed to get into her warm bed and hold the soft, downy head of her son. To smell his hair, which was warm and soft, like milk.

I really think I should get back now.

Oh. He was crestfallen. He didn't know how, but he had hoped to make love to her tonight. But then, perhaps he would wait until the marriage.

Driving back in the taxi, she thought of the guy from high school, Mike, who sold cars. They had gone out once, to Pizza Hut. He had picked her up in his green pickup, which smelled of Brut cologne when she got in.

He drank Southern Comfort mixed with coke in a plastic UVA cup, which he held down by his feet. At Pizza Hut they had a deluxe pizza and he talked about going to Padre Island, which was in Texas. She remembered they laughed politely. It wasn't much. He kissed her and he tasted like Sprite. He never called again.

Now all the Mikes would be gone forever, she would be in the arms of a foreigner, who smelled strange and ate weird things. Odd spices would line her cupboards. He might have her wear a covering over her whole body. What if wasn't nice to Trevor, what if he converted him to a foreign religion. Despite all these fears, she didn't know what to do. Her only option was to clean toilets at the hotel. She fell into her soft bed, after the babysitter left, and grabbed the small curled ball of her son. She held him, and loved him, and thought of Khouri, dark and safe, a stalking animal with kindness.

Meanwhile, Khouri battled with himself. What are you doing, he asked. He went down to the Caribbean lounge and had a rum and coke, extremely out of character. A worn looking woman, in barrettes, served him and asked him where he was from. The manager, a man with spiky hair who Khouri thought perhaps was gay, asked him if everything was OK. The entire bar seemed unkempt and disorderly. He answered perfunctorily, but he was so shrouded in doubt, he seemed rude. He tried to imagine his life with Patricia and couldn't. He saw his life alone, he saw his empty house and felt sadder.

THIRTY-NINE

Just six months before he had orchestrated the estate sale of Meryem, his sister and Ali, her husband. He had to go to San Bernardino, where they lived comfortably in a large Spanish mansion, and tour the rooms without their presence, but he felt the warmth of Meryem in all the details, the gold, the brocade, the spring green, the coral she had just decorated with. Tassels, so many of them, hung on all the curtains, the ends of the couches, on doorknobs, and how many Persian hand-knotted rugs did they own? He counted twenty-five. In their bedroom, he smelled her perfume. In her stainless steel refrigerator, old cartons of juice, jars of pomegranate jam from their mother, Torshi pickles, yogurt, leftover kebabs from a take-out, vitamins, teeth whitener, a special facial cream made of sea algae, their life in microscopic detail. This was a sick role he held and he detested it, and yet it held a valor: who else should sell your belongings and mill through them, but a loving brother? It was the duty, the payment of love. Love was a liability, you sped towards pain as fast as you sped towards pleasure, you would suffer eventually because death would come at some point, and so, as he has to pack Meryem's bras into boxes, or throw out her contraceptive pills (and wonder when she was planning to discontinue these and have children, and another wave of sadness, this was never happening) or go through her letters which he tries not to read, but must skim perfunctorily to see if it is important (and learns painful truths of how she feels about her husband), and as these are done, each act makes him sadder and sadder to lose a sister he apparently barely knew. Eventually, it is all too much. Khouri goes and calls an auction company who comes and takes the whole house contents for a mere five thousand dollars while he sits in a Chinese restaurant and eats Plum chicken. And when they call on the cell phone to say, the job is done, he comes over and gets the check (which he donates to the local Baha'i center in their name) and walks through the house in the waning evening light, and it is all empty, soft and quiet padded by the creamy Berber carpeting. And yet, in the middle of the living room, lay one golden tassel, discarded, and Khouri picked it up, and felt himself buckling over and curling into small ball, clutching the tassel. Sobbing, he lay for hours as it darkened outside and he could hear the ringing of children's bikes fleeing by and the revving of motors and leaf blowers and then it was quiet, and he felt very ill.

Since then, since the wooden flight back in the airplane where he felt nothing and the months at home, he has not been able to sleep well, waking at three, four and not being able to sleep. And it is because of one persistent, terrifying thought. He kept the tassel, for some reason. It hangs from his dresser. So he awakes sometimes, looks over in the dark, sees it's quiet gold fringe, and again, the thought, the feeling, will descend. He sometimes tries to warm milk and drink this, like a baby. It doesn't help much. Or take a warm bath. Sometimes, in desperation, a sleeping pill. Still, as the artificial curtain of sleep pulls his eyes down and then, the thought. The thought. The thought:

Will I die alone?

Only tonight, drinking this rum and coke in the lounge, the thought ringing through his brain changes. It begins with the above and mutates and obsesses and coalesces with all the reasons Patricia will not marry him. She did say so but American women say things and mean nothing, they have short memories, like dogs. If he doesn't stay by her constantly, she will fly like a bird quickly to another. He is sure of this. He has heard this said many times, his friends claim that to date an American woman is foolhardy. They are fickle, undependable. They will divorce you quickly as soon as you do any little thing. Is it true, he wonders? Aren't the hearts of all people the same. This takes a while to scan for comparisons. He has no solution. He thinks of his Baha'i upbringing:

The world of humanity has two wings; one is women and the other men. Not until both wings are equally developed can the bird fly. Should one wing remain weak, flight is impossible. Not until the world of women becomes equal to the world of men in the acquisition of virtues and perfections, can success and prosperity be attained, as they ought to be.

He is sure that the heart is the same, that there exists good and bad, and not by culture. The problem he is experiencing is simple: he is alone and sad. It is not a good state to be in. He is in mourning. He sees the face of his mother, her creased face, black short hair, her eyes as deep as tiny blackened wounds. When he hugged her, her bird delicacy in his arms. How was it he was small in her arms once? How life reverses itself. Her soft, muffling voice, always telling him what to do, with love:

Can't you find someone other than this girl? Why this girl?

He is asking himself the same. What has he done? He hasn't been to work this whole week, calling in sick. His boss has called repeatedly on his cell phone. Is he throwing everything away, his career, his education, for this folly? His paper on for the conference in Frankfurt is due on Tuesday. He could call his boss and tell him he is marrying, but this would seem insane.

His house sits alone in another city. He has spent money and time foolishly pursuing a girl who is not right for him. He is an idiot.

The night is long and fitful. He doesn't call Patricia. He plans to leave in the morning and never return. The question doesn't plague him so terribly during the night. Yes. Yes. Yes.

He will die alone.

FORTY

In the morning, after she drops Trevor at the babysitter, she takes a taxi over to the Toyota dealership and sees Mike in the large window and he is talking to a customer and he looks up, surprised. He comes over to her.

Well, hey.

Hi.

You looking for a car?

Well, no, I just. Was around here, came to say hello.

Hey, cool.

He stood awkwardly, smiling.

Would you,hmm, like to get a sandwich or something? she says, I'm kind of hungry.

Lunch? Sure, sure. Let me get my stuff.

She is out of breath. How absurd she is, and foolish. What is she doing? She just, just wants to talk to an American guy, a normal guy to see something. She is checking. Her life is a shambles.

He comes lumbering back, he is a large man, six feet two for sure, he leans way over as compared to small Khouri. She prefers a large man. Or does she? She doesn't even know. After the gym teacher, the pregnancy, she has pretty much avoided all men. She has been a mother, writing her poems. They are not good poems, they are vents for her frustration. They tend to be arduous and clunky vehicles of her emotions, but she labors over them with her pencil, late into the night.

So, how's, what's, your kid's name?

Oh, Trevor.

Yeah. Trevor.

He's good, he's four now.

That's a good age. There's a place up here, a deli.

In the shop she has a tuna fish on rye and Mike has a Rueben. He tells her about fishing. How he uses chicken liver wrapped in pantyhose as bait (*she remembers the dark complexion of Khouri, a burnished gleaming color of light wood, like cherry perhaps. She saw cherry cabinets in Home Depot, it was almost the same pinkish brown, could she write a poem like this?*). How he sits on the bank early in the morning when the sun's coming up, the smell of the river coming up slow. You can smell the mud and the algae, real strong, on the bank. Sometimes you hear turtles snapping on the bank. If you're real sharp, the hissing of river snakes can be heard (*she could write about that cherry wood skin, and those eyes, those black eyes*). You be surprised how awesome it is, the river. You like that, fishing? Camping? I'll tell you (*when they danced, he was so perfect the way he turned her. He knew how to spin her, how happy it felt to dance that dance with a person she liked. Loved?*) I do some camping come summer, that's for sure. Whoa. A camping fool. Got me a good tent. Big one. Practically sets itself up. Schwing! Just pull a little doodad. (*Was it love, love, love? She was feeling sick and strange. She barely knew him and yet, and yet, and yet. This Khouri. This Khouri*) And when I get the grill going, now that's something good. I take those catfish, rub them with cajun spice. You know the kind you buy up there in Safeway? (*maybe she could write a poem and it would be a real one, because she would write about Khouri. She needed to see him. Where was he?*). Hey, earth to Patricia. You listen to anything I said, girl?

She snapped to and looked in his blue eyes. They seemed transparent and faraway.

Can you give me a ride? To the Royale hotel?

Sure. I don't see why not.

FORTY-ONE

In the morning, Khouri wakes early and packs his bags quickly. All of his toiletries he likes to lay out carefully on a washcloth on the counter, and he undoes these and pops them into his bag. His face looks worn and yellowish in the light and deeply sad, and worse, he feels like he has acted like some ridiculous fool, chasing around this girl, neglecting his job, his house, his friends, his whole life. What he will do is simply throw himself into his work more. He will work until ten at night, come back, watch some TV, and sleep. *I will sleep and sleep as much as possible.* But his heart is so heavy and painful. He doesn't know what to do. It is proper to call Patricia. To explain.

He has no idea what to say. He does not know what he feels.

It is something like this: There is a way, a code, a system he is used to. It involves his mother (*dark hair, bony body, sharp bird crevice eyes, smell of sumac and roses, and when she smiles, all crevices around the eyes as warm and loving as sunshine, and all the love comes toward you at the same time, she is angry for my disgraceful behavior, for letting her down, for not being good, for not being Baha'i, for not being a proper Iranian of whom I should be proud, we are the original Aryan race, after all*) and the lack of his sister, Meryem and her husband, Ali, and his other sister, Nour, who was lost early, and his first wife (caramel hair, soft skin, an American,) and his Iranian fiancé (Kimiya) and it has left him a hole in his chest he is seeking to fill with this girl because she has somehow, somehow touched him inexplicably, deeply, somewhere, but he cannot fit her into the above patterning, she does not fit it, it is confusing. He lies on his bed, a mess. He is longing for her, hating her. Somewhere in the hotel she is cleaning rooms. He needs to find her, speak anything to her. See her. Say something. He leaves his bags and leaves his room. He starts at the top floor, gets on the burgundy elevator. It is playing Josh Groban, again. Always this music is playing. He goes to the eighth floor, runs down the hall, looking for the cart. He sees it at the end, and he rushes into room 823, only to encounter an older Peruvian woman pulling a bedspread across the bed, she looks up, hello. Oh, he answers and leaves. He is out of breath now. Why is he rushing, he asks himself.

He runs down the stairs to seven, searches again for the cart. This one looks like hers, as if they are personal. He pushes open the door and goes into 733.

FORTY-TWO

Our Jedra ran through the halls of the hotel, sweating now through his nice pullover and trying to ignore what his brother had told him, but still he had heard the words, *I have something to tell you* and he couldn't ignore this.

His brother hadn't wanted to go. But he did. He did. He remembers.

Suddenly Montague was looming in front of him, coming out of room 542.

Hey Jedra man. Fixed the circuits you know. Coded them down. You know. Hey.

Jedra stood in front of him, shaking.

Whoa. Whoa man. Calm down. You Okay, little man?

Jedra caught his breath, gulped some air. Tried to make his face stiller. OK.

Yeah, because. Whew. Sit down, take it easy. Like I said, you know that break on the fourth? Got her running good. Where you tools man? Where you little jean bag all cute and all?

Jedra just pointed downstairs as he wiped his forehead with his palm, wiped his cheek.

You don't look too good. You sure you OK? You sure?

Yes, yes.

Yeah, come on. Sit down here.

No, I—

Sit down, for a bit.

Please! He yanked his arm away.

Hey, calm—

Get off! Yelled Jedra. Leave me alone now!

Damn, I'm just.

I have to go.

Jedra man, what's up with you—

I'm going. Going. Jedra ran down the hall. He could hear Montague, though, as he ran to the stairs.

Damn. Damn. Damn

But he didn't care. He had a mission still to accomplish. He didn't want to run into anyone he knew. He ran up the stairs, two stairs at a time, his legs quivering. Got to get there, he said. Got to. He ignored the idea of the field. He would think of this later. He had ten more flights to go until the top floor. He could do it. His lungs were burning. He tried to think of Phyllis, his life with her. He got to the top and gasped for air. There were skylights everywhere and he looked pale and dusty now in the light. He saw the door of the boss and he went towards it. He was drenched in sweat. He smelled slightly of Feta cheese and mildew. His hair was soaking wet and he trembled.

He came to the door and he knew he now walked in the steps of heroism. He had lost all things that could matter, like dignity and pride, but he could gain by this act. He knocked on the door, the door of Mr. Edward S. Feinstein, President, of the fine and revered Royale Hotel. A perky *come in* responded and Jedra opened to face the desk of his secretary, Marge Wallace, a plain brown-wrapper type of woman. A slip dress bound in the waist by elastic in pea green. Hair short and curled and water-colored. Large oatmeal arms squeezing out of the dress. A few hairs coming out of her chin.

Good afternoon. She frowned slightly, he was so sweaty. Can I help you?

Appointment with president, please.
Yes, you have one?
Appointment please.
I don't understand. You *have* one or *want* one.
Having one now please.
Well, your name.
Mr. Jedra Abdullah.
I, I don't see any Jedra Abdullah, here, maybe—
Having one now please.
I hear that but.
Now please.
Well, Ok, he's free. One second.
She pressed the intercom.
A Mr. Jedra here. OK. Yes. Uh, he says.
But Jedra had already passed her,
Mr. Abdullah,
And had gone to the door

FORTY-THREE

Mr. Feinstein had plans to leave early for Passover that night. His wife, Doris, had called him five times today to ask him to buy extra parsley, did he think four quarts of matzoh ball soup was enough considering the Schwartzes were coming and bringing their annoying Aunt Miriam, and could he possible stop and get some more Chardonnay at the liquor store? He had said, calmly, yes, Doris, yes, OK. I am at work and I am busy so give me a break. This is seder, for God's sake, she had said. I'm doing all the work, after all. I'll be doing stuff when I'm there, he said. Did you practice your speech? she said. Yes, he lied. It would be the usual banter, *I am so honored to have my friends, family in our home, this year has been so*—

A small, sweaty Arab looking man fell into his room. He seemed greatly agitated. He shook. His eyes looked fierce and dark and concerning. Mr. Feinstein recognized him somehow.

Can I help you?

He heard the intercom, heard his secretary bleating, a man has just *insisted*—

—OK, thank you, He's here. Joel Feinstein. He stood up, offered his palm. How can I help you?

It is. (he was breathing so hard.) A matter of great urgency.

Urgency.

Importance.

OK. Well.

Sit?

Please.

Sir, I am Jedra Abdullah. I come here from Iraq. I am working hard here. I am in the boiler room, your technician with Mr. Montague, I am working all the time.

Yes. Yes. (that is how he recognized him)

I try and do the good job—

Well, I certainly recognize that, who is your supervisor, Jedra, is it Timsom Parks?

Yes, Mr. Timson.

Couldn't you have gone to Timson, for your questions, I have to—(he looked at his watch)—I have to run here shortly, it's a family holiday—

Is not questions I have—

Well, I'm sure Timson can handle your issues quite well, you see, anyway—(he started to rise)—I'm afraid I'm going to have to see you out—

Please!

Timson is your supervisor, any problem you have he can deal with most professionally—

Are you not the president?

Of course, but you see each manager has their jurisdiction and is actually much more knowledgeable in those areas than I, I really deal with the budget, and other matters, now if you'll excuse me—Carol—he buzzed his secretary—

Please—

Mr. Jedra, I am sure—

Please!

Now, calm down, we're adults here.

Please! He was shrieking. He had risen in his chair. Veins bulged on his neck. His eyes were watery.

Please! Please! Urgent!—

Mr. Jedra—

Please!

I'm going to have to ask you to—

IT'S GOING TO BLOW.

I beg, what, what,

Blow. All Up. Soon.

I'm sorry, I'm not understanding.

Everything. Blowing. Finished. Destroyed. Dead.

Mr. Jedra, what are you saying?

This was said in a muffled squawk. All blood had drained from his face. He remembered 9/11 distinctly. He remembered his wife calling, crying. His college friend was killed in the blast, a stock analyst. He attended the memorial. He remembered the sight on TV, the giant walls falling. He felt powerless, the fire, the crying. The long search. Now, an Iraqi man was in his office, screaming of explosions. The man was crying. He was yelling:

GONNA BLOW. SOON. GONNA BLOW.

Calm down sir, let's discuss.

ALL THE HOTEL GONNA BLOW, THE WALL CRUSH IN. ALL THE PIPE GONNA BURST.

Jedra was shaking, his face wrinkled like brown paper. He saw his mother, her kind smile, her dimples, the tea in the afternoon, her apron, her bread song, her smell of lilies, he saw his father, his slippers, his white heels popping out the back. He saw them breaking fast together, eating bread, laughing and celebrating through the night. He saw his brother's body in the field. His whole family away from him, his parents suffering without electricity and food and bombs falling everywhere and Jedra comfortable in a country he didn't belong. He belonged with all of them.

He ran out of the room, embarrassed he was a grown man crying and when would it stop, when would he be listened to and respected and loved? He ran down the hall, sobbing. He had told him and he hoped he understood. He must find Phyllis. He must hold Phyllis. But maybe now she would hate him or die or leave and he would be alone as usual in the boiler room and the walls would blow and he would then be drowned in the waves and then he would see his dear family in another place and this sadness would be gone. Oh, my Allah, dear one, I pray to you.

Doris was calling again, Joel Feinstein picked up, stunned, Another thing, she began. More matzoh. Pick up one or two big boxes, too. Joel?

Doris. He whispered.

What. *What*, Joel.

I gotta go. Crisis.

Crisis?

Oh My God, I don't think I can get those things. There's something—

What is it, Joel?

A crazy Arab. Threatening explosions.

Get out, get the hell out.

I'm going!

God sakes!

OK! I'm calling the police!

Honey!

Bye!

Joel was trembling. He could be a hero or dead meat. Hurry. He called Loss Prevention.

He stumbled and hyperventilated. *Kyle, There's an emergency*—he began.

He ran out to his secretary. Go home, that guy is threatening a bomb—

Oh, Jesus Christ—

Leave.

Feinstein ran down to the executive offices, talked to Morgan and Bimbley, told them he called L.P., talked to the front desk manager. People were running, packing papers. Leave, they screamed at each other. They remembered how people didn't leave the building during 911. There was a scurry, frantic activity. Wastepaper baskets, files, cups of coffee were knocked over. A vase of lilies and roses was overturned. Someone screamed. They rushed to the elevator. The smell of sweat was animal and desperate in the air. A secretary looked oily and disheveled. Bimbley was

on his cell. Morgan kept pushing the button frantically. Feinstein ran down the hall
and yelled:

I'm taking the Goddamn stairs Jesus Christ fucking unbelievable on Passover no less.

FORTY-FOUR

M r. Kyle Logan of Loss Prevention had just eaten a slice of pizza. The biggest event of the last six months had been the robbery of a diamond tennis bracelet last November, but it was actually suspected the victim had left it by the side of the pool, but she claimed insurance on it anyway. Her name was Vicky Druthers and he had interviewed her for hours and then described the tennis bracelet in a lengthy essay in his report, and, yes, Goddamnit, he would admit his life was Lordy-to-hell dull as dirt. That's where the kayaks came in, the extreme kayaking he had taken up lately. He had not told Sally, his wife, he nearly drowned last weekend on the Susquehanna, that he was underwater for awhile and the kayak hit a rock and pounded him against it, and his friend Terry had to pull him, blue and cyanotic, out of the water and give him mouth-to-mouth. When he came to, he saw the sky and thought he had died. Terry freaked out and shook him. He spurted a bunch of river water up and coughed and threw up a bit. Jeez, man, Terry kept saying that night, when they ate at a Mexican restaurant. Jeez, you were almost dying, you fuck. There was an awkward silence after that. The truth was, neither really knew much about kayaking, they were not experts. Both were pushing themselves, pushing the boundaries for the thrill it brought, but the thrill was afforded by a quick slide by disaster and then back again. It made no sense. It somehow allayed the diapers, the cable TV, the tennis bracelets. It was something deep and pitiful that Kyle couldn't explain. There was a lot of shame involved, but both men now were too addicted to the weekend suicide attempts to care. There was an erotic edge to the adrenaline. They just said it was fun. They never talked much, beside *shoot the shit*, as Terry would say. But they were silent coming back the next day. They came to artificially when Kyle's wife, Dani, greeted them at the door.

When she asked about his trip, he said, pretty routine, wouldn't you say, Terry? Not bad, said Terry, coughing in protest. The coughing reminded him of the gush of the river bilge that came flooding out of Kyle's chest, when he came back to breathing. He shuddered. Are you cold, said Dani? Let me turn down the AC. The kids ran in from outside where they frolicked on a slip 'n slide. Life became sweet and careful again. The dark water would loom up again, another weekend. He dreamed of the Colorado, the Nile, the Yangtze.

One would think Loss Prevention would involve more danger, thought Kyle. He got to carry a gun. He had a direct line to the FBI. He spent a lot of money every month on the biggest SUV he could find. It sat daintily overnight on his immaculate black paved cul-de-sac, where it should've been parked askew on a cliff in the Rockies, covered in mud, while he kayaked below in grade four conditions, but it would be, yes, it would be. One of these days.

He had always felt, always, always, that the Iraqi dude was trouble. He probably worked for Al-Qaeda. They all do, somehow. He felt they didn't do proper backgrounds on all the foreigners that worked there. You just never knew. These days. You never knew.

Feinstein had made the call. It glowed red and then he was all out of breath and Kyle got the hell up off his ass. There was no suspected site. He called the FBI and local law enforcement. They brought in the dogs. One wasn't sure if it was biological or plastic or what. One couldn't say where the dead zone, the red zone was, without a suspect device. Where the hell was the suspect device?

These days he'd taken to hanging around the Caribbean Lounge downstairs, drinking a sex on the beach, when Mario the bartender would slip him one. This would've gotten him fired. he was having a weird thing with a waitress, Carla, for two weeks now. It hadn't become a full fledged affair yet but they had kissed in the supply room on two occasions. She might go Fatal Attraction on him at any moment. Between the killing waters, the drinking, the waitress, he knew he was screwing up. He was kind of out of control and wasn't sure of his motives, but he knew he wasn't bad. He knew he was lost, scrambling around looking for something that felt like himself .

FORTY-FIVE

Jedra Abdullah ran down the stairs to the boiler room, his little sanctuary, and sat on his red crate and pushed in the sooty boombox in the corner and listened to Josh Groban sing about falling, again, for the thousandth time and tried to eek some comfort from it, but it felt like poison. All was dark around him and he sat there, sobbing. Whining through the air, he heard the dim screech of sirens. All around him he could feel the pressure from the water. He wondered why all he tried failed miserably, why Mr. Feinstein refused to hear his plea and turn him into a hero and now what would he do, no doubt Phyllis had left his house forever and he would come home to an empty house and all his family were dead now, too. There was no reason for him to continue on in this existence. His small denim bag lay at his feet.

A task force was pouring into the hotel through the back entrances. People were being escorted out of the building. Hotel customers were being woken from their naps, interrupted in lunch, the lobby was a mess. People were starting to run. There was chaos and cacophony, rushing herds of people, terrified and senseless.

Jedra Abdullah, downstairs, unaware.

When the men in the suits, some kind of special task force, crashed through the boiler room, they saw the small red crate, overturned. The dogs were whining, high-pitched, crashing into the crates and breathing hard. Drool splattered from their wet mouths in all directions. There was a small denim bag with tools, and the dogs had overturned a small paper plate containing some olives and a bit of Feta cheese, and one was licking the cheese and an officer, yelled, SCOUT! and the dog stopped. The boombox still was on, and Josh Groban was singing through all of this. This man couldn't be far. Their flashlights crisscrossed the dark like white lines of paint, and they tromped around, yelling inane things that made no sense, and they yelled in Arabic, with Oklahoma accents, to *come out immediately. There will be severe repercussions*, they added.

They were not good searchers, really. The men had not learned the art of tunnels.

In a far corner, slid into a small vent were Phyllis and Jedra, like two tiny mice, wedged into a crevice. Their hearts battered against each other's thin carapaces and they breathed shallowly. Phyllis smelled of sweat and coconuts and Jedra smelled of onions and creosote, and then the boots all crashed through a next room and yelled and screamed and they sat in the cool, dark, quiet for awhile as moles.

Then Phyllis suggested they climb the vents, all the way to the top and get out on the roof, so they did. It was extremely hard and she was barefoot. Each time she stepped she had to hang on a bent section of tin and hang her toes on the same below and they were throbbing, and Jedra's nails were burning, but he did the same. And just when he would get a grip and lift up he would bang into her buttocks and she would almost laugh and yet this was not a laughing situation, they were being hunted down. They would put him in jail again, forever and this made him sad and he didn't know why when all he tried to do was help this place from exploding, and that's another thing, it would explode and they would die. When he was down in the boiler room, he could hear that the pressure was even greater, it was whining, and pinging and soon it would snap, and then death would be fast and victorious, he was speaking fast in Arabic about all of this and Phyllis said please, sshh. So, he was quiet. Yet he could still hear the Josh Groban ringing out, which made everything seem surreal. And it always made him cry, so once again, Jedra Abdullah was crying as they climbed, like giant unwieldy spiders, through the silvery vent system of the Royale.

FORTY-SIX

Khouri pushes open the door of 732 and just as he sees another anony-mous maid emptying a wastepaper basket, he hears an alarm of sorts and the maid looks up askance. What's that, she says.

> I don't know. Where is Patricia?
> Patricia?
> The young maid who works here, blond one? Small?
> Oh. Patty?
> Perhaps.
> I don't know.
> The alarm again. The sound of lots of running.
> Something is going on out there, she says. Get out my way. She push-es past him.
> He feels strange.

As he enters the hall again, a mass of executives tromp by and by now, Khouri realizes something is truly amiss. He will go down to the lobby. He runs down the hall.

He is running and running, looking for her and the people are pushing him in all directions and he climbs up to the top floor and hears a sound in the supply closet and he opens it to find the woman from the front desk and that small Arab who fixed his room before, standing disheveled and ragged and covered in dust.

And Jedra, Jedra who is beside himself, tells him to close the door and go away,

And Khouri is angry, have you seen Patricia, he says, she works here?

No, says Jedra in Arabic, leave us alone.

I don't speak Arabic, I speak Farsi, you know that, says Khouri.

I know very well where you are from. You are my enemy.

I am not your enemy, my friend. I am a man looking for Patricia, who is in danger. What is going on anyway?

The hotel is going to blow, said Jedra.

The world is ending, said Phyllis.

We are going to the roof, said Jedra. through these back stairs over there.

So there is a bomb in the hotel?

The pipes, the water, it will blow.

Khouri looks at him. For this, people are running like this??

Trust me.

Khouri laughs. A few water pipes to break is not so—

Be quiet, you idiot! yells Jedra.

There is no time, says Phyllis. The end is coming.

I have to find her, says Khouri.

In his mind, he knows how it will end. He will never find her. She is hidden somewhere. He will search and search and she will be in some small corner, afraid. And then perhaps there really is a bomb, maybe this small Iraqi fool made a plastic bomb in his spare time, and it will go off and the old hotel will blow up in one large crash of cinderblock and dust and glass shards and she will be crushed. He will stand outside the hotel and watch another person leave his life. He will then drive in his car and lie on the steering wheel and cry and hold the gold tassel of his sister and see his mother's monkey eyes, and maybe his chest will cave in, implode from all the pain he has suffered. But then, there is the boy, Trevor. Another orphan. So he will go get him and hold him and then maybe his life will some meaning. He will take care of the boy. It will ease his heart. It will be orphan with orphan. Perhaps this is the meaning God has bestowed on him. Another being who can understand the windy feeling of no family.

Phyllis grabbed his arm. Jedra had gone running ahead.

You have to help us.

Me?

They are after Jedra, they think he put a bomb here, but he didn't. They are searching for him now.

And what do I do?

Talk to them?

Talk to them. Say it is a mistake. Say there is no bomb.

They will suspect me. I am Middle Eastern as well.

Please.

Phyllis! I am going to the roof!

Jedra had found the door and was leaving. Phyllis looked at him and ran off. Then they were gone.

FORTY-SEVEN

Kyle of Loss Prevention has the place emptied and pretty much evacuated. He worries he might've overreacted here, after all there is no actual detection of a device, so no red zone, or dead zone, no site of combustion, so to be on the safe side, he just pulled everyone out. I mean, what if he veered on caution, and it had biological aspects and everyone got sprayed with sarin and nerved out and convulsed and died all over the place, how would he look? Like a dumb fool, that's what.

Evacuate. Get them out. He didn't care if it was chaos, which it was. People were in pajamas, half naked. Some actually naked. Or with shaving cream on. Disheveled. But where was the device?

A special task force is still in there searching for the guy. Was he operating a whole El Qaeda network right from the hotel? Wouldn't be surprised.

Hey, there, sir, says Kyle to Mr. Feinstein.

Kyle, what's the situation. Any luck on locating anything here?

Not yet, sir. Dogs are in...

Ri—ight. Hmm.

You talked to the guy, right.

Yeah. He was pretty incoherent. He was saying a lot of stuff. Lot of Arabic. He was out there, maniacal.

Probably a key player.

Who'd of thought at the Royale.

May be a whole network at work.

You think?

Possible.

Don't get it.

So, it's that little guy, down in the boiler room. The technician. Jedra, right?

Yeah, little guy. Got that knapsack.

He seemed nice enough.

You never know.

This was a crisis Feinstein had never known. Doris wouldn't shut up about the seder. How could this happen. Something about the fact that she rented so much for the event, and that so many relatives were down, really set her off. At least he didn't have to stop for all that crap now. Ha.

Then he felt guilty with that last thought. Inappropriate.

FORTY-EIGHT

Patricia has been dropped off at the back by Mike, the service entrance. He says, you know we could go fishing sometime, up on the river, if you like, and she just says sure, Mike. I'll call you. I have your card.

She watches him drive off and then she says, that's the end. That's the end of you and all of you, forever. All of you Mikes. And Toms. And Carls. And Bobs. Goodbye.

And then she enters the hotel.

There is a room she has always loved, for some reason. It is suite 333, a room of roses.

The wallpaper is a rose pattern and the bedspreads and the curtains match. It is a corner room and she always cleans it lovingly. It is the hotel's honeymoon suite. Patricia has her master card for opening the doors, and so she takes the service elevator to the third floor. All is quiet around her. She cannot hear Jedra Abdullah and Phyllis in the vents or hear the growing chaos of the hotel. In fact, all is peace. She comes to the room, opens it, and is flooded with the scent of freshly cut roses. The room has been occupied. The bed is still unmade and roses, bunches of roses are every-where. Rose petals cover all the floors and the bed, and an empty bottle of pink champagne floats in a pool of water in an ice bucket, and yet the people have left, there are no suitcases or belongings. Someone has written, *I love you forever*, with red lipstick on the mirror. She lays on the bed, which smells of the lightest floral perfume and she closes her eyes, and all she can see is Trevor.

Maybe she slept, maybe she just went into a daze, but when she awakes she wants to write a poem. She has been burning with this for hours. She finds the hotel stationary and a pen and she begins to write. She scratches out words, and chews the pencil. She dreams of Khouri's skin, his eyes. The exact color. She writes:

Love me in a field of roses and thorns,
   you of the wounded eyes and sandalwood skin.
   Where the angels leave their soft, sweet feathers for me to find
   and I brush one across my lips
   I am the huntress who seeks your heart
   like the baby dove in my palm, it's black eyes blinking up, it's mouth so red
and wet,
      love me like we're in a field where things never change,
      where day never comes, just the lovely fog of all the stars,
      of your darkened arms around me, crushing the grass
      love me like you'll never leave me again.
      Oh, the field of your desire opens all around me,
      and fills me with the sweet scent of broken skin.
      I am the huntress who seeks your heart.
      I am diana in the field, carrying a spear of shame.
      I am the shadow you turn to find
      has faded in the light.
      Hold me before the last gasp of dawn.
      the wheat is crushed under the weight of your heart, so heavy
      and ready to love me again.
      I close my eyes and summer roses are fading on the wind,

but the birds wings sound velvet in the sky,
and the ground holds us naked and hidden in the broken reeds,
I am the huntress who has taken your heart,
such a lovely heart it is,

sweet and sad, like your self, like the dove's own falling from the arrow.

Then Patricia sits back and laughs. She wrote a poem, finally. It means something. She lies back in the bed of roses and holds it, and she is happy. Even when she hears hundreds of people running through the halls, screaming, she doesn't move. She lays back in wonder at herself. The room is thick with the attar of rose, and she never wants to leave. Slowly, she takes off all her clothes and throws them to the ground. She lies naked in the bed and loosens her hair from her habitual plain rubber band. She takes the rose petals that are everywhere and throws them up, and it is then she hears him, calling from the hall, Patricia! Patricia! Patricia! Only with his deep accent it is:

Pah tree SHAH!

Pah tree SHAH!

Pah tree SHA-AH!

Khouri's voice, ringing out from faraway, down the hall. She calls back, Khouri! And then there is silence. She hears him running. She calls again. He calls, he's gone down the other side. So, she calls again. He responds, he's coming closer, she's calling, suddenly the door bursts open and he is there, running in the room. He looks at her, her blond hair spread out all over the bed, her body covered in petals, the bed disheveled, the room full of roses, the perfume heavy. All the cautions and voices of his past are forgotten. The people of the hotel are terrified, herds of elephants, children are crying, and the shouts are indeterminate, muffled, desperate. The poem flutters to the ground from her soft, pink hand, an alarm has sounded, brill and sharply piercing the air, Phyllis and Jedra are entering a small corridor from the vent, Leslie Downing and Daniel Espritu's heads have bounded up, listening quickly, like two small animals in the brush.

FORTY-NINE

Leslie downing and Daniel Espiritu were at the window and saw the crowds.

It seems the beach has something going on. I know what it is, what's all the excitement.

You do?

Oh, yeah. I guess I'd forgotten. Is it January already?

No. It's March.

No. You're wrong. It's January. This is the festival of Iemanja. Look how many people are in white.

She looked. Many people were wrapped in sheets from the hotel, to cover their nakedness or underwear, but she gave up arguing.

They're wearing white, it's her color. They wear white and they carry all things for her favor, combs, powder, rum, flowers. All gifts to give her. She is the mother of all Iemanja. She's the mother of the sea and of boats and of all things of water.

But it was clear to Leslie the crowd was of desperation, that something terrible was happening in the hotel. There were police cars, and Hazmat vehicles, and media littered everywhere. People could be seen running out and the stampedes could still be heard from the other floors and then the alarms started whining.

Daniel, I think we need to leave.

I can't.

There is danger here. Something is wrong.

Leslie started putting on her jeans and her sweatshirt and Daniel just sat there, naked and wan in the drab light.

I see them putting the boats on the water now. It's the tradition. Everyone makes a little boat and a note or a wish about what they ask for and they put them on the water, and then if it goes to sea Iemnaja has listened, but if it comes back, she spurns you. This is the best time when the water is green like emeralds and the sun is shining and the people dance and they. And they...

Daniel?

They...

Are you OK?

I don't feel so well.

Daniel, put on your clothes. Something is wrong.

She helped him put on his shirt and pants and slippers. He seemed vague and distracted.

I thought I saw my mother out there in the crowd. Tall and in dark clothes, looking up at my window. With her Brazilian, Terinho. They were waving at me.

It's possible, hurry. Maybe there is a fire.

There were more shouts from the halls.

I want to get out of here, fast.

I haven't been out in three years.

It will be OK.

Can we walk down to the ocean. I want to make a wish to Iemanja.

OK.

Let's write one down. Can we write it down?

I'll do it.

She took a piece of paper, from Hotel stationary and wrote carefully on the top:

Dear Iemanja

What do you want to ask, Daniel?
I want to ask. I want to ask her to live again. Ask her to help me live again.
OK.

Please help Daniel Espiritu and Leslie Downing to live again.
We are grateful, thank you,
Leslie and Daniel

After that, she folded up the note into many pieces. She put it in her pocket and she took his hand.
I want you to come with me.
I don't know if I can, Esperanca.
You can try.
He stood up.
I think I am ready.
She led his hand to the door, she opened it and led him past the door. When his feet hit the burgundy carpet, he gasped.
I'm out!
It'll be OK.
Hold on to my hand.
I will.
She led him to the elevator. There was a man hurrying down the hall, his shirt untucked, his hair askew. He pulled a suitcase.
What's going on?
They say it's going to blow. They say some employer hid a bomb or something. An Iraqi or I don't really know.
Good lord.
In Brazil, no less, said Daniel.
Pardon? Said the man. I'm taking the stairs. And he ran off.
Daniel, it's a bomb scare. We should take the stairs.
She led him through the clanking metal stairs, all the way down, and

they both got dizzy. Finally they emerged into the cacophony of the lobby, where hordes of policeman were running and a guard said, right this way, come on, come on, and led them to the door. The rest of the lobby was cordoned off with police tape. The door was huge and glass and cameramen lined each corner.

We're going outside now, Daniel.

His eyes were glassy and faraway. She pushed on the doors. There was a huge rush of chatter, of microphones rammed in their faces, of screams and yells, of probing questions thrust in their faces, but they walked on. She held his hand tight and he looked down, his face grimaced. They went through the throngs of people, yelling, oohing, shouting. She could feel the tremors in his body through his hand and she held on tight. She put her arm around his waist. He fell against her and held her.

She led him across the street to a small park in front of the hotel, the same little park they could see from his hotel window, and she carefully sat him down and said there, and he looked down at the ground and shook. And she continued to hold him.

And then finally, he picked his head up and looked around at the people, at the hotel, at the little park. At Leslie. He looked around, his face frowning and tears began to come from the corners of his eyes. She held him and told him he would be OK. And he cried more and more. And then when he was done, he said to her:

This. This is *not Brazil*.

Leslie held him and said nothing.

This is not Brazil.

She was thinking about what to say, what she really thought. In so many ways, it was Brazil, at least to her and him, whatever Brazil could mean to a person. When a place can mean a state of mind, an atmosphere. In essence it was Brazil and by being Brazil it had saved some part of her so she didn't want to ruin everything and have it go back to the cold land she had voluntarily inhabited before, where the only jewels she wore were the hopes of some kind of culinary fame, and where she had traversed in the fields of loneliness and despair as if it was a comfortable vocation she had chosen, when really she could have the comfort of living life and enjoying it's fruitfulness right now, right now she could be loved, and happy and fine.

This is not Brazil, is it, Leslie?

And what would it do to him, to lose this dream? Would he now implode and accept the loss of Esperanca and Brazil, perhaps the only time in his life when he was happy and well, and would he now crumple and die slowly, like a transported tropical plant, slowly suffering without it's native soil and light, and finally, die? Or was Daniel ready to heal? Had the effect of Leslie slowly regenerated his heart and mind and brought him, little by little to the real world? Was he in essence, ready to live again?

No, it is not Brazil, Daniel. it is Washington, D.C.

His face was very dear to her, with its expression right then of deeply fought composure as he allowed himself to look around in a three foot circumference of their bench. It was as if he wore his scientist guise one more time, as if he were studying the effects of this non-Brazilian environment clinically, and yet, in his paleness and elfish features that looked so removed form the tanned, hardened world, he looked fragile and sad.

It was then that the woman in white approached them. Where she came from, Leslie did not know. She wore a large spreading skirt, and blouse, with lots and lots of colored beads. She stood in front of them. She came and held Daniel's face. She spoke to them in Portuguese, but Leslie understood every word:

I stole the child in the night.
Had no choice.

It all started long time ago when I go working there. I saw it coming from the start, when I worked up the hill. I cooked stuff, shrimp in coconut, fish in palm oil, all them things they love. I washed the clothes in the bathtub and hang it out on the grass to whiten up. I scrub those floors while I hear them laughing on the porch, and while I hot and sweat trickles down my cheek, I hear the ice crackle in their glasses, fresh cane rum mixed with smashed limes, and I think,

I could die of thirst but I keep on. I work on. And I love they child. The truth is, I loved the boychild. His eyes were sweet and fragile and brown as dirt and he want me to hold him, and I did, much of the day, sometimes all the day instead of do my work. The house in those days had the sweet, ripe smell of old mangoes from the back garden and always a pile of avocados on the kitchen table, which the children liked me to mash up for them with sugar.

In that time, the Mrs. and Mr. were fighting, yelling sometimes behind the closed door. I heard all fierce whispers, crashing things. She say she dropped her vase by accident later, all the flowers crushed up on the floor, but I could tell from the way the Mr.'s dark lashes look down for one quick second that Mrs. threw it at him, and when I walked by reaching down on the floor, mopping up crystals of glass and dirt and petals, a big thought comes up to me, a pretty picture of a young man with green eyes and rake in his hand, in fact I know the boy, Emerson, pretty thing who work the garden, and you don't have to tell Esperanca nothing, my friend. Because I see and feel everything and I trust my vision. He took up with that boy. Mrs. don't like it. She threw the vase.

When I want to figure a thing out, this is what I do. I go in the garden and set on a log under the porch and I look up in the treetops where the sky is. I watch just that spot where the leaves meet the sky and I let myself go, a soft, dreamy feeling like you're about to fall asleep and let myself see things. I see people and things happening and I don't put no judgment on those things, I don't think what's right or wrong, just take it in, just hmmm, what do you know. Isn't that something. But I see things that going to happen and it's a gift but it gets me in trouble. It's a power and a sadness but it's a true thing. People sometimes say it's not real but there are so many things around you can't see that are more real than even yourself. Love is real isn't it, but you can't see it, unless you count the way it slaps it's way across a face when a person don't want it too but you can't hide love people no you can't. All these things around us all the time, other worlds, other places, other beings, the orishas, dark things, and all some people really want to say is bad luck, but it's more than that. There's a thin veil between this world and all the others and when you know that, the world makes more sense.

There's another thing I don't tell anybody, besides the fact I see things others can't. It's my secret, but I'll tell you, because I trust you two. Another comes through me sometimes. I hear her speaking and see her walking and then I go away and when I come back, she gone. Her name is Fufu Otufa. She live in 1453 in Congo by the base of a river and a man, a Portuguese man named Don Rufio De La Vasquez came and put her on a boat. She got a sadness to her and a kind heart and she suffered, that one. When Fufu come up, you listen, because she tell some truth. She like to drink Palm wine and rum and she love men. She get me in trouble because I'm a shy girl. There's been some times I wake up in some poor fool's bed, hair all mashed up, stinking of palm wine.

This happened once. Mr. and Mrs. had me make Caipirinhas for their guests, a Mr. and Mrs. Foster from California, North America. Theys more big Americans like the Mr. and Mrs, all big bones and teeth and freckles and wear too many clothes and plaids. I mix up some caipirinhas and I get a buzzing sound and I know Fufu coming up, she smell that palm rum and she get all crazy, ohhhhh, crazy, give me some of that. I don't want to but it go up in my mouth and down me and she laugh laugh laugh, almost giggle like a girl, her hips start swaying, and we dancing in the kitchen and she's speaking in her African tongue words I don't know, and boom, I'm out of there. Next thing I know I lying naked in a big man's arms in a smelly bed, sun coming up, roosters crowing, scratching, me trying to figure out which side of Rio I on now, which favela, which side of the mountain Fufu done dragged me. All left of my memory of it all, the feeling her skin has, it so much smoother than mine and her laugh peeling out my throat, and the doorway, the doorway where I could see Mr and Mrs. entertaining their guests from California, North America, grew blurry with their figures, and I could taste more caipirinhas swishing down my throat, and then it goes black. That fufu crazy. But she know some stuff, girl. And just before I lose down that black tunnel with the caipirinhas and laughter and the North Americanos growing fuzzy in my eyes, she whisper from my own lips up to my own ears, That boy ain't right. Shango got hold of him and going to turn him all wrong. Watch the pretty world fall down.

Fufu never wrong.

That's why I took that boy, hid him. When I looked up in the trees for something, I saw it all. I saw Mr. going away, leaving Mrs. I know he don't want her. I saw the house with a big crack in it, like the family fall apart. And I saw the boy all ruin in his head. I saw it worse and worse. I saw sadness on that house like a cloud. And the worse thing, I saw that boy take his own life. I saw it. He would've done it. In the garden, with the gun they kept in the cabinet. I saw the tears, the mess. I did only thing I knew how to do, take that boy up the hills to the people. They knew what to do. They push out the Shango from his head. When they find us, he clean. He ready. That Mrs. get a new man. Everybody happy. They sent me away, up north. I go to Recife. I work on the fishing boat up there. I don't care. I don't want to see my pretty boy sad.

You was OK for awhile but then it all come back. Shango come back. I was afraid this going to happen, he get jealous of happiness. He want to feel that human happiness, you know. When you was in school, he come back and take over again. Well, I say to him to go on now. You don't need this anymore. Time to live again. Time to let go of me. I got places to go. But I love you child. I do.

She kissed him.

I got places to go. Fufu's got some ideas in her head. I need to get to the beach. I need to go.

Then she was gone. She didn't disappear. She walked away into the crowd.

Then he said:

Quantum Query and Non-deterministic Query on a Punctured Surface, with a long-range Electron-Phonon Interaction.

And then, he laughed. She thought that it was good to see him laugh.

FIFTY

Stupid Iranian. Always to think they know all of everything. But they do not.

Jedra felt maligned. Phyllis and he were running up the stairs and Phyllis said, don't worry about him.

I do not worry about this one, I am angry that he not knows, not seeing danger of this situation. All is going to blow.

They had reached the rooftop. They pushed open the door and the wind was sweet and warm.

And there, there in the middle, lightly toeing a soccer ball, was his brother Jalil.

And he spoke:

In the name of Allah, the merciful, the compassionate.

Praise be to Allah. My brother.

So many people are outside the hotel, brother. They are gathering like a storm. I am wondering what is happening.

Jedra came out and the heat buffeted around them, disfiguring the air in waves.

There will be an explosion, brother. All the years these pipes in this old hotel have endured much, but now they will suffer no more.

As it says in the Qur'an, *all that happens is what God has decided for us.*

And will there be hurt people, brother?

I am hoping not but it is very possible. At least they have listened to what I have said.

And are you the woman that Jedra loves?

I am.

And what is your name?

I am Phyllis. We have met before.

Yes. Outside his building.

Yes, I remember.

You are the boy who plays soccer.

He was such good player, you wouldn't believe. You should play teams, brother.

Now, I cannot. Play teams. You make me laugh.

Why are you here, why do you always come around.

I want to rest.

Then, rest.

He sat down and looked over at the people, I cannot, he said.

And what is it you want to tell me before?

They are coming for you, brother. The police. They will not listen to you. They don't understand what you tried to do. They will grab you forcefully and you will cry, it will blow, but they think you have made a bomb. They think you are evil.

Is this what you wanted to tell me?

No. I am telling you this so you can run and not be captured again and again. You will be put in jail again, my brother.

Tell me then, what is so important.

I don't have the words.

Well then. Start somewhere.

I cannot.

In the meantime, she saw them. Phyllis saw them, from the right side but the two brothers did not. She saw the sky filled with them. Perhaps she now allowed herself to see, finally. Perhaps it was the child that had opened up her eyes again, after shutting them through all the years. They were part of the clouds, and they spoke words to her and she heard them, and she tried to say, Look Jedra! And his eyes turned to her and said, look at what, my love? And she said, there! And his eyes were only reflecting the clouds and he said, do you mean the clouds, and she said, no, no. But there are only clouds, my Phyllis. Do you mean birds? I saw a bird?

No, she said.

Something is going to happen, Jedra.

Yes, It is going to blow.

No, something else.

Could he not hear the wings? It was almost too intoxicating. The strong rustle was heavy and whipping through the air. She had to cover her ears. The wind was warm still but sharp. She could smell overpowering that smell, the vanilla, the rose attar, the salt, the smoke, myrrh. She couldn't breathe.

Tell me brother! Tell me what you've come to tell me!

You remember the morning, that morning?

Of course. In all my times, I remember it all the day.

It was cold. I didn't want to go. I told you, yes, that I supported it, but my stomach was full of rocks and I was sick. It felt wrong.

We had no choice. We were living in hell.

We always have *choice*. I saw you wrap bread around the newspaper. I went down the hall and saw Mother sleeping. Her hair dark, in a braid. Our father, his hand on her back. It was so early. No roosters had called yet. The fire still smelled from last night. You were leaving sesame seeds on the rug from the bread. You packed lentils in pockets on our back. When were we going to cook those?

I don't know.

Then we went through the street, crawling like babies. I had a gun in my boot. It felt cold. I was so scared my teeth jarred. I wanted to throw up. I was too scared, brother. I was a coward.

You are the bravest.

Then we got to the Tigres. It was beautiful, black and shiny like a rock. But we were to swim it across. Oh Allah, I wanted to run back. So much I wanted to run back and be back in our bad life.

I made you go.

It was my idea.

It was never your idea, you are right. I made you go.

I would do whatever you would say, my brother.

I am sorry.

In the water, it was terrible, remember. As cold as knives. We swam across. We had gotten maybe two miles down the road—

Please! I can't relive this again and again!

And then they came from nowhere. How did they know where we were? Suddenly all around us I heard the click of brutal metal guns. I was kicked down, I saw them kick you too.

Yes.

And then they took me out to the field—

No, Please, my brother, spare me.

You were screaming.

Please—

You were screaming, me first. Me first.

O, God is good. O God protect us all.

Then Phyllis heard sirens and police horns. They saw them on the roof and they were calling to them. They said, Please surrender. Men were running up the stairs and in the meantime, through the throng she saw enveloping the clouds, all the crushing wings and feathers, all the beauty of these beings, she saw him, Ismael, he came towards her again. He said to her:

This is about Truth, as the only invariable, absolute need that all seek. In all you do, find and speak the truth. Make your life a vessel of truth. Choose work that reflects your own truth. Do not lie! Don't lie to yourself, don't lie to others! Don't lie to your lover. Make your lover a sacrament of all that is love and truth. When you wake in the morning, and you are lying next to the one who has held you all night, who has kissed you with open eyes, whose heart has opened unto you, this is truth.

And she said, I know what you say is right.

But the brothers didn't hear anything.

Allah aqbar! Allah Aqbar! yelled Jedra. Please, my brother.
I must finish.
Please.
Jedra, I must.
It is unbearable to live this again, always.
You were saying, me first, and those words were the last ones I heard, and I loved you brother. And then it tore through my chest, and I was pounded down and above me I floated. And I saw them shackle you and drag you. I saw you sob for me. I saw them drag me to the field where they had dug a shallow grave and they threw me down in it. I did not hate those brothers then. And I saw you put in the truck with the sheep. I saw you lying in the shit of the sheep and you were sobbing and I felt sorry for you, my brother. And I saw the two men who had shot me get into the second truck and I saw you drive off in the first truck, and they went forward towards the city, to the border, away from Basra, and the second truck I watched cross back over the river. I went with the second truck, back to our village—

What are you telling me.
I saw the truck cross the road by our friend, Um Nour and her family. The yellow house. And I saw it turn right into our driveway—

Jalil.
And it stopped there, the truck.
No.
And the men, these two that had killed me, Omar and Sayed, are their names, though I hold them no grudge—

Please no.
They walked in our house, broke down the door, actually. Which woke mother, she heard the loud crash and woke father, and she put on her robe, it was flowered with lilies, and she smelled of lilies from her powder. And she whispered to our father, who told her it was Ok, to be quiet, and he, brave one, went first and came to the front of the stairs where the soldiers had started to ascend the first step. He had put on those old slippers

he always wore, the leather brown ones and his heels, so whitened, and he couldn't put in his fake teeth even, it was so fast, and he said, who is there? Yet he saw the soldier, and the soldier said, is this the home of Jalil and Jedra Abdullah? And father did not know what to say, he thought we were asleep in our beds, please, he said, we are peace-loving, we mean no harm, please leave our family. But the soldier Omar said, your sons were caught and killed in the uprising this morning. And Mother screamed and father said, no, it is not possible and the soldiers marched upstairs and stormed around and found our rooms and dragged our parents in and showed them the empty beds and they cried. Our parents, and everything got knocked down, our schoolbooks, your science books, my soccer magazines, and my trophy, and the soccer ball rolled out, and Omar said May Allah forgive all of us, and he pushed mother on the bed and—*crack, craqk, crack!*—shot her in the head and father screamed and he held him forward and did the same and then there was an awful silence—

Jedra had fallen down forward into his arms. He lay on the roof.

—and Sayed said let's go and they dragged the bodies bumpily down the stairs, trailing blood—and they put them in the truck— And the neighbors had come out and they were all crying but trying to hide and not get shot— and they drove through the town, by Um Nour's sleeping house and our Uncle's house and— through the cold river and to the field where I lay—

Ohhhhhhhh, said Jedra, ohhhhh.

Phyllis had gone and held him. Ismael filled the skies.

—and they put them, my mother and father, on me, and they covered us with the dirt. So what I had to tell you was not what I wanted to do, but I had to tell you, that they are in the field, my brother. But it is with love I come to you, Brother. And it is with love I tell you all of this.

Jedra stood up and saw all around him with eyes of pain, in a blurry kaleidoscope of clouds, of screams from the crowd, of beautiful Phyllis who stood in front of him, of his dusty brother, who smiled at him. It was then the police came crashing through the doors, like animals all dressed in the same color, but they were not animals, they were simply men doing what they thought was right, trying to help keep peace, trying to care for their families, they held guns, they knew no other way, they had names: Jeff Landham, Ben delfuego, Harry Pscietcik, and others. they saw the perpetrator and warned him to be still, they said, do not move, they said, you need to surrender, where is the device located, they said.

But Jedra said nothing.

In a dream it seemed, Phyllis told them things. She said, this is all a mistake. There is no device. And yet Jedra was not really listening. He was following his brother, who walked toward the edge. He was watching him kick the ball with the edge of his foot, the way one does when they play. It was the same dusty, dirty ball he always used. Jedra came towards him. And yet, he said nothing.

He was seeing his mother, in her house dress, cooking the lentil soup she made. She had taught him how, he often would stand by the stove as she cut onions, garlic for this soup. *Another thing, spinach is good to add*, she would say. Her hands are brown and thick, with cuts here and there from all the cooking. It is Ramadan, this memory. It is almost time to eat, he is drooling at the sight of the soup. His father has come home, he is sitting at the table. The places are set, the soup is ready, the tea is brewed, the lanterns are lit to greet the holiday, now the *muezzin* calls for the breaking of the fast, there are prayers said by father and they break the bread, and laugh and eat the soup. It has a taste you cannot imagine when you are that hungry. There was a lot of singing that they liked to do. His mother, her broad face shiny, liked to sing and rub the cheek of Jedra.

Where is the device?

And his father's face had become small and folded through the years like a small raisin, dark and creased. His eyes were hidden in the folds of his wrinkles. He was much older than their mother, by fifteen years. He was a man who repaired shoes. Often Jedra would walk into his shop, which was in an alley in the bazaar in town and ask for a few ditmars to buy ice cream or a pastry and his father would be hammering at his small stool, nailing the heel of a boot. The smell in this room was of the smoky, cured warm smell of leather and dust and apple tobacco from the hookah his father would smoke from. Occasionally, it would be tea time and his father would make a dark glass of tea for him and he would smoke some of the apple smoke and it had a sickly sweet taste which made you cough. But he never said much. He would only ask if Jedra had done his schoolwork and his prayers. And Jedra always said yes, and he would reply, good son, and that was the end of it. If Jedra and Jalil misbehaved, he was called to punish and he did so unmercifully with a thin, snappy piece of willow.

Where is the device?

Jedra turned to them.

I am telling you there is *no device*. The water is going to blow the place. The pressure is too much. All is going to blow.

Noone is going anywhere until we locate the device.

His brother, Jalil, had now gotten on the edge of the building and walked upon it as if it were a tightrope. Jedra came towards him. Phyllis was behind him. The men were surrounding them.

I think we should go with these men, Jedra.

The air was so thick with the flush of the wings of the angels she could hardly breathe.

I cannot, Phyllis, he said. He smiled at her. I don't want to be in a prison ever again.

You won't be. You did nothing wrong.

Believe me, I will be in prison forever, I know. Everything is useless now. Everything is over.

No, Jedra.

Please.

He stood up on the edge.

Jedra.

Come down off the edge please, booked the megaphoned voice of one of the men.

I know exactly what I do, said Jedra.

My brother, said Jalil.

Are they there, he said. Are they there?

Yes, said Jalil. They've been waiting.

Then tell them to wait not anymore. I will be coming. Please forgive me.

We all forgive you.
Jedra, said Phyllis. She held his hand.
You have to go back, he said. Go with the men.
I can't.
Please!
I am with you!

She wanted to go back. She wanted to be free. She wanted to go back to where she knew. There was a buzzing sound, a large motor sound that got louder and louder. It sounded like an engine that was revving way out of control. Some people were holding their ears and the policemen started screaming orders to each other, and some ran down the stairs towards the sound. The crowd milled in swirls and started running backwards. The fire engines arrived loudly with their bleating horns. The Buzzing seemed to be almost clanking.

It was then Jedra saw them, his family. They stood in black, the cloth of their clothes flapping in the light wind. The tears stung his face. He had cried so much these years his face felt raw and naked, and yet these new tears were a balm, soothing the craggy folds of his face. His mother stood large and round and smiling, her face round and shiny as always, and his small father, his face burnished, tea-brown, along his mother, not smiling but dreamily looking beyond all of them. They seemed dusty and old, and yet, even the smell of them came up on the breeze, lilies, dust, a soap his father used, waxy leather, onions. It hit his stomach like a punch and he turned to Phyllis and he grabbed her hand and he pulled her, and he shouted, *they are here now*. And she knew what to do, she held his hand, the men were yelling, the crowd held their breathe in shock, the angels stormed around them, the wings as fierce as a clutter of scared doves in the grove, or the thunder of a wild herd surprise. There was a deafening cacophony of sounds so beautiful and harsh, so quick and stunning, in the few seconds of this moment that became a life of moments as they watched, they gasped, they cried, they yelled.

The moment of courage is simple and direct. The heart is beating, the knees are quaking, but one reaches for it all the same. Like scrambling out the window at four a.m. with burlap wrapped around your legs to make less noise as you crawl. Bread wrapped in a roll stuffed in your pants. The water around your island appears dark and oddly pretty, as if beauty has no place in danger, and when you reach a boat, you are over there, and your younger brother laughs and cleans his tooth with his pinky nail, you see the same eye tooth he has flashed from that large-lipped mouth since you were very small and this is the same one who takes a bullet in his back—*craqck, crack, crakc!*—as you run in the alley of the town where you are captured and that is the end of him. The end of him. *I have noone.* So in the sandstorms of your captivity, as voices in the next room speak of logic science and philosophy and argue, suddenly you are whole and alive in another place, reaching again, despite all odds which say *never* and *foolish*, which warn of and promise you death and destruction, everything, everyone, everywhere, take notice, you must not fall in this trap again. There is no exit door. There is no safety net. We will all die. Do not enter. Do not ignore all the learnings you know. Do not break free.

This is all about love.

Jedra Abdullah held the hand of Phyllis, and they ran into the air towards his family, out over the crowd, towards the clouds, as his family cried and his mother's sweet voice sung the bread song to him, and everyone else screamed. it was then the sound deafened, it was then—*crack, craqk, crack!*—split the air and water surged from the crevices like a tsunami as Jedra had always said. The walls were ripped and shredded and the lobby sprayed and gushed. The crowd was splattered with the crescendo of water and ran backwards, as they looked up and saw water from all directions, buckling and tumbling the hotel, breaking forth. Then, their mutual eyes pulled up toward the sky, and saw the unthinkable:

Jedra and Phyllis jumping off the building, holding hands.

FIFTY-ONE

Khouri Karimi's perpetual mourning had ended in a pile of rose petals.

The *narahati*, the pervading sadness, of his life was tossed aside in a rash movement and he would never inhabit it again. Now he would shed the black he had draped himself in psychically, he would shave and bathe again in the waters of life. He would ignore his mother's Persian demands, his ancient warnings, gone is the house of his dead sister and brother-in-law and the tassel, gone is his mother's sad eyes, gone is the smell of his empty house, his failed marriage, his broken heart:

Khouri falls on the bed, smiling, and buries his head in Patricia's hair and rose petals. He picks Patricia up in his arms, all of her naked and unabashed, and lifts her, and she is light. She smiles. Then he carries her through the hall, running. She is only looking up in his black eyes which are darting this way, back and forth. They are glittering with light. They are full of sparks and glint like water. She will only look in his face, she ignores the crowds, the yells, the stampede. He is running down the stairs. He has reached the lobby. It is a mess. She is naked and doesn't care. He flings open the doors and runs out into the warm air of spring where the crowds have gathered. He takes off his coat and puts it around her. He still holds her.

Like this, they watch the hotel blow up in front of their very eyes. It is like a strange apparition, a mirage in the desert. He holds her and once again, when he turned to look at her, his eyes were so glittery and black, the crashing hotel's light bounced back in them like two miniature explosions.

A new world danced in that light, where things acted differently, where physics became so miniaturized it lost all sense of our normal physical laws, where neutrons and gluons broke apart and danced in waves and particles and nothing was until you decided it was, until you saw it, in his black Persian eyes, that moment, her child was safe, her home was safe, her heart was safe, Khouri's eyes, reflecting the windows of the hotel falling down, were safety.

And Khouri was all about bravery. He held her back from the explosion with his body in front, guarding her, saving her, though it was mainly water, which came crashing out and splashed on everyone, as if all the tears from the decades of hardship had gathered strength from being held back, and at this one particular moment could hold back no further and burst through and disintegrated all the feeble boundaries that had kept them in, all gushing heartaches, all thackered pain, all plaintive cries, all watery sorrows, the sea of tears, that could no longer be held back.

* * *

In the later years he would stand over the cradle of their firstborn, Hafez, who came surprisingly soon, he would rock his cradle and murmur in soft Farsi some words of the poet Rumi, whilst Patricia cooked in the kitchen and Trevor did his homework:

Tu niz delkabadi darman ze dardyabi gar gerd-e dard gardi, farman-e man gerelfte.

(You are broken hearted too, you shall find cure in love, if you listen to me and pursue this ailment.)

And the baby would awake, his small dark eyes blinking. And Khouri would tell him again the story he loved, about the building aflood with the water of tears and the angels, two angels, that fell from its rooftops and floated, to the miraculous eyes of all who watched, high above the heavens.

EPILOGUE:

THE FOURTH TALE:
THE END

Introducing, Bostitch.
People person.
Motivator.
Highly Effective Individual.
Manager Extraordinaire.

Bostitch = excellent judge of people. Normally. Case in point: new employee, name of Frances T., hired this week in The Caribbean Lounge at The Royale. Consistently seven minutes late, often reeking of vanilla beauty product and menthol cigarettes. According to The Royale Manual, verbal warning will be in action soon. This is not a party or something.

What we got here is a philosophy of life. Hard work gleans results. Bostitch keeps it simple. In his left hand pocket is the manual, in the right hand one is a well-worn funeral home folder from his Grandpa's death. They contain lots of advice for living. In fact, you'd be surprised how informative this folder and The Royale Manual can be. They are chock full, *chock full* of good stuff for your life, and a person would be amazed.

On a Wednesday evening, Bostitch stands outside the swinging doors for a second and hears this new waitress talking to Joan K., another employee. Bostitch doesn't like it. Bostitch mad.

Hard to make ends meet, you know.

I'm telling you.

Yeah, so Desiree, my oldest, needs shoes and she's screaming for those Sketchers, and, you know, now that Tommy's gone, and all that—

Oh, yeah, Sketchers. Sixty bucks a pop—

He won't fork over a dime, him.

Your ex?

One and only—

Ahem, Ahem, AHEM, Bostitch says, pouring through the door in in the manner of, say, a hellblown avalanche, *Table three is looking around!* He holds up The Royale Manual and reminds them of *Directive Number Sixteen: An employee must always, at all times, be present to greet customers as they enter the lounge.*

Similarly, *Directive Number Eighteen* could be utilized. *An employee must always stand on guard, hands neatly clasped in back, in order to provide the customers with instantaneous service. Roving eyes are a polite customer's beacon of need.*

Bostitch says, diamonds are only chunks of coal that stuck to their job, you see.

Employed persons stare and nod heads in perfect timing.

If they'd, you know, petered out, they'd just be chunks of, uh, dirt or rock. So keep on
trucking!

Bostitch is in control. Employees back down.

People do not slouch at The Caribbean Lounge. *Busy, busy, busy.*

At four thirty, when staffage come in, they have to move fast, lugging steam trays from the kitchen to the front for happy hour. Well, 1) they light the sternos underneath, then 2) they go to Thuog in the kitchen and ask for the food, carrot tempura, fried wontons and jalapeno poppers 3) All the food must be out by five, along with sauces, toothpicks and spiraled piles of napkins 4) Bostitch says, no loitering or chitchat 5) Am I making myself heard here?!

The Caribbean Lounge sells quite a bit of concoctions from the *Island Dreams* menu on the table. The Maui Colada is quite a hit as well as the ever popular *Sex on the Beach* (Bostitch's personal favorite) and occasionally, as will happen, people get drunk. *Directive Number Twelve: Inebriated customers must be disallowed to purchase more alcoholic beverages and, in extreme cases, may be escorted, with security, out of the hotel premises.* Two weeks ago, though, inebriated couple copulated on a bar stool in the left corner. Bostitch felt powerless to enact managerial duties due to romantic nature. Bostitch cares about people. :)

New employee Frances T. has potential. Note: style in evidence, like her hand-tooled cigarette case with a "F" carved on it (along with a compartment for a lighter). Two, she is always neatly dressed, no runs in her stockings, though Bostitch may have to comment on the butterfly clips she wears in her blond hair as it is definitely not Royale.

Bostitch notices woman fidgets.

He says, Frances T., you seem distracted.
I'm. I'm just tired, Sir.

Bostitch lives on the west side of town, in an apartment building called River Run, with an obese cat named Mr. Charlie. Bostitch is concerned about that new girl, because after work, when driving back from a bar he frequents (*it's called Jellicoe's after, you know, that Cats thing on Broadway. Bostitch goes there. Vodtons. Talks to Carl about irritations in life, and such. Gas Prices. Things That Piss Us Off*), when he turns on Connecticut, he sees a person walking along the side of the road and then realizes it's Frances T, (At 2:14 in the morning) with her shoes in her hands and a messed up face. Bostitch slows down, calling out *Frances T., Frances T.,* until she turns and says, *Oh, hey, Sir* and Bostitch says, *can I give you a lift?*

I'm fine, Sir, just going to the 7-11.

And yet she stops, looks at the mirror on his car for a bit, really studying it,

You know, a cup of coffee *would* be kind of nice.

Despite misgivings, Bostitch cares. Bostitch buys Frances a large, with four Amaretto creamers.

She pulls out that cigarette holder, flips it with her small hands, and Bostitch said, so, um, why, what are you doing?

Hunh? Smoking.

No, what are you doing, I mean, now?

Oh. Just walking.

Taking a walk?

Yeah, sir.

This Frances T. sucks in her cigarette hard, stretching the skin around a bruise under her chin. When she does that her mouth crinkles up and Bostitch thinks she looks like Granny from the Beverly Hill Billies. Just the mouth, though. The rest is not Granny, more Ellie Mae. Then she says, how about we split a Snickers and Bostitch says, well, Frances, It's been a long night and I work brunch, attempting to get back into professional manager space, but she insists on hovering in it. Bostitch has noticed that some women of the straight orientation think gay men hunger for them as friends. They get real chummy, real fast. Bostitch doesn't have a problem with that, but he's trying to draw some lines these days. It's a professional thing.

Just a damn Snickers, she says. I didn't ask you, you know, buy me a diamond or nothing. We're talking *candy bar*, fifty-nine cents.

So, Bostitch buys a Snickers and light is popping up over the side of the valley and Frances T. starts to nod out on his shoulder, much to his discomfort. She says in his ear,

I don't even *like* Snickers.

Me, too. I prefer Skor.

You're looking to score?

I said, I like those *Skor* bars. You know.

I seen them. Figured they sucked.

They're darker. Toffee, or something. You like toffee?

I can't go home, sir.

And that would be because? he says, shifting his body, smelling her hair.

He'll be waiting, he caught up with me at Shooter's, shove me up against the hood, and now he's waiting in my house and he'll do stuff, he gets in by breaking a window and sits on the couch. In the dark and shit.

And we would be talking about?

My *husband*, duh.

Bostitch gets out spare sheets for female employed companion, who will sleep on couch. A Royale representative will be in tomorrow at The Caribbean Lounge, and Bostitch has draped manager's outfit over couch and buffed shoes by the La-z-boy that Keith had left, and naturally new female employee, Frances T., comes in and immediately notes the picture of Keith and Bostitch in Cancun and she says, boy, that's a hunk.

Yes, he is attractive. Would you care for sleep garments?

Yeah, a T-shirt'll do. Is that your brother, the hunk?

Bostitch notices her lack of personal hygiene, displayed by chipped toenail polish.

He's, uh, a friend named Keith.

So, who's the other guy in the pic, with him?

That. Actually. That, that would be *me*, says Bostitch.

Bostitch is uncomfortable with personal appearance issues. Bostitch feels considerable weight loss is irrelevant to a manager's performance.

There was a pause for about thirty seconds, and then Frances T. says in a chirpy way:

Hunh. That's you.

Me. Yes. Well.

She was silent.

I used to be. Quite muscular. Strapping, you could say.

You just look, I don't know, different. Not in a bad way, I mean.

Bostitch prepares guest's habitage. Double sheets with cotton blanket, quilt added for extra warmth. Bostitch's romantic nature enable him to be silent while Frances T. continues to look at picture, and think of friend in picture who left Bostitch with much, quote, emotional baggage, unquote. Bostitch says, I wish he'd take the couch.

Female employee looks up.

I wish he'd take his couch. And his socks. And the pants. The toaster. His underwear, not to mention his toilet bag and his CDs. I mean, when a person moves one should take their personal belongings, it seems proper, don't you think, if a former waiter, who has barged into your life, taking advantage of your romantic nature, does not wish to continue said friendship, then said waiter should evacuate and, uh, diminish proceedings.

Bostitch's face is quite pink.

And, and, take *that damn* Mr. Charlie, also—

—uh, sir.

People like that should be aware—

—I think I'll hit the sack, says Frances T.

—that *other* people have feelings, despite their highly professional demeanor, and, and, may have feelings that require a certain delicacy—

—I'll just get some water—

—a certain *care*, to enable quote, *closure*, unquote.

Bostitch realizes he may have been shouting. He stands strangely in his own house, looking around for an out. Frances T., though, does that instinctive mother-thing some females do, in awkward times, and she rubs his shoulder.

Easy there, boy.

And so, Bostitch calms down.

Bostitch has trouble sleeping with others in his house, and finds himself lying in his bed, his heart beating. He thinks he made a fool of himself. He has problems distinguishing borders. He almost wants to draw a square in the air when he says that. He shuffles around in the bed. He hears Mr. Charlie meow loudly and run in the room and then all of a sudden it's Frances T. in his bed, I'm sorry, she says, I get real scared. I hear the window opening all the time in my sleep and I wake up. Shit. I'm fucked up, she says. I'm sorry. Let me just, lie here. OK?

Oh, Frances, Bostitch whispers, I don't think so.

But she doesn't move. Bostitch is, alarmingly, aroused. He lays still, but his heart is loud and thumping. A hand moves. It covers his. He sweats. She drapes her arm on his. He moves closer. He is throbbing. She is on him. They kiss. He drinks adrenaline. Frances doesn't talk. Nor he. Bostitch moves all over her, stunned by the soft thing she has going on with her body and the animal smells and stuff. Bostitch hears himself moaning. Frances T. whispers, I got a rubber, and she gets up, and Bostitch freezes. She comes back and Bostitch tries to explain his situation to her but his voice goes nowhere in the night. What you mean is, safe sex and that's why I got this, she says in his ear, the cold foil on his stomach. And Bostitch shuts up, hears it rip open and she gets on him. His last thought before he falls asleep is how *not* different it all is, how slippery and fun, how everything *goes, goes, goes* toward a moment. There were girls in high school, of course, before he came out, but that was rigid with performance anxiety, and now, Bostitch is still a manager, despite, the intimacy of said moment.

In the morning, Bostitch is embarrassed and doesn't know what to do, and feels quite terribly confused, but she, she is perky and says, you know what?

She wears one of Keith's bathrobes from the closet.

This is a real fine couch, sir.

Bostitch finds the *sir* oddly comforting, so he goes with the mood.

Well, Keith had fine taste in furnishings.

If you don't mind me saying, sir. But you may want, you know, to get rid of some of the Keith stuff, to move on and such. Might be easier.

Bostitch says, I think you're right, Frances.

And he would've analyzed that further but responsibilities loomed.

You're absolutely right.

Frances seems pleased by the answer. They did not touch further, to his disappointment and relief.

Bostitch washes Frances T.'s clothes while she wears a large shirt of Keith's and she lounges most of the day and reads Keith's book *Will Do: Success* and he tells her she could get a uniform from the stock room and today she could skip the name tag, but she'd have to tie the apron all the way up, and Frances T. says, this job is your life, isn't it, and he says, it's been very important for my sanity. He considers for one quick moment begging her to be naked again with him, but that was only for a second and then Bostitch regains composure and coughs.

When Bostitch and female companion go to Royale later, he drops her at the curb and goes to the garage, tells her she would have to hightail it to get Happy Hour out on time, and she said, no problem, and then Bostitch immediately set about checking the tables (four needed sugar, salt and were dirty), checked the glass supplies and sent Marco to replenish (a nice fellow from Honduras with gleaming shoes and watch), then realized it was five and the Happy Hour food was not out, people were starting to come in and the steam poured from the uncovered trays. Bostitch was outraged, and went to the back and found Frances T. talking to Laura K. and said, The happy hour, girls? It's *Five*.

And Frances T. said, OK, we're coming, sir.

And Thuog in the back says, Boss, I am waiting for them to pick up, his face wet with sweat and he looked quite displeased, so Bostitch went back to the station and female employees were still gab-gab-gabbing away, and he said, Frances T.! Laura K.! You need to move now, and as he yells he can see Frances T.'s eyes are puffy and teary—red alert to feelings!— but it is now *five fifteen and there is a line of people in front of steaming empty trays*.

Bostitch is not too cheerful.

Employees to front station! he says in an urgent voice, which comes out as a strangled squeak.

Oh, Lloyd, I don't know if I can manage, I've had a problem with my ex, *Tommy*, you know—

Professional atmosphere, Frances T.!

She's had it *rough*, Lloydie, said Laura K., putting her arm around her, in a looped fashion.

And then it is *five twenty two*, Bostitch goes and gets food, seven trays of it, sauces, sesame-soy and ginger-chili, the Jalapeno poppers, people are grabbing tongs and taking food from the trays even as he holds them mid-air, they are empty in seconds and he drags more from the kitchen, and Frances T. sits in the back on a milk crate and Bostitch's normally neat hair is damp and stringy, and in the midst of this all, the loss prevention manager, Kyle, is there, with his southern warm voice, spiky hair, diamond pinky ring, *Hey there, Lloyd*!

Bostitch says, Hello, Kyle, glad to see you.

Loss Prevention manager says in a friendly and convivial tone, about the *damn fine weather we've been enjoying, did you get a chance to enjoy it? Do you partake in any sports?* and Bostitch is having a hard time answering him, lifting the hot trays, empty except for the greasy crumbs of tempura, and hot water drivels off the edges of the pan on his tuxedo front and he had to use a whole pile of spun napkins to mop up shirt and table. *Me, I'm a kayak guy*, says Kyle, following him to the kitchen as Bostitch balances three trays on his arms. *Give me some white water anytime*, then using his most cheerful, pep-filled voice by the coffee station he starts in on how he *can't help but notice that it seems like you aren't running a tight ship here*, just as Bostitch drops a tray of tempura hunks on the floor and they bounce all over the carpet, *kind of some loose gears, if you know what I mean, I mean, the food's slow, and you got a line of people from here to hell and back, and*—

Well, a girl had problems—

Of course! They all do! Don't we all, son, don't we all! But Royale needs our professionalism, bud. We're an A Number One Team here.

Well, it's a special case, see—

Special, schmecial. We just can't allow this kind of *mess*, Lloyd. Teamwork! Teamwork, fella! Because, see here, Lloyd, and he leaned down and whispered fast in Bostitch's face, in the kindest manner, see here, there was some, some *negative press*, some jabberwockies on the case, so to speak, last spring about your, uh, fraternizing with some of your staff, you know what I mean, Lloyd, but I said, leave the man alone, I said, I really did, Lloyd. Because, you know, I don't care about your private life. That's your affair, so to speak. In other words, we take care of our own.

Will do. Kyle. Will do.

Well, there you go. That's my bud. Who's my main man in The Caribbean Lounge, eh? Will I see you June at Ramadaland, Buddy boy, down in Tampa. Catch some rays, my man.

Hey, you losing weight? Atkins, dude?

Well, I'm not certain—

And I'll tell you what. I'd be happy to show you the ropes, on that Kayak thing. I think that's the ticket, Joe. Kayaks. Test yourself. Challenge yourself.

Loss Prevention manager's hand is tight on his shoulder, crablike. Bostitch feels a horrible knot growing in his stomach, a whopping compulsion to fall into Kyle's chest and sob. He looks down to the ground and tears fill his eyes. So he keeps looking down and folds his arms across his chest and says *yeah, yeah* a few times. *Kayaks. Yeah.*

I'm telling you, dude.

Yeah.

Kayaks.

Yeah.

Then, thankfully, Kyle slaps his back really hard. I, he guffaws. *Onward. You got a whitewater future, boy.* He walks off, his trousers making a swish sound as his thighs meet.

Bostitch wonders what the hell Kyle does with his time. How does Loss Prevention gives him the right to asshole him around repeatedly, on a daily basis. Where are the disasters he needs to attend to? Is Bostitch the only disaster the man can find?

After he leaves, there are crumpled napkins around each table like dropped blossoms, and the tropical plants have cigarettes stuck in their soil, and the Happy Hour table is smeared with lakes of Orange-Mango Salsa and Pineapple-Mint chutney (this is supplied in giant five gallon Ziplocks) and half empty plates litter the tables, and Bostitch cleans up by himself. Frances T. comes over and asks him to sign her card. She looks at his face the whole time he does it, Bostitch could see her from a corner of his eyes. When he looks up, though, she looked down.

Sir, uh, Lloyd, uh, I was wondering.

Bostitch noticed she needed powder.

It was a rough night here, Frances T.

Maybe I could cook dinner for you, you know, one, one time or another. I do cutlets. Pretty decent.

The Loss Prevention manager was in tonight.

That fat jerk? He stared at my tits.

The Caribbean lounge was, was a *disgrace* tonight.

I bet you like spaghetti. You like spaghetti?

He started to say, *The Manual*, but she had already slid next to him at the bar and asked Marco, the bartender, for a *Sex On The Beach* shooter and Bostitch could hear the muzak playing, it was a tape number six, The Beach Boys segueing into *Day-O!* and as she lit up a cigarette.

Hey Marco, says Bostitch.

Hey boss, rough night, eh?

Well. Not too pretty, no. Hey. Have I told you The Knotty Log story?

Well, I think so—

I *know* I've heard this before, says Frances T.

—*Well*, there was this boy who was supposed to chop this knotty log, someone said to, you see—

(Again, another favorite tale from the small funeral folder of his Grandpa's he kept in his pocket for inspiration. It was amazing how much info they had managed to cram in those few pages, that G. Irvin Van Scyoc funeral home company. Sometimes people ask Bostitch, what you reading these days? And he would like to say, a funeral folder, but then they would think he was, well, touched, so he says, *this and that*. It's a good answer, seems to satisfy them. Bostitch drinks his drink)

—I think I know this story, too, says Marco—

—So this boy works *real hard* on it, Marco, just chop-chop-chopping away and yet the log would not split. It wouldn't split, Marco—

—Is that right? Hunh. What do you think of that, Marco? Frances T. says and Granny-mouthed her cigarette.

Tell us more, Mr. Bostitch!

— Just then as he wants to give up an old man comes along, he says, you're wasting a lot of good time hitting around that knot. Try hitting it squarely next time.

Bostitch catches a glimpse of himself in the bar mirror, alarmed to see his face appears hollow and worn under his vaguely optimistic hairstyle, appearing puppet-like for a brief second.

—So you know what, Marco? You know what? Give me another shooter and I'll *tell* you what, my friend—

—Okey dokey, boss—

—That boy did what the man said and that log broke at the first strike! You see, Marco, successful men and women keep plugging away at a goal and nothing gets in their way, Marco! They also have a knot, as everyone does and they hit it squarely. Point here being, Marco, everyone, and I'll top that off with another of your fine beverages, is that we all got some kind of knot, yet we can persevere, by hitting it *squarely*—

There a lot of things I'd like to hit squarely, I'll tell you that, Lloyd. Lot of fuckers in this world, says Frances T.

Bostitch nods. Bostitch goes to the bathroom with his leather backpack. He wonders whether he would need a *Depends* tonight, in case of accidents. He decides the answer is no, images of naked Frances T. spin in his head, so he sprays Country Freshin' Day potpourri in the air and a double dose of Armani For Men in his pants and unfortunately a small trace of feces had landed on an edge of his garment, so he wipes it down, now the tape plays Margaritaville, Bostitch pulls his belt super tight, wipes his face which was rather wet with perspiration, and respikes his hair. Then he goes out to the bar. He finds a sensation of happiness is oddly lodged in his chest.

Actually, Frances, says Bostitch, I *do* like spaghetti.

Ok, OK, I'll keep it in mind, says Frances T., putting on her patch-work rabbit-fur jacket, you ready, Freddie?

Sure thing, say Marco.

Oh, manages to come out of Bostitch's mouth, but it practically has no weight, a simple puff of air without sound or effectiveness.

Yeah, old Marco here's going to give me a ride home, how about that?

When Bostitch looks up, Marco gives him a big wink, OK lady, says Marco, let's go.

You good here, boss?

I'm fine.

I brought up two case of white. And two Kahlua, too.

Good, good.

A lady is waiting! Frances T. yells out as she places change in the cigarette machine.

Coming! Hey, Boss, maybe I get lucky, Marco whispers, a big blast of Kahlua breath in his ear, you know?

Bostitch drinks his shooter, Marco turns smiling, the clock strikes eleven.

Fuckheads.

What's that? Marco grapples with his jacket, his eyebrows up.

I *said*. Fuckheads. Both of, *all* of yous.

I don't think I caught you there—

You're a damn fuckhead. And *you* are a damn fuckhead!

Lloyd, you better—

—*Whoa*, boss—

Bostitch lunges out with his bony hand and tries to hit Marco in the stomach, but he crumbles forward and falls on his face. The carpet smells terrible. He remembers he should've called the carpet service as it is the end of the month. That's something he's supposed to do.

Bostitch finds himself getting up and thanking Marco to their appalled silence, and then, grabbing his backpack, funeral packet in his pocket, he goes to the parking lot. He takes the big circle of Royale keys and flings it out into the empty field next to the dumpsters. He sees Kyle's humongous SUV and pisses on the license tag. Then, he takes the Royale manual, spits on it, and rips the pages out in chunks. He sprinkles them on Kyle's car until it flutters softly in the hot air of the parking lot. Then, happily, he walks to his car, just as he sees Kyle coming out the service entrance. Bostitch panics and runs over to Kyle's car, picking up the papers desperately.

What in hell you doing, son?

Some *persons*, some *idiots*, starts Bostitch.

What *are* these papers—

Hoodlums, or—

Hoodlums?

Fuckheads—

Fuckheads? Do I smell piss? On my car?

So Bostitch pauses. A witness, if there had been one, would note the serene expression under the mawkish spiked hair, his stiff, tiny body.

You *do* smell piss on your car. And spittle. Of myself. I *spitted* on your car. And, and I ripped up the dumb book, because it and you, basically *suck*. Because you, you majorly suck, and so do you all, all you, fuckheads.

Jesus—

And you look dumb. Your butt is big. I reject you.

When the hotel blew up before that was last straw, because he wasn't there. He was dealing with Keith and all that. But he wishes he had been. Wishes he had been caught in it and blown away, washed away like some of them. And those two that cast themselves from the roof, like two lost birds without wings. He could've been with them.

Bostitch walks to his car. It is not a sports car. It is a what you'd call a generic, air-toned vessel. It has the *swagger* of an economy rental car.

Backing up, he almost hits Kyle running. He tries to do one of those cool, high school peel-outs, but steps on the brake really hard and stops. Kyle buckles across the hood, you *mother*, he yells. And just when Kyle is up, coming at him, then he accelerates.

And so Bostitch flees in the night, screeching tires from The Royale parking lot.

Another broken heart cracked—*craqk, crack, craqk!*—in the halls of the hotel, like all the others. Some find love, some find it and lose it, some always search, like Bostitch.

And the people come and go. Through the night, the people come and go.

They say it is not important. It always is. They say you can't buy it. You can't. They say it comes quickly, like a tidal wave. It does. Suddenly, it is here. They say you have no control, that there is no mercy. There is no control or mercy. We are all it's victims. We all surrender. We all succumb.

You are thinking of it now, wondering where it is, where it went. It is behind you or in front. It is elusive. It will come when called.

Be ready. Be alert.
Your time is coming.